DOMINIC'S
PARK

ANNE CALLANAN

CRANTHORPE
MILLNER

First published by Cranthorpe Millner Publishers (2022)

ISBN 978-1-80378-021-4 (Paperback)

www.cranthorpemillner.com

Cranthorpe Millner Publishers

For Sean and Jackie,
Thanks for being delusional enough to chance reading
my first draft.
Love you both.
XX

The catalyst

It had been five hours and there was still no sign of the little boy or his dog. The whole town was out searching as the fog descended and darkness fell. Torch beams shone in the blackness, their white lights flickering in the distance throughout the surrounding countryside.

"Harry?" "Patrick?" were the names that resonated again and again, as voices carried in the cold, still air.

Volunteers with their dogs and sticks continued looking long into the night; their knitted hats dampened by drizzle which formed perfect round droplets on top of the wool. With scarves wrapped tightly over chins and coats buttoned high to protect from the elements, they searched without success. It would seem as though Harry Regan-Hennessy and his service dog Patrick had disappeared into the mist.

One by one, weariness and despondency got the better of the volunteers and they reluctantly returned to the warmth of their homes for food and rest. Many prayers and good wishes for Harry's safe return were sent out that night; the communal grief of a missing child weighing heavily on their hearts. Harry's parents, JJ and Niamh, searched into the early hours until a combination of exhaustion and the constant pleading of Niamh's parents to stop, eventually forced them home too.

"Why hasn't Patrick brought him home?" It was the third time Niamh had uttered those words since trudging back through the door, only thirty minutes before. "He hates the rain. Where are they?"

It was no night for a child, let alone their eight-year-old autistic son to be out in the elements. Wet to her core, she paced the floor while her parents and sister fussed around her. Offering her a mug of tea and encouraging her to eat a slice of toast, they tried their best to help, reassuring her that everything would be all right, imploring her to sit, to rest or get some sleep. Yet the more they mollycoddled her the more agitated she became.

Sleep? Are you kidding me? she thought. *I should be back out there looking for Harry. Nothing is OK. If you weren't here, I'd still be out searching. Jesus, would you all just leave me alone!*

Earlier that evening, following a frantic phone call to her parents, Niamh's family had arrived to assist with the search, and initially she'd been very appreciative of their warmth and hugs. The feeling of being encompassed by love and concern had been comforting and reassuring. Yet as the night wore on and with Harry still missing, her earlier feeling of solace had morphed into something else. She wasn't exactly sure how she felt, but she knew discontent was creeping in.

Why did I ask them to come? she thought to herself. *They can't really help, and now they're just in my way and telling me what to do.*

Her pain was becoming unbearable. Overwhelmed by the number of people around her, Niamh needed a bit of space without their concerned, watchful eyes following her back and forth across the room. Resentment and gratitude rumbled within her in equal measure.

Unable to express her mixed feelings because she didn't want to appear ungrateful, she offered a weak pretence of a smile while they consoled her, and as often as she could walked away to pace around the furniture for a few moments' peace. The whole situation was surreal.

Leaning against the door frame, Niamh looked across at JJ, her estranged husband. He was dozing fitfully, laying rather uncomfortably across their son's bright red beanbag; the one Harry used to watch television.

He shouldn't be there, she thought. *That's Harry's spot*, and she had to suppress the urge to tell him to leave; to go back to his rented house in town. It took every morsel of her self-restraint to stay silent, knowing full well that asking him to leave would be spiteful. Harry was, after all, his son too. She continued to scan the room. There were bodies everywhere. These were the people she loved, but she hated the sight. None of them should be in her home like this. She only wanted Harry and Patrick. In her head, she screamed, *Get out! Get out, all of you! I don't want any of you. I just want Harry.*

Niamh loved her family dearly, but from a distance. They, including her, were all high achievers, used to being in control of their emotions and environment. She neither wanted them to witness, nor did she think they could cope with, the raw and exposed emotions she was feeling right now. All her strength was being sapped trying to maintain her composure. She wanted to wail like a banshee or kick and punch until she was black and blue from her efforts. She didn't want to be in control of herself, but with them there she couldn't let go. Confined in her home, her tired eyes continued to flit about searching for clues as to what might have happened, until eventually they involuntarily closed for the briefest period of rest.

JJ watched her despair from a safe distance. He could see Niamh was distraught but he didn't think she would accept any comfort from him. Only six months separated, they were still testing out the boundaries of their new alliance, and that relationship was rather raw. He concluded the last thing either of them needed was a misplaced word, so he stayed back, doing his best to conceal his own emotional rollercoaster; sincerely believing it was easier for them both if he pretended to doze.

JJ also wished he could escape the watchful eyes of her family. They were not happy about the separation and were naturally siding with Niamh over the split. It was uncomfortable being in their presence.

As he rested on Harry's beanbag, he could detect his faint scent; a floral washing powder ingrained in the fabric, and he hoped that by that time of the night, Harry was sleeping soundly, oblivious to his surroundings.

Niamh, JJ and her family stayed like that for a few hours – scattered about, sleeping on and off in various chairs around the living room. At five a.m., unable to rest any longer, Orla, Niamh's younger sister, started to cook breakfast.

Niamh felt awful. She had only slept for an hour, and the smell of the sausages and scrambled eggs made her heave. But she desperately needed to fill the time until she could go out searching again, so to occupy herself, she offered to help Orla prepare the breakfast. Orla turned her down, wanting her sister to rest, and although her rejection came from kindness, to Niamh, it was unwelcome.

Niamh tried but couldn't go back to sleep, and moved from the armchair where she'd most recently been resting to a chair at the kitchen table. There she sat anxiously jiggling her legs up and down, watching her sister work and feeling her stomach churn.

By five forty-five a.m. the family were all gathered around the table, trying to eat. Not one of them had an appetite, and a large basket of toast sat untouched in the centre of the table. They looked bedraggled and bleary eyed. Too tired to make conversation, they ate in silence.

The doorbell rang and Niamh sprang from her seat to answer it. It was two Gardai, a male and female. They, like all police officers across the world, looked officious in their uniforms, with their heavier outer jackets emblazoned with GARDA. Seeing them on her doorstep, Niamh hoped they would live up to the English translation of their name 'Guardians of the Peace', giving her back the peace of mind she had experienced before Harry disappeared. She showed them into the living room and was quickly joined by the rest of the family. Orla offered tea to the Gardai, but they politely declined.

It was immediately made clear that they wanted to discourage the family from going straight back out. They offered assurance that enough people had volunteered to engage in the search, including members of the local GAA club (Gaelic Football Association); their parish's club apparently having joined forces with the neighbouring club.

"There are plenty of people to assist us with the

search today," the male Garda said, "Willing and able volunteers, almost too many to coordinate. You should stay home and rest up as best you can. There's bound to be media attention, and with any luck, you'll soon have Harry back at home."

The search area the evening before had been very concentrated, it being hoped that Harry had only wandered off. Yesterday, even though Anna his childminder had promised that the back garden gate was locked, the questioning Gardai had hoped she was mistaken, and the child would be found somewhere close by with his dog.

Niamh and JJ knew that was unlikely, as Anna was vigilant about keeping the gate locked, well aware it only took a moment for Harry to decide to run.

Niamh had listened intently when Anna explained to the Gardai that she had detached Harry from Patrick's harness – as she always did when he came home from school – to allow him to use the swing in the garden while she prepared dinner.

"It's the activity that helps him transition between school and home. I always detach Harry from Patrick when he wants to use the swing," she had told them. "I thought he was safe in the back garden," and then she had begun to cry.

If only Anna were less reliable, Niamh had thought, *Harry might still be here*.

Harry's numerous sensory issues meant that he often

became distressed or distracted by his surroundings, and as he had grown older, he had become a constant flight risk. To provide more safety when out walking, it had been recommended he get a service dog. Patrick, the large German Shepherd who had arrived into their household two short years previously, was that dog, and he was loved by them all for his patience and loyalty.

Harry and Patrick could be attached to each other via a tethering system, and in his role as his service dog Patrick became an anchor by sitting down if Harry tried to dart off. Harry rarely tried to run these days, preferring to lean in to Patrick if he was feeling distressed, and over all, his stress levels had significantly decreased since the dog's arrival.

Anna had also told the Gardai that Patrick was still wearing his service harness when they had disappeared. They'd all hoped it's fluorescent orange colour would make it easier to find them, but now with no clues or sightings overnight, everyone was concerned something more sinister had happened to them. Niamh just couldn't imagine what that might be and clung to the hope that they were together, as the Gardai told them about the different areas to be searched that day.

Despite her attempts to remain calm, she began to have great difficulty controlling her thoughts. Frightening and dreadful images tortured her, and talk of a search by the lakeshore sent her mind spiralling. If she sat at home, there was no way she'd be able to dispel the distressing images of Harry's limp body laying lifeless, covered with sand and grit on the beach with his wet hair plastered across his forehead as the water gently rocked him back and forth, white as a ghost, still and dead. And Patrick, wet and shivering, lying beside him with his head resting on his chest, whimpering. She simply had to fill her head with other thoughts. She had to get outside and active otherwise she might lose her mind completely.

In the end, ignoring the Gardai's reassurances, both JJ and Niamh insisted they would rejoin the search party if Harry was not found by mid-morning.

After the Gardai left to help coordinate the volunteers gathering at the town hall, Niamh's mother tried to get her to eat some more breakfast.

"Come back to the table, Niamh. I'll make another pot of tea. Eat a little more."

"No, I can't, Mam. I'm going to have a shower," she said rather dismissively. Noticing her mother's upset face, she added, "Maybe later."

Taking her mobile phone with her, she went upstairs, and once inside the bathroom, she telephoned Louise. Louise was the veterinary nurse assistant at Niamh's veterinary practice in town, and also her best friend. They'd been working together for six years.

Having also been out searching until late the night before, Louise was woken from a deep sleep by the call. Arranging her pillows to support her head, she sat up in her bed, hoping Niamh had some good news.

"Louise, you have to help. I can't wait about here anymore. Will you pick me up? I'll tell them we have to organise the closure of the practice."

"Niamh you can't do that. Stay at home. I'll organise the clinic. You've enough on your plate."

"No, you're not listening to me, Louise! Listen. I have to get out of here or I'll go mad and say something I'll regret. I know you'll do the organising," she emphasised, "I just want somewhere to go. Please help me."

It was so unlike Niamh to ask for help that Lousie agreed.

"OK, OK. What time will I get you?"

"Would half an hour be all right? Thanks Louise, I owe you."

There was a brief silence on the other end of the phone while Louise rubbed some life into her face with her free hand.

"OK, see you in a bit. Hang in there, Niamh," she said, as she reached for her clothes on the chair beside her bed.

Downstairs, back in Niamh's house, JJ had decided it was time he left. The tension in the household was palpable, and he knew his presence was only making things worse. Heading for the door, he used Niamh's earlier excuse, saying that he needed to go home and shower, before seeing himself out. He would rejoin the search later.

Much to Niamh's relief, by the time she came back downstairs, he had already gone.

"Louise will do most of the work," Niamh said to her horrified parents, explaining that she was going to sort things out at the clinic before heading back out to search for Harry. "I'll just help and tinker about. I need to do something. I can't just sit and wait. I need to fill the time."

They tried to reason with her but Niamh was clear. She needed to get out of the house. Sitting at home and waiting was driving her mad. In the end, her parents had to agree. She wasn't going to be dissuaded, and they wanted to be supportive. Perhaps keeping busy was better than rest.

Niamh almost ran out of the house when Louise arrived, leaving her parents behind, consumed with concern for her wellbeing and their grandson's safety. They were condemned to spend the day at home with their youngest daughter, listening out for the ominous ring of the telephone.

Cold and weary from their sleepless night, the two friends spent a while just sitting side by side in Louise's car, staring at the road ahead. Louise put the heating on full to give them a bit of comfort, but it only added to the dryness of their tired eyes. It was another drizzly and foggy start to the day; the kind of fog that sneaks dampness into your bones without you noticing, silently dropping its fine mist on your shoulders before slowly seeping downwards. The windscreen wipers intermittently swished back and forth. Louise spoke first.

"Are you sure you want to go in? I can follow up with the clients you know."

"I need the distraction, Louise. I can't cope. I have to do something."

"Sure." Louise left it at that. She didn't want to resort to empty platitudes. She'd heard enough of them herself in her time.

She was older than Niamh by almost twenty years and, at sixty-four, was considering retirement. Niamh was not looking forward to replacing her – Louise was a very competent assistant. She'd completed her veterinary nurse training in England before a similar course existed in Ireland, and had worked there for many years, not returning to Dublin until she was in her thirties. Louise had been fifty-eight when she moved out of the city to Niamh's clinic in County Wicklow. At the time, she'd worried she was too old to change jobs, but recognising her vast experience and knowing her 'salt of the earth' personality would make her a natural with all the clients, Niamh had been keen to employ her. She was right, people found it easy to engage with Louise's humble, down to earth character, and she was a good sidekick to Niamh who found it difficult to present anything other than a perfect front.

Clients generally took longer to feel at ease around Niamh; she came across as being a bit aloof, despite her efforts to be polite and professional with a friendly, caring manner. Niamh often needed a little bit of distance from others. She wished she didn't, but it gave her security – a safe zone in which to live her life. Louise was one of the few people she regarded as a friend. Even though they didn't really know an awful lot about each other's personal lives – their bond for the most part cemented by work banter – they both knew they had each other's backs and felt secure in each other's company. They were a good team professionally and personally.

The surgery was a haven, and once they arrived, Niamh went straight to her cramped but well-organised office. There, no one was watching her, telling her to rest or asking her how she was. It was such a relief. Louise didn't follow, instead giving Niamh some space while she started re-organising appointments. The phone calls were awkward. It was difficult to avoid being pulled into conversations about the whole horrid ordeal, and Louise was acutely aware her conversations could be overheard by Niamh.

She watched Niamh through the open door, moving some papers around her desk, and it wasn't long before Louise noticed her rest her head on her folded arms. Niamh only meant to close her eyes for a moment, but instantaneously she was asleep.

Louise knew her friend wouldn't sleep for long. She remembered the nights from her own past, many years ago, when sleep came to her in short fits and starts. She'd wake then, feeling shaken and anxious, having relived her trauma once more through her nightmares. Wishing she could help her friend, she knew only too well there was little she could do; there'd be no peace until Harry was found and nothing would console Niamh until then. Being there to support her in whatever way she could was the best she could do.

Louise continued to make her calls until Niamh jerked herself upright as if electrocuted. Wiping the back of her hand across her face to rub away the saliva which had trickled down the side of her cheek, she gazed at the spot on her desk where she'd been resting her head. With frightened eyes and muscles tensed ready for battle, Niamh looked about her. It only took a second before she recognised where she was, and why.

"Louise," she called out groggily, "How long have I been sleeping? What time is it?"

"Only fifteen minutes," Louise whispered, covering the mouthpiece of the phone.

Niamh waited for her assistant to finish the phone call before saying,

"Let's go check the forest road again, Louise."

"OK," Louise responded, "Just let me put a message on the answering machine and cancel this last appointment for today."

14

Fifteen minutes later, the pair got back into Louise's car and drove the short distance to the forestry carpark. There, they searched the same areas they'd covered the night before, but this time with the advantage of daylight. As she walked, Niamh prayed to a God she didn't believe in that her son was sheltering somewhere with Patrick; that he at least had him for company and warmth. She knew if he remained outside his chances of survival decreased the longer he was missing. Looking for clues, assessing footprints, shouting and listening, they tried to stay expectant, but the tracks Niamh, Harry and Patrick regularly enjoyed for weekend walks denied Niamh any sign of her son or his service dog. Her fear and frustration deepened.

Niamh and Louise decided to return there again in the evening, hoping that Patrick might bring Harry back to a familiar place, if not home, and the forest was a favourite of theirs. Deep down, they both knew this eventuality was becoming increasingly unlikely as more time wore on, but they clung to hope and said nothing.

By ten a.m. they'd left the forest paths and joined a group who were about to begin a search of the fields and farmlands at the back of Niamh's house. The inclement weather was relentless, but everyone maintained a positive exterior, while secretly fearing the worst.

At the town hall, the epicentre for the search operation, groups of volunteers gathered throughout the day, warming their backs against the radiators that hung along the walls. They spoke in hushed tones while cold hands encircled hot mugs of tea or coffee and hungry mouths bit into ham or egg salad sandwiches, filling the void in their stomachs so they could keep searching. As each group left to make way for the next set of tired and wet volunteers entering the hall, they let out shouts of:

"Thanks very much ladies."

"Fair play to ye."

"Jesus, Theresa you make a grand ham sandwich."

"Keep that kettle on the boil now ladies, we'll be back for more tea later."

And with the easy banter came occasional quiet laughter; tiny snaps of humour to lighten their moods.

The dry and re-energised volunteers streamed back out into the cold with new vigour, while inside the ladies from The Irish Country Woman's Association (ICA) scurried around gathering used cups and plates for washing, chatting away as they did so.

No time was wasted – steaming teapots and re-filled plates of food were repeatedly passed back through the kitchen hatch and put on the freshly wiped tables in readiness for the next group's arrival. The local ICA was a well-oiled machine in the community, a vital cog in any crisis. This same scene was consistent all day long: a parish pulling together as one in the search for Harry and Patrick.

Meantime, JJ was across the far side of town, doing all he could to ensure Harry's safe return.

Eugene

Eugene was up earlier than his usual mid-day rising time. He filled his small backpack with the few supplies he thought he might need – batteries, a torch, phone, iPad, leads, toothbrush, a change of t-shirt and some extra socks. Oh, and of course, his needles and stash. He couldn't do this job without his heroin; he couldn't do any day without his heroin.

He walked from Dominic's Park to the local bus stop which brought him into the centre of town. From there, he headed for the Liffey quays where he waited for the ten thirty a.m. bus out of Dublin with a handful of other passengers. Large seagulls, the renegades of the Dublin skyline, were swooping overhead, occasionally dropping down onto the riverside barrier. Some of the birds people-watched from their perches, waiting for bits of chips or crisps to be dropped on the pathway, while another pulled vinegar-soaked paper from one of many overflowing bins that were evenly spaced along the pavement.

Eugene had been to this bus stop before as a young teen with a few of his friends. It had been a hot summer's day, a school day, but they'd not felt like school that day. While they'd waited for the bus, they had flung the crusts of their school lunch sandwiches into the sky, watching as the gulls snatched them up. On that occasion they had travelled to a village in Wicklow, thirty kilometres from the city, well known for it's beautiful lakes, to steal a boat for a few hours of fun. Rowing about the lake had indeed been great fun, no one had caught them. All-round, they'd had a very successful day.

This time he was heading to a cottage in the same area, but he wouldn't be stealing a boat; instead, he'd be hiring a bicycle to cycle the route that circled the largest of the lakes.

The journey from Dublin was not pleasant. Eugene was still feeling sick from the night before. The road was winding and bumpy and the bus was constantly swaying to and fro. Keeping his eyes closed and trying to sleep was the only way he could avoid vomiting. He was very glad to arrive at his final destination and get his feet onto solid ground.

The chill on disembarking from the warmth of the bus helped to clear his head a little as he walked the short distance from the main street, out the graveyard road, to the leisure centre where he'd previously stolen the boat with his friends. That time it had been a busy spot, but on this March day, ahead of the tourist season, there were only a few people about.

After hiring his bike, he began to cycle towards the track that followed the lake shore. Once there, he read his instructions again to check how far to go before he should leave the track and head out onto the road.

It was a cold but pleasant spring day, and even this hardened city youth was entranced for a while by the combination of water, sky, trees and rolling hills. Eugene was as close to being appreciative as possible for a twenty-one-year-old with a sinister agenda on his mind.

He cycled for about a kilometre as instructed, before branching off onto the lake road which hugged the shoreline. He didn't know it then, but he cycled right by the spot where his body would soon be dumped, left to decay.

Not accustomed to pedaling a bike, he could feel his calf muscles begin to hurt after about twenty minutes, and seeing another hill ahead of him he decided to get off the bike and walk for a bit. At the top he rested briefly to look back across the expanse of lake. Five minutes later he was back on his bike.

There were bright yellow gorse bushes and ferns delicately uncoiling their new fronds lining either side of the road, but Eugene was tired now and all this went unnoticed – he no longer enjoyed any of the scenery, more intent on counting the dips and elevations that lay ahead of him, cursing the rolling hills that Wicklow had on offer.

An hour later, having circled the lake as far as the cottage, he approached a closed entrance gate. He'd been warned to avoid being noticed so made sure no one was watching before crossing the road. It took some wriggling about to open the latch of the battered old gate, but much to Eugene's relief, he managed it. The gate swung open onto a rough gravel laneway. Shutting it behind him, he walked his bike up the hill which led to what would be his home for the next few days, glad to be at the end of his journey.

The cottage was very secluded. *Shame I have to babysit*, he thought, *this would be a great spot for an all-night party with no bother from neighbours.*

Eugene stowed his bike in a shed at the side of the cottage, then he unlocked the back door using the key left for him under a stone. The interior was very dark, the windows to the front blacked out with bin bags and the rear windows shaded by the hill behind, the cottage almost set into the hillside. He noticed a strong smell of paint but it didn't bother him; the fresh air and cycle had eased the worst of his nausea.

The back door opened directly into the kitchen, which was the central room of the house. Off this were two bedrooms and a tiny bathroom. His bedroom was intended to be the room on the right and the child's to the left. He wasn't allowed to turn on the main lights and noticed the light bulbs had been removed in case temptation got the better of him. Glad he'd brought his torch and spare batteries with him, he left the backdoor open while he located and switched on a small lamp in each room. Sparsely furnished, the bedrooms had a bed and bedding, with a small bedside table. The one to the left also had a low table covered in playthings for a child's amusement.

Eugene thought the darkness was a bit excessive – the house was in the middle of nowhere. Still, he knew to do as he was told.

Through the open backdoor, he could see the little yard behind. This was the secure place where he was allowed to let the child or dog go out into when needed. It backed onto the rock of the hill and was gated at both ends.

The body heat he'd generated from the cycle was fast evaporating and the cottage was cold. Finding the central heating switch inside one of the cupboards, he flicked it on. It wouldn't take long for this small cottage to warm up. As the oil burner ignited outside in the backyard, he saw puffs of smoke rise from its metal housing.

"Shit," he said as he quickly snapped the switch off, the smoke instantly stopping. He'd not tell anyone about his mistake.

Looking around, he saw a gas heater in the corner of

the kitchen and one in both bedrooms; the one in the child's room had a large fireguard surrounding it, secured in place by clips attached to the wall.

After some fumbling he managed to turn on the heaters, and with the smell of the gas revolting him, he left the back door slightly ajar until the fumes had dispersed.

Eugene then dumped his rucksack on his bed and returned to the kitchen. Looking in the fridge, he was glad to see milk, butter and fizzy drinks. A cupboard was also stocked with basics – bread, tea, beans, tins of stew and a supply of various sweets. That was all he needed; he rarely ate a full meal anymore. Halting his exploring, he gulped down some of the milk and when his thirst was quenched made himself comfortable on an old couch in the corner of the kitchen, next to a tiny TV no bigger than a portable one. Switching it on, he lowered the sound so it was only barely audible.

"Jesus, it's black and white!" he said aloud, "What a stingy bastard. How long has he been hanging onto this old thing? Bet he still has his communion money in the post office too."

The picture was grainy with an occasional diagonal line slowly cursing its way from bottom to top.

"Probably a coat hanger on the roof for an aerial," he surmised, as he switched it off.

Retrieving his iPad from his bag he plugged it into the nearest socket to charge it up. When he switched it on, to his absolute dismay, there was no internet connection, so he tried plugging it into a socket at the far side of the room. There was still no connection. He tried the bedrooms too – the same.

What the fuck am I going to do with no internet access? Eugene didn't think he'd ever had a day without internet access in his entire life. He was seriously put out, and to his surprise, it made him feel anxious. Walking around the cottage, he tried to find something to occupy his mind. Agitation was setting in.

In Harry's room, he found another tiny TV connected to a video player, and under the low table were dozens of video tapes. Rifling through the bundles, he found them to be mostly children's cartoons, which were of no interest to him. There was also a home video. On top of the table was a large jigsaw, some paper, crayons and a watercolour paint box, but again, none of this would keep him amused.

A bundle of blankets lay on the floor beside the bed. *That must be for the dog*, he thought. He wasn't that keen on dogs in general, and even less so on German Shepherds. Despite being assured he'd nothing to fear from a service dog, he was still apprehensive.

Wandering back into the kitchen, he looked inside the last two kitchen cupboards. One was full of dog food and dog treats. Taking a handful of the treats, he put them straight into his pocket in case he required them later to keep the dog at bay. The other cupboard was empty apart from a few dead flies.

The silence and the isolation of the place, along with having zero access to the internet, was all starting to make him feel very on edge. He wished he could have some of the heroin he'd brought with him to take the edge off, but he dared not, afraid that the tell-tale signs would be recognised when his temporary new boss arrived. He told himself he was better off saving it for later anyway, when the kid and dog were asleep.

One hour passed, then two, then three. Feeling less anxious, but very bored, he resorted to sleeping to pass the time until the smell from the gas heaters triggered more nausea. Sitting up, he noticed signs of condensation on the polythene used to black out the windows, and became afraid he'd be gassed in his sleep. To err on the side of caution, he re-opened the backdoor, just a crack to let in some fresher air, then curled up on the couch again with a blanket for warmth as he tried to nap.

In the late afternoon, he was awoken by the crunching of a jeep's wheels on the gravel outside. Eugene instantly jumped up and stood alert, waiting for the door to open, anxious to see the child and dog he would be taking care of for the next few days.

They entered through the back door, the same one he'd used to enter the building earlier.

Shit, he thought. *That dog is HUGE!*

Finn

The blue light which shone over the Garda Station on the main street in town exaggerated the dark circles under Finn's eyes. Finn, the caretaker at Harry's school, looked tired and much older than his forty-five years, standing there for a moment to pull his coat about him before setting off home. It was later than he thought, still drizzling and starting to get dark, but he didn't care. He was leaving the station and the rain meant there'd be fewer people around. The hardier ones would be out of town searching for Harry, while the rest were most likely back in their own abodes by now.

He hoped no one saw him as he stepped into the street, head lowered and hands in his pockets. His cold damp shirt clung to his back as he began his walk home, the nervous sweat of an evening spent with the Gardai chilling him to the bone. Shoving his hands deeper into his pockets, he clenched his fists; humiliation, anger, and most of all fear, were held tightly in his grip.

He wanted to be back in his own house, sat in his own front room, even if it was no longer the welcoming home of his younger years when his parents were still alive. He'd have no one there to greet him this evening – not even the love and affection of his dog Twitch to look forward to. But it was still somewhere to retreat to when the world was harsh.

A few years ago there had been times when Finn hadn't left his home for weeks on end, only emerging for essential trips to the supermarket. Getting Twitch had changed that, as the dog needed walking twice a day. His little dog did much to improve his image in the town, and he was very aware of that. Having a pet had seemed to make him more approachable; he had found it was easier to talk to people with Twitch at the end of his lead. He didn't understand why, but it was just so, and now he missed him.

Being asked to come into the station by the Gardai to help with their enquiries had raised emotions and memories that Finn worked hard to keep buried in the recesses of his mind. He'd not expected them to be so abruptly brought back to the fore this way. Nor had he expected to see anew the inside of a Garda interview room, and once more be considered their subject of interest.

Many years ago he'd made a humongous mistake, and today reminded him of that fact. His mind continued to race as he walked.

How in hell did I get landed in the middle of this mess? he thought. *What are they doing listening to some cock and bull theory of JJ's? JJ the bastard. Not content enough murdering my Twitch, now he's trying to implicate me in Harry's disappearance!*

"Revenge." That's what the Garda had said.

Harry, sweet Harry. They really think I'd abduct a child for revenge? Why did JJ suggest it? Is he trying to get me to drop the case? I'll have my revenge all right but in a court, watching JJ's face when he's found guilty and loses his licence, gets a hefty fine or better still both!

"Fuck you, JJ," he muttered to himself.

Finn walked quickly, almost trotting at times, so intense was his desire to get home. He kept his head lowered; even saying "How are ya?" or "Thank you" to people as they turned slightly to allow him to pass by on the narrow pavement was beyond him.

Ahead he heard a group of voices, the sounds of chatter and laughter getting louder as they came closer. Local youths, wandering aimlessly around the streets. As they approached, he kept his head down. *Feck this,* he thought.

One of them had heard his father talking earlier about Finn being taken in for questioning. He was an astute young man and noticing Finn's defeated-looking body language decided to take the opportunity to impress his friends; he deliberately knocked into Finn's shoulder as he went by.

27

Under normal circumstances, this would have provoked a catalogue of abuse from Finn, but the vigilant young man was betting he wouldn't respond tonight for fear of getting into further trouble. He was right; Finn just kept walking. He heard the nervous laughter once the boys had gained a little distance but still chose to ignore them, not even turning around to give them one of his infamous glares.

Finn had a reputation in the community and this youngster was enjoying the rewards of having a little inside information. His timing was perfect. He was a budding opportunist who might perhaps go far in life and he'd enjoy the bit of veneration from his friends while he could.

Shortly after, and much to his relief, Finn arrived at his home. Up the garden path he stomped, past the overgrown front lawn with the remains of a lawnmower long since departed from this life. Arriving at his front door he searched for the key, his fingers stabbing into the far reaches of his pockets.

"Where are the fucking keys? Shit, shit, shit," he said aloud, only just then remembering that he'd been told to collect his belongings at the desk.

He stood looking at the ground and gave the front step a sharp kick, the force reverberating up his leg.

Well, there's no bloody way I'm going back there tonight; no way I'm letting them snigger at me. The bastards must be loving this – stupid, weird Finn. I'm not going back, he told himself.

He looked behind to see if anyone was watching, then turned to his left and walked to his side gate. Swinging it open, he stepped by his bicycle and the bins overflowing with black plastic bags. Finn regularly forgot to put out the bins.

Approaching the backdoor, he hoped by some miracle he'd left it unlocked. He knew he hadn't, he never left the house unlocked. In fact, he usually checked repeatedly as he left. Yes, he knew it would be locked, but Finn like anybody else in that situation still hoped in vain and tried pushing down the handle.

Eight months ago he'd have been greeted by Twitch jumping up at the backdoor's half window: up-down, up-down, excited to see him home, the little scrawny terrier yapping with delight. Not tonight though. Tonight there was only darkness and silence from within his house, and a growing sense of rage from without.

He took another moment to peer at the ground as he thought, then walking back past the bin and the bin bags, he picked up a bristle-free brush which was leaning against the wall behind his bicycle and returned to the back door. Raising the brush to shoulder height he rammed the handle into the glass pane, reasoning he could lock the inner kitchen door tonight for extra security after boarding up the outer one.

One quick sharp jab was all it took. A cracking noise

like a firework igniting and the task was done, the broken shards of glass falling to the ground. He worked quickly, like a burglar, pulling at the sharp shards that were left stuck in the edges of the window frame. A small piece of the broken glass pierced his thumb and drew blood. Shaking his hand he swore and sucked it clean, then reaching inside, he unlocked the door.

Finn didn't stop to attend to his thumb, instead going straight to the cupboard under the stairs he pulled out a piece of chipboard, four screws and an electric screwdriver.

The job was completed in thirty minutes, Finn's backdoor boarded up for the night. The damage had been a small sacrifice to make; much better than having to return to the station. Standing back and sucking at his thumb to stem the bleeding, he admired his handiwork and ten minutes later, after much rifling in drawers to find a plaster, he began to prepare some supper. Nothing fancy, just tea and toast.

As the smell of fresh toast filled the kitchen, he stood up and walked around the table, tapping its corners as he circled it. Then he folded his crumpled tea towel on the countertop and re-arranged the cooking utensils in the ceramic jar next to the cooker, all in an effort to settle himself. Anxiety was coursing through him. He didn't want to go back to prison; he couldn't cope with that. Yet right now, the sense of it invaded every part of his being. *How have I found myself in this position again. What the fuck? What the fuck is going on*? he thought.

"Jesus, please bring Harry back soon," he said aloud, gazing up towards the ceiling as if looking for answers from Him up there.

Finn wasn't a religious man. His faith had waned over the years, but right now God seemed his only hope, and once a Catholic always a Catholic. No harm in touching all bases in a crisis. 'Never say never' his mother always told him.

He became aware he was still wearing the cold, damp shirt he'd put on to smarten himself up for going to the Garda Station and sniffed at his armpit. Smelling his stale sweat, he tugged at the buttons to get it off, and retrieved a hoodie discarded over the back of a kitchen chair the day before. The hood caught on the chair back and he pulled it sharply to release it, eager to replace the cold cotton just discarded with the more comforting fleece fabric.

Yesterday he and his neighbours had searched for Harry and Patrick. They'd only been missing for a few hours at that time and everyone had thought they'd be found before bedtime. He'd been saddened when there was no sign of them, but it was also one of the few times he'd felt included and part of the community and it had made him feel good. Now, what were people going to think and say?

Sitting back down at his table, he looked at his hand

31

resting on its edge and noticed it beginning to shake. A swell of emotion rose up within him; a sensation of heat rising from his feet to his head. He banged on the tabletop and let out a deep guttural grunt.

Finn's nose was running and he sniffed. Knowing tears were close he could have cried, but he pushed back what he perceived to be that unmanly urge. Instead, when kettle boiled, he got up from his seat and with great ferocity stirred a teabag around in the hot steaming water that he'd poured into his mug. The boiling water splattered over the mug edge unnoticed. A drop of milk was added, and taking a gulp, he slumped back down into his seat. His toast popped up from the toaster on the kitchen counter beside his chair. After spreading on a thick layer of butter – the butter having been left out on the table since his breakfast – he took a large bite. This morning he'd thought he'd be spending the day looking for Harry. This morning felt like days ago.

It was a lonely picture: Finn sitting in his kitchen by himself staring at the boarded-up window, munching his toast and gulping his tea; the only sounds of his own making – chewing, swallowing and breathing. With nobody else to keep him company, the questions in his head kept coming. *How can they think I have anything to do with Harry's disappearance? What would I want with a child? Am I supposed to be a paedophile now too, as well as a murderer?*

"Fuck," he said aloud, imagining the neighbours, the

village and indeed the entire country talking about him, bringing up his past and using him as the scapegoat; someone to blame. What was he going to do?

He wished he had a drink in the house, but he'd given up alcohol years ago, believing it was to blame for the manslaughter conviction he had received when he was nineteen years old. Since then, he had been afraid to get drunk; not wanting to risk losing control of his temper like that again. A sip or two, alone in his house this evening, might have helped calm his nerves, but he had no intention of heading back outside to get some. He didn't need it that much.

Finn sat at the kitchen table long after he finished eating, thinking about his parents and wishing he had them there for company and reassurance. The pain of their loss remained with him, his feelings of grief no less than when they had each passed away. Fantasising they were there with him, he imagined them telling him all would be fine and he heard their voices saying to him,

"Don't worry, have a shower and head to bed. Harry will be found, he'll be OK. They'll apologise for suspecting you. You're a good lad and we love you."

They would tidy up the kitchen table and he'd hear the TV from downstairs as he fell asleep in his bedroom.

"You're a sad bastard," he said to himself, and he got up to clear his own table before heading into the sitting room to try and distract himself with some TV.

A while later, someone knocking at the front door roused him from his sleep.

Could it be?

By twelve noon, Niamh, Louise and the group of volunteers they had joined earlier that morning to search the fields behind Niamh's house were heading back to the town hall for an update and a much-needed warm drink. Despite Niamh's dejected state of mind she was putting together a few words of thanks for the volunteers in her head as she walked. It would be difficult, but she wanted to let people know how grateful she was for their support. At the town hall, she was brief and dignified. People were surprised and appreciative of her visit and talked about her bravery after she left.

Typical Niamh, Louise thought. *If it was me, I'd be so totally wrapped up in my grief that I wouldn't even think of the sacrifices others were making to help me until much later on. I'd be lost and unable to function. I wish I had her strength and confidence.* Louise often wished she could be more like Niamh; she greatly admired her strength, but life's experiences had shaped them in very different ways.

The day wore on. An update from the Gardai bore no good news and Louise watched as Niamh's resolve began to falter. One after another Niamh repeatedly pulled her fingers, stretching them as far as they could stretch, trying to release some of the tension in her hands. Louise pretended not to notice but she could see desperation and despair were close to the surface and there was nothing she could do other than observe and be present.

By six p.m. they had finished their search of two more areas close by and were in Louise's car travelling back into town. En route they would pass by the clinic, so they decided to drop in and check for phone messages before heading out to Harry and Patrick's favourite forest walk one more time. Niamh couldn't let go of the feeling that this was the most likely place they would turn up. Harry loved the softer clay paths under his feet and the patterns created by the shadows of the trees on sunny days. Louise wasn't going to tell her any different. If that was what she needed to believe then they would look again.

They expected the carpark to be empty but as they emerged from the narrow alley that led to the clinic from the main street, they noticed two women standing by a blue jeep, both talking on their phones. Niamh was suddenly excited, high with expectation that they might have some news of Harry, but all hope was instantaneously dashed when they introduced themselves as reporters. Louise was annoyed when Niamh agreed to talk to them.

"The more publicity the better," Niamh said.

They were still there at six-thirty p.m. It would be dark soon. Torn between whether to return to the forest with Louise or finish up with the reporters, Niamh, as usual, decided to follow logic and not her heart. She trusted Louise to be thorough in her search efforts, and she decided that their splitting up was the better use of their time.

Louise left, saying she'd pick her up when she was done and bring her home for some dinner. Even though Niamh had eaten very little, she wasn't hungry, and wasn't looking forward to forcing down more food just to placate her parents.

The streetlights began to flicker and switch on as Louise got into her car. Looking into the back seat, she checked for her raincoat. It sat in a sodden lump, still damp from earlier, and she wished the dismal weather would let up.

It was a typical cold March evening; so different to the previous day when the few hours of sunshine had promised better weather to come. Today the sun hadn't appeared at all and as Louise set off, not even the warm orange glow from the street lighting was able to give the illusion of warmth. Worse still, black clouds overhead indicated a heavier shower was on its way.

She drove lost in thought, guiltily aware that she was

relieved to be on her own, away from the sadness and stress she'd left behind at the clinic. Longing for the left-over macaroni cheese waiting to be eaten in her fridge at home, she briefly questioned if this meant she was an uncaring person. Accepting that her head ached and she was tired and hungry, she forgave herself. *I'm exhausted, not selfish*, she thought, knowing she would do whatever it took to help Niamh.

Louise hated driving at dusk. Missing the perfect twenty/twenty vision of her youth, varifocal glasses were like her best friends now; she hated to admit it, but she needed them and was lost without them. Cursing her failing eyesight when she met the full beam headlights of a car after a bend in the road, she flashed impatiently and the lights ahead dimmed obediently. Then just as the car reached hers, in a defiant act of revenge, she flicked up her headlights again. *Don't cross Louise when she's hungry, stressed and tired!* she thought to herself.

Recovered from her momentary blinding, at the furthest reach of her vision she thought she could see the outline of a child and a dog. Her heart jumped. The outline looked so familiar. Then she saw a glow of rainbow-coloured lights. Gripping the steering wheel more firmly, she leaned forward, her face as close to the windscreen as possible. Hardly daring to hope, she squinted to try to get a clearer view while the wipers swished back and forth.

It can't be Harry, can it? How could he suddenly appear, so close to home? That other car would have stopped. Surely the whole country is aware of the story by now? Louise increased the windscreen wiper speed to try and get a better view. Her headache and hunger pangs disappeared and a rush of adrenaline removed any thoughts of tiredness.

She followed the silhouettes as they moved under the lights at the edge of town. Four hundred yards further on and they'd have been in darkness, beyond the bounds of urbanism on a country road, with no footpath and no lights. The shape of them was right, so too the little rainbow-coloured display of light – the colours matched those of the fidget spinner Harry loved.

But he doesn't have that anymore so it can't be him, can it?

Closer now, and from within the range of her headlights, she could clearly see, without doubt, that it was Harry walking in the direction of home with Patrick.

"It is Harry, oh my God it is!"

They made an odd-looking pair as they stepped in and out of the shadows beneath the streetlights, a slight boy trekking along behind a large German Shepherd who seemed determined to keep walking.

Harry was wearing the same clothes he'd been wearing the day before, when he was first reported missing. There was a stain on the neck of his blue jumper, splattered baked beans perhaps, and his trainers were noticeably scuffed and mucky. Those who knew him would correctly guess he'd recently been sitting on a chair somewhere, swinging his legs and banging his feet against a wall. He liked the *thud*, *thud* noise – it calmed him.

A sleeve of his faded but favoured orange coat was also stained. With his nose running, every so often he lifted his arm and wiped it across his face, leaving the tell-tail silvery trail of snot behind.

Harry's hands looked raw with the cold, but he seemed unperturbed. One held the lead that attached him to Patrick's harness and the other held his colourful fidget spinner. Patrick was focused on his job: getting Harry home. He was the one in charge. Harry wasn't even watching where he was going most of the time, too engrossed in trying to keep the spinner turning. Just before Louise reached them, as the drizzle turned to rain, Harry hauled Patrick to a halt one last time and pulled his hood up, tugging it as far forward over his face as he could. He hated the rain.

Louise felt her blood pressure rise, tingling with excitement. She could hardly believe her eyes. Her empty stomach lurched up into her throat.

"What in the hell?" she said aloud in her car, "Sweet Jesus, it is Harry!"

There they were in the flesh, in the beam of her headlights.

"OK Louise, get a grip," she told herself, pulling in ahead of them. *I have to be calm*, she thought, *Harry doesn't respond well to stress.*

"Hey Harry, how are you young man?" she said in as normal a tone as she could manage while getting out of the car and keeping a little distance between them.

Patrick, pleased to see her, had stopped in his tracks. He was frantically wagging his tail and rubbing up against her looking for some affection. Although drenched and strongly smelling of wet dog, she didn't care, she was delighted to see him and briskly scratched his shoulder, all the time keeping a close eye on Harry.

He looked tired and his cheeks were rosey red. It was hard to tell if it was from exertion or just the cold. *Maybe he's been crying?* Louise thought.

"What are you doing out here on your own pet? Are you on your way home?"

There was no response. Louise didn't expect one – she was talking aloud to herself as much as to Harry, trying to normalise the madness of it all.

Harry and Patrick were both very wet. Wherever they'd been, they had clearly been out in the fog and drizzle for quite some time. Louise was also getting wet; in her excitement she hadn't remembered to grab her coat and it still lay across the back seat of her car.

"Harry, I'm going to give you a lift home. It's getting dark and your mammy will be worried about you. Will you take my hand?"

41

She knew this could go either way; Harry would quickly decide if he was going to cooperate or not. To her great relief, he held out his hand. She clasped it gently, feeling its coldness, and hoped the warmth of her own hand would seep into his as she led him to the front passenger seat of her car. Noticing he was tied to Patrick by the lead, she separated the two and helped Harry in first, fastening his seatbelt as quickly as she could. Just as she shut the door, another car pulled up.

"Is that Harry?" a voice said.

It was Mrs Nichols, a regular client at the clinic. She'd been out looking for Harry with all the other groups of people and was heading to the town hall to report back. Louise held Patrick squirming excitedly on his lead, her legs sodden from his wet hair.

"Yes, isn't it fantastic? I just found him, here on the road. He looks OK, I'm going to bring him straight back to Niamh."

Mrs Nichols clapped her hands together and began to cry with delight, muttering praises to the Lord, but Louise ignored her emotional response.

"Will you let the Gardai at the town hall know?" she said as she moved away to put Patrick into the rear seat of her car, his wet wagging tail still lashing the back of her legs while she spoke to Mrs Nichols. Then she sat back into the driver's seat, clicking on the child lock as she closed her door, not ready to lose her precious find. Mrs Nichols managed to stifle her sobs and disappeared into the distance to convey the good news.

Louise's heart was thumping, pounding in her ears, her initial shock turning to joy. Harry was OK! He really was OK. She glanced across at him and felt another flash of guilt, this time about how quickly she'd lost hope of finding him alive.

Louise didn't even think of phoning Niamh to prepare her for this unexpected find as she swung a U-turn in the road to travel back the same couple of minutes' journey she'd just completed.

"Right, let's go," she said, feeling quite ecstatic.

The car started to steam up as they drove on, and the air was heavy with the scent of wet dog. Louise opened her window slightly and turned up the heat as high as it would go. Harry lowered his hood and rubbed a little circle in the passenger window with the sleeve of his coat. He sat looking out and continued to play with his spinner while Patrick, unable to contain his excitement, moved forward from the back seat to plant a sloppy lick on the side of Louise's face. She reached towards him to push him back.

"Good boy Patrick, we'll be home soon." Louise was glad to see he seemed fine too. "Sit Patrick".

Patrick whimpered a little in protest but obedient nonetheless he sat himself back down on the seat on top of her coat, muddying the already damp material.

All the lights were on in the clinic when they drove through the front gates as though they were open for business. Niamh was in her office, the reporters having just left. What a miss this was for them! As she drove into the carpark the security lighting burst into life. It was only then that Louise thought, *I should have given Niamh a little warning.*

Reunion

Sat inside the clinic, Niamh noticed the external lights come on. She walked to the side window half fearing, and at the same time half hoping, for an emergency referral. The reporters had been a good distraction but she needed more. Surprised to see Louise's car back so soon, she thought she must have forgotten something and grabbed her coat and keys to head for the door to join her.

As Niamh unlocked the door, she stopped to listen. She could have sworn she heard Patrick bark.

In her car, Louise had quietened him with a, "Shush Patrick," as she came to a halt.

Pulling in to her usual parking space out of habit, she clicked off the child locks. Within a second, Harry's seatbelt was off. He hopped out of the car, followed by Patrick who jumped up and over the passenger seat in his haste to exit. Louise fumbled with her seatbelt and shouted as she opened her door,

"Wait, wait a sec. Harry, hold up!"

In the meantime, Niamh had unlocked and opened the clinic's door. She stood motionless, a featureless figure backlit by the waiting room lights behind her, unable for a second to take in the reality of the scene before her.

Another second and adrenaline took control of her body just as it had done with Louise only minutes before when she had found Harry. Niamh raced across the yard, calling Harry's name. When she reached him, she dropped down onto her knees. The sudden jolt of pain when she hit the tarmac slowed her momentum enough to allow her stop and momentarily reach out to gently hold her child at arm's length. She looked him up and down, examining his body, checking every little part of him, and then even though she knew he might recoil, she couldn't resist pulling him in to her. Niamh clung to him, her head buried in his nape.

Harry seemed surprisingly calm about it all and let his mother hold him, his spinner still turning in his hand. Louise stood over them, a spectator, with tears streaming down her face while Patrick jumped around Niamh in excited circles, lunging in to give her sloppy licks as he danced about. The rain continued to fall, glistening like fireflies around them; the tiny droplets of water reflecting in the brightness of the security lighting, bouncing off the tarmac as they fell.

Harry's hand softly swept across the side of Niamh's

46

face as he pulled back. He really did hate the rain. She turned towards him, cherishing the gentle stroke and he looked right into her eyes. Niamh searched deep inside that look, then he pulled away and she released her grip. Checking his path was free of puddles, he stepped sideways, and putting his hands over his head to protect him from the rain, he made a run for the clinic door and the dry interior, Patrick following behind.

Niamh sank back onto the ground, all her strength now gone. Louise reached for her.

"Where? Where did you find him?" Niamh sobbed.

Louise tried to pull Niamh up from the wet ground but Niamh couldn't move.

"How did you find him Louise?" her voice raised and more urgent now.

"Niamh get up," Louise begged, "You're getting soaked. Come on, get up and come inside."

Rolling sideways onto her knees, and with Louise lifting her from under her armpits, she managed to stand up. Arm in arm, they headed back into the clinic where Harry and Patrick were already settling in.

Harry sat on his favourite chair in the corner of the surgery; the chair he usually sat on when Niamh worked late. Normally, he'd be wearing his little handmade green scrubs, a present from his grandmother, which matched Niamh's. He'd almost outgrown them but Niamh knew he wouldn't like getting new ones. Harry got very attached to certain articles of clothing and his

47

scrubs, like his coat, were a favourite. Niamh hadn't had the heart to start the process of introducing better fitting ones to him yet.

Flinging his wet trainers and socks to the floor, Harry twirled his spinner and swung his legs as though it was just another normal late evening at the clinic.

Niamh knelt in front of him admiring his beautiful blue eyes, soft wavy blonde hair and round impish face. Still dressed in the same clothes she had last seen him in, he was a bit grubby but fine. Once again, she inspected him for signs of harm, noticing fresh bite marks on the back of his hands. The bite marks indicated he had been stressed and biting himself and she wondered what had happened to him. Holding his free hand – so cold – she looked again into his eyes. As he looked back at her, she touched his face and then he looked away.

"Oh Harry, I love you so, so much."

Niamh leaned in to hug him again. He didn't resist but as always he didn't hug back. She didn't care. He was safe and he was home.

Louise was speaking on the phone in the background when Patrick landed a heavy paw on Niamh's shoulder. She turned to pat him and then, concealing her face in his soft, wet, smelly coat, she began to cry. Unable to control the gasps, she let her tears fall freely. Patrick just sat, his tongue dangling. Louise hung up.

Feeling faint, Niamh stood up, then leaning forward

with her hands on her thighs she suddenly vomited. The relief was intense. Louise grabbed a chair and sat her on it.

"Put your head down."

Niamh sat for a minute with her head in her hands before looking up and smiling,

"Happy sick," she said and began to cry and laugh at the same time.

Louise didn't understand the joke because she hadn't known Niamh when she had morning sickness in the early stages of her pregnancy with Harry. She didn't know that Niamh had regularly vomited at any hour of the day, each time ecstatic to be pregnant and announcing, "Happy sick," to herself, or to whoever else was with her.

Grabbing a large roll of surgical paper, and with a couple of well-executed swipes, Louise made short work of the mess. Her veterinary nursing experience stood her in good stead on such occasions; she was in no way squeamish.

The colour began to return to Niamh's face and getting up, she walked across the room to where Louise was washing her hands. Encircling her waist, she leant into her back.

"Thanks Louise."

Louise continued to stare into the darkness of the window, following the tracks of rain as they wriggled down the pane. In the glass, she could see their reflection mirrored in the background, embraced in trust. She felt the warmth and sincerity of that hug and wondered what Niamh would think if she knew the whole truth – the truth she'd been unable to tell her. The truth that shamed her to her deepest depths. She was weak and always would be.

She turned when Niamh released her and watched her pull a chair as close to Harry as she could. Niamh ran her fingers through Harry's hair. Some days he liked this, others he didn't. Today, he liked it.

Turning back, Louise filled the kettle with water and flicked on the switch. The hissing kettle echoed in the now quiet and peaceful room. Little Harry was home, having appeared at the side of the road just as mysteriously as he'd disappeared the day before.

A few moments later, a blue flashing light announced the arrival of the Gardai.

The confession

A short time after the Gardai arrived, JJ burst through the door. He looked tired, dishevelled and stressed. His hair was still damp from being out in the rain. Wearing a baggy t-shirt which hung loosely over his jeans and displayed an obvious sweat patch between his shoulder blades, a smart pair of brown leather shoes were the only nod towards his more typical stylish attire.

Despite his unkempt appearance, he looked younger and fitter than his years. At sixty-five he could be mistaken for being in his mid-fifties. Like many men who take care of themselves, he was ageing well. In fact, he felt he looked better with age. He preferred his broader shoulders and his face now that it had lost its boyish soft lines. He fancied his jawline as chiselled – the look of a movie star. Even his greying hair contributed to his air of distinction. JJ was also far more assured these days – less defensively abrasive than he had been in his youth.

All in all, he often joked, "Much sexier as an older man!"

Like a strong wind, he blustered his way into the room. He was always a presence.

"Oh thank God," he roared, shattering the calm that had enveloped the surgery. A sudden cacophony of noise amongst the quiet and hushed voices gathered around Harry.

"Harry," he said as he headed straight to him, "Harry, you're OK!"

Unlike Niamh, he had no gentleness and pulled his son right up out of his seat.

"My boy, you're OK!"

Harry immediately stiffened and Niamh bit her lip. They both knew what was coming next.

"Oh fuck it, sorry, sorry Harry, I didn't mean to startle ya. Daddy didn't mean to startle ya. It's OK."

Yet it wasn't OK. Harry began to cry and scream. He moved his hand towards his mouth and bit into the back of it, pulling at the skin with his teeth. JJ snatched his son's hand away.

"No, Harry, no."

Harry screamed louder. The two Gardai who had arrived looked on, not knowing how to respond. Niamh found her voice.

"Jesus, JJ."

"I know, I'm sorry, I was so relieved to see him."

He started to stroke Harry's head while holding on to

his arm to keep his hand away from his teeth. It appeared to be having some effect, so he kept going. The little fidget spinner which had fallen to the floor when Harry had been so rudely pulled from his chair was returned to him and JJ gave it a twirl. Harry's cries lessened. JJ lifted him back onto his seat and continued stroking his hair until he was completely calm.

"He's been biting his hand again Niamh," he said looking back at her.

"Yes," she replied.

Niamh felt her blood boiling. She wanted to pull JJ off Harry and shout at him for being so insensitive to his son's needs but that wouldn't help matters. As always, she let it go to keep the peace. It was this – and JJ's complete inconsistency in following through on behavioural plans – that had ended the marriage for her. JJ just never quite got it or was it that he didn't want to get it? She was never sure.

Behavioural plans were a constant, but often slow, process and JJ always agreed to, "Give it a go," (his words) but then inevitably he'd resort to his own way of doing things. This generally meant treating Harry like any young child who needed reprimanding for misbehaviour.

Initially, Niamh hoped that given time JJ would recognise his son's needs were different, but over the years she grew increasingly frustrated. Eventually, she had been forced to concede to herself that JJ was never going to fully accept Harry as he was; that he honestly thought it was Harry who had to adjust to him, not vice-versa. She felt there would never be any movement forward on this and she'd been proven right. He continued to hint to her that Harry was often pulling the wool over her eyes.

With Harry sitting quietly, JJ moved away a little and turned around to face everyone. He began to speak, the bluster now gone, his tone contrite.

"There's something I have to tell ye," he said, looking down rather sheepishly. "I couldn't tell ye before, but now I can see Harry's safe, and well... I'm sorry, I hope I did the right thing?"

Louise was making some tea and the mugs clattered as she put them down on the table they used for lunch break. She paused to give him her full attention.

JJ's voice broke; this surprised Niamh – she'd never seen him cry and she wondered if he was about to. Generally, he was very restrained when it came to displaying his emotions. Perhaps this was what had attracted her to him in the first place. He was similar to her in that way; his restraint was something she understood. It meant neither of them had to deal with the other's true emotions apart from the times when things bubbled over. She looked at him. What was it he had to say?

Pulling a chair from under the table, she sat down. One of the Gardai indicated to JJ that he should sit too and directed him to the only other available chair. JJ was unable to look Niamh in the eye as he took his seat opposite hers but that didn't stop her scrutinising him, trying to glean a clue from his stance as to what he was about to disclose.

Louise pulled up two swivel chairs from across the room for the two Gardai to sit on and then stood further back from the group, leaning on the doorframe that led into the waiting room.

JJ and Niamh were now facing each other across the middle of the table, with only a few mugs between them. It felt like the mediation sessions they'd recently begun which were uncomfortable and tense, intended to help them sort through their family and financial affairs. They were so close they could almost feel each other's breath.

"I've been blackmailed," JJ almost coughed out. "I couldn't tell ye before, it's been going on for months. They said I'd never see Harry again; said he'd disappear off the face of the Earth. I couldn't risk it. I'm sorry."

He glanced up to see the reactions of the faces about him. There was a short lull and one of the Gardai suggested JJ take his time but Niamh interjected.

"What? Why? What did they want? What did you have to give them? I don't understand. JJ what are you saying?"

Confusion was evident in every line and crease of her face.

"I gave him nothing. I don't know why he let Harry go. This guy," he said, looking across at her now, "You don't know him Niamh, but I knew him when I was a young lad back in Dublin. He said he didn't want the development the company's working on to go ahead. He didn't say why. He thought I could stop it. I told him I couldn't."

JJ was desperate to get it all out in one go. He didn't give Niamh a chance to interject again.

"I tried to stall the development plans. Work thought I was mad, having a nervous breakdown or something. I told this guy I was a major supporter of the project and my boss would find my change in stance strange. I mean, it was a great plan, our best yet, but he didn't care. They were really getting pissed off with me at work Niamh and then, well… Harry disappeared."

He took a short breath.

"I was frantic Niamh. I told him I was nearly there, about to get the whole thing halted, and asked him to give me Harry back. Told him he had special needs and well… well, he must have listened. I don't know…"

It was one long rush of an explanation. Niamh was silent; she didn't know how to respond. Blackmail? She just couldn't get her head around it. They were normal people, living normal lives. Blackmail and kidnap was for TV – for gangsters – not for them.

One of the Gardai had taken his notebook out and begun to record JJ's words as he spoke.

"OK Mr Hennessy, you said you knew this person you spoke to, can you give me their name?"

Niamh couldn't help herself, "You knew who it was! You should have told someone! You should have told someone you knew who it was!" She was reeling.

"His name is John Williams," JJ said, avoiding Niamh's glare and directing his response to the enquiring Garda. "But us young lads, we knew him as Long John."

"OK," said the Garda, "Did he speak to you by phone or in person?"

Niamh interjected again from the far side of the table.

"I don't get it, why didn't you tell? He could have been killed!"

Astonishment had given way to anger, a steely tone creeping into her voice.

"By phone," JJ said continuing to keep his gaze firmly directed towards the Garda and not Niamh. He knew he was in trouble; he could feel the hole Niamh was burning into him from the far side of the table.

"OK great," the Garda said again, scribbling the name down and underlining it for emphasis. "We'll need to access your phone records. Was it your work or personal number?"

"Work," JJ replied.

Niamh couldn't take any more. She stood up, pushing away her chair with the back of her legs as she rose. It scraped on the tiled floor like chalk on a teacher's blackboard.

"Do we have to do this now? Can JJ answer your questions later? We still have to get Harry checked over; it'll be a late night for him. God knows what he has been through. Blackmail?" she said again, in disbelief.

She was angry and close to tears. JJ reached across to touch her but she recoiled.

"I don't understand why you didn't tell me or the Gardai? Anyone? They could've killed him," she seethed.

His hand slid back to his side. Sounding like a repentant child he said, "I'm sorry Niamh, I'd no choice."

Aware of the rising tension between the couple the Garda stopped his questioning.

"OK, emotions are high and everyone is tired. We'll need more information, Mr Hennessy. Would you accompany us to the station to give a full statement? The more information we have early on the better."

Niamh was still fuming and ready to confront JJ there and then. The pot had boiled over.

"Why did they pick you to blackmail? Why not take the boss's kids?" she spat out, unable to stop herself.

JJ ignored her and responded to the Garda's request.

"Of course," he said. Then, looking across the table to Niamh, he added, "Are you OK to head to the hospital with Harry? I'll meet you there later."

"Yes," came the curt reply as she violently shoved

her chair back under the table.

Trying to lighten the atmosphere with their departing words the Gardai spoke of their delight at Harry's safe return home, but Niamh wasn't listening. She was observing JJ, who was so keen to get away at the same time as the Gardai that he almost stood on their heels going out the door.

He blew a kiss to Harry as he went and said, "See you later," to Niamh.

They were all gone and the mugs and tea were left sitting on the table untouched.

Louise walked over to Niamh, who was standing in the doorway watching the cars as they departed the carpark. She put her hands on her shoulders and Niamh crumpled as she turned towards her. Sobbing, Niamh held on to Louise for support, trying not to drag her to the floor. All she wanted to do was curl into a foetal position and rock. She'd never felt so physically weak before; her legs barely supported her. It was one of the few times in her life she relished March's invigorating, cold evening air.

"I'll come with you to the hospital," Louise said after a minute or so, gently pushing Niamh a little further back from her.

"Sure, yes, great, thanks Louise," she said, wiping her eyes and quickly regaining some of her composure. They gathered up Harry along with some snacks and a drink. His trainers and socks were still wet so Niamh put them into a bag to bring with them and found his plastic surgery clogs to wear instead. *He'll be warm enough with them inside*, she thought. *Hospitals are always stiflingly hot anyway*.

After Niamh had checked that Patrick was in good health, she lovingly sent him to his bed in the corner of the room, thinking he deserved a break. Then the three set off to A&E where a different Garda would meet them.

It was still raining as they left.

A moment to reflect

The trip to the hospital was as awful as expected. The doctors and nurses were wonderful and so patient with Harry but it was a difficult few hours nonetheless. Harry hated the lights, new sounds and smells and had a rapid series of sensory overloads – which Niamh referred to as meltdowns – with short periods of respite in between.

Louise left as soon as JJ got there. Unlike Niamh, she was delighted he'd arrived so quickly. She had somewhere she needed to be and made a speedy exit.

JJ was quite uptight after his visit to the station. Sitting quietly in a hospital corridor was the last place he wanted to be, but he could see how tired Niamh looked. All her nervous energy had expired. He knew he'd not been there for her over the past couple of days. They'd both coped separately as always, and on top of that he'd upset Harry in the surgery. Wanting to be supportive, he tried his best to speed things along, ignoring the fact that Harry could not, and would not, be hurried. His efforts were less than helpful.

The atmosphere between them remained tense. Every time JJ tried to 'help', Niamh either responded with criticism or a judgemental looking glare. As far as she was concerned, he was interfering rather than helping. He suspected Niamh didn't want him there, and he was right.

Hasn't he done enough already by putting Harry in danger's way? she thought. *He's so wound up too, and Harry's picking up on it.* She bit her tongue for as long as she could before eventually snapping.

"Just leave us to it JJ. Go home and take a chill pill or something would you."

Huh, he thought begrudgingly. *Niamh's better off on her own as usual. I'm just a nuisance. Well, I'm not staying where I'm not wanted.*

"Harry just wants you anyway," came his dejected parting comment.

Forty-five minutes after he had arrived, JJ left the hospital, frustrated by what he perceived as Niamh's possessiveness of Harry. She had no time in her life for anyone else.

He wouldn't admit this to himself, but he was also relieved to be given a legitimate excuse to leave and eased his conscience with thoughts like, *I can't do anything right by Niamh where Harry's concerned, and she's just waiting to have a go at me anyway.*

In truth, they were both glad to get away from each

other. Neither had yet learnt to disengage from their marital relationship. It was a hurdle they regularly crashed into when they were together, especially around Harry.

After he left, Niamh thought about her family waiting for her at home. She wanted a bit of peace but they'd fuss around her and Harry and she didn't think she had the energy left to deal with that. Convincing herself that it was the right decision, for Harry's sake as well as her own, she phoned her mother to ask them to leave. Niamh asked as nicely as she could, but laid it on thick and heavy, using Harry as the excuse to avoid hurting her parents' feelings.

"Harry's all out of sorts, Mam. He needs the house to be normal. He doesn't like crowds at the best of times. No, Patrick will be fine for a few hours on his own and thanks for collecting him from the surgery... please Mam, you know the longer Harry's routine is disrupted the worse it will be."

Eventually her parents relented.

In the end, Niamh didn't get home until after eleven p.m. Harry had been unable to cope with the new environment and demands being made of him. He'd even refused to put his clothes back on when it was finally time for them to leave. In desperation, Niamh had to borrow a blanket and wrap it around him so she could get him into the taxi and home. Mick, the taxi driver, hadn't blinked an eye. He lived near Niamh and knew them well. He was the only taxi driver she ever used. It felt more like asking a friend for a lift home than using a professional service.

Poor, confused Harry fell asleep almost as soon as the car started to move. He didn't even wake as she carried him to his bed. After tucking him in, Niamh stood to admire the soft fuzzy hair on the side of his cheek, illuminated by his night light. Curled into a tight ball with his heavy weighted blanket pulled right up to his neck, only his adorable head was on view, a head that Niamh knew every part of right down to the freckle under his chin.

The arrival of that blanket two years earlier had given her great hope that Harry could be helped. His sleeping pattern had quickly improved. They no longer had to take turns to settle him every two hours, it was just once most nights now. Indeed, he was making progress all round – sometimes two steps forward and one back – but nevertheless, at the end of each year notable improvements were obvious.

Her tears started to trickle again, one after the other, a stream of salty water down her face as she stood there silently observing her son. She loved him, adored him. How would she have coped without him?

Five minutes later her bath ran deep and hot, steam filling the room. She left the light off and the door open so she could hear Harry if he woke. Patrick slept contently outside in the hallway between them both.

Lying back, Niamh breathed in the scent of roses and slipped as far down into the water as she could, luxuriating in the bubbles and enjoying the dim light. Inevitably she thought about Harry and JJ, but surprisingly not about the kidnapping. In her mind, she went back over how their little family unit had disintegrated.

She'd been in awe of the polished businessman JJ when they had first met. He was significantly older than her, but handsome and confident. Unlike many of her previous partners, he had seemed comfortable with her independence and had lacked the possessiveness she'd often encountered with younger men. She'd enjoyed the calm this new love brought with it.

Her parents had loved him too. They thought he'd guide her on the straight and narrow and rid her of what they called her 'romantic notions' about her business; as a businessman himself, they hoped he'd encourage her to expand her small, intimate-style veterinary practice into something larger and more profitable. Something more like the chain of veterinary practices they had in Dublin. Niamh always insisted she favoured intimacy over profit and they'd always worried that dream would lead to her insolvency.

She thought back on how short-lived their newly married life had been before she became pregnant. Although unplanned, they had been delighted and excited and had looked forward to becoming parents.

JJ had been so proud when his son was born; his 'little man' he'd called him, enthralled by the small person he'd made with his wife. Niamh had also secretly taken great pride in producing the first male on her side of the family; two granddaughters preceded him.

She had kept her maiden name when she married, not wanting her branch of the Regan name to disappear, and although Regan-Hennessy hadn't a great ring to it, her family and friends had taken great pleasure from the anagram of Harry's initials: HRH. Priceless, everyone had said, a little prince.

Combining parenting with work had not been easy. Harry was a poor feeder and sleeper. Millions of other parents have similar experiences, they'd thought, but slowly it became clearer that Harry was a little different in his development. He just wasn't making the same gains as other children his age.

Fiona, the Public Health Nurse, was the first to broach the idea of a developmental assessment with her, but Niamh had not been ready to have her concerns discussed out loud. It made it all too real. Indeed, initially she'd been quite annoyed when Fiona suggested one for Harry.

Then there'd been the long waiting lists. Those were some of the worst months – the waiting, the worrying and the not knowing – watching the vitally important early months and years of their child's life when the most development took place tick by.

Both of them had been stressed about their son, but neither shared their concerns. Instead, they had tried to stay upbeat and positive for each other's sake.

After all that waiting, suddenly there was one assessment after another. Numerous appointments followed with the Early Services Team, psychologists, physiotherapists, nurses, doctors, speech therapists, occupational therapists and social workers. These professionals became part of their lives. Some team members were a welcome part; others were just tolerated for Harry's sake.

When they had eventually received a diagnosis of autism, both Niamh and JJ had tried to deny it, hoping there was another possible explanation. It provided a reason for the difficulties they were experiencing with Harry, but the enormity of the diagnosis had taken some time to accept.

As he got older, more behaviours began to emerge. There was self-harm in the form of biting and pinching himself. He also began lashing out at them; there was endless kicking; his repetitive behaviours increased, and sometimes he refused to eat. It was a very difficult time.

Niamh recalled it had been quite early on when she'd decided that she should attend all the Early Services Team appointments. Even now she resented JJ for forcing that decision. He had never relayed enough information to her after he'd attended meetings or assessments, and he'd sometimes forgotten to ask a question she thought vital but he considered trivial. He hadn't seemed to care about the details like she had and Niamh wanted every detail, not a general, "Yeah, we saw everyone today, they just said xyz." She'd needed to know how hopeful or despondent they'd looked, but he had never been able to tell her that.

Although their words were always encouraging, she hadn't trusted words alone. She needed the other clues they unknowingly gave as to how much progress Harry had been making, revealed through their facial expressions and body language.

The constant criticism for not having all the information she wanted because of their differing perspectives frustrated JJ and became the cause of their first major row. The beginning of the end began that day. Niamh went into fight mode and JJ took flight. It had been as simple and as complicated as that.

Before they knew it, Niamh had acquired the dominant position in relation to Harry's care and JJ had been side-lined. He no longer maintained an equal status in the parenting game. As the parent who held all the information Niamh had to teach JJ what the team were teaching her, but because she'd been so emotionally invested in her son's welfare, she'd had far less patience than the team. And so it was that Harry became more dependent on Niamh.

Niamh saw JJ disengaging. Logically, she'd known what was happening – she'd not been ignorant to the effects of her actions – but emotionally she had been unable to give him a way in. She'd been a driven woman who had to ensure the best for her son. What Niamh hadn't known was that JJ had also seen what was happening, but he too felt unable to respond. He knew he shouldn't have relinquished his responsibilities without a fight, but he'd been so overwhelmed by his emotions that he gave up. Niamh had backed him into a corner and he had considered himself to be in a no-win situation. When he had tried to help, he was criticised. When he had tried to give Niamh a broader perspective, he was told he didn't care and when he had tried to reassure her that Harry would make progress in his own time, she'd said,

"So now you can't even be bothered to put in the work?"

If he pushed Harry to do better, he was told he lacked understanding. Nothing he said or did helped. In his eyes, he had no choice other than to retreat and let her get on with it.

Niamh resented him even more when he gave up, and in turn she started to notice a part of him resent his little man. He told her she was too soft with Harry and she watched him begin to compensate for that. He became less tolerant and more demanding of him. That had been the straw that broke the proverbial camel's back. It broke their marriage in two.

They'd clung to the edges of their black hole for as

long as they could, doing their best to hang on, but each crisis had pulled at their grip until sadly weariness won. They stopped trying to understand each other's responses, letting go and falling into the abyss instead. Despite living in the same house, they ceased communicating with each other, and had operated like robots about Harry. Eventually Niamh asked JJ to leave. There'd been no big final argument; he'd been ready to go and agreed to temporarily move into a rented house in the town.

In those first weeks, until their lives began to settle into new routines, there was genuine sadness, but it soon became clear the sadness was less consuming than the differences that had emerged.

When Niamh took time to reflect like this, she sometimes wondered whether they should have sought counselling. Would it have helped? Did she want help? Did he? Or had they both realised the mistake they'd made in the first place by getting married?

The more time that elapsed the less she worried about it. She felt she'd made the right decision. She and Harry were doing better on their own. There were no more arguments about the best route to take or the best therapy to follow. No more arguments about whose turn it was to do Harry's occupational therapy (some of which he had initially hated, like skin brushing). No more competitions about who was the most tired.

The water was starting to cool but she didn't want to

get out and continued to lie there, thinking. *Where had Harry found his old spinner*?

When they were in the hospital, she'd noticed that the spinner Harry was playing with was an old one, and she'd thought about the battle she would have trying to get it off him again. He'd been addicted to it and had been weaned off it months ago. The newer versions were less flashy with no lights and were mostly used for bedtime to help him settle and reduce his nocturnal activity of occasionally pinching his arms and legs. It gave him something to occupy his hands. Niamh still kept spinners on standby during the day but he was becoming much less reliant on them since she'd got rid of the ones that lit up.

She allowed herself to cry again, a little self-pitying this time. Quietly sobbing, careful not to disturb Harry, she watched her tears disappear into the rose-scented water. After she pulled the chain, she remained in the bath as the water lowered, willing the cold to give her the impetus to stand.

Blackmail, she thought as the last drops of water disappeared down the plughole. We're better off on our own.

Blast from the past

Finn couldn't have been asleep for long, it was only nine p.m. Startled by the knocking sound, he groggily made his way to the front door, switching on the porch light as he opened it. To his surprise, Louise was standing on his doorstep. He knew her from the veterinary surgery but he'd had no need to visit there in the last few months. She'd been very kind when Twitch had died, as had Niamh.

"Harry is back," she gushed. "I heard you were helping the Gardai with their enquiries earlier and thought you'd be relieved to know he's back."

Her breathing was audible, almost gasping as though she'd been running, but he could see her car at the side of the road from his doorway. She was beaming.

"He's back," she repeated, "Niamh's still at the hospital getting him checked over but he's fine. Cold, wet and tired but fine. I thought you should know."

Finn took a step back, still baffled by her presence as

news bearer on his doorstep. What to say?

"Oh good, that's great."

There was an awkward silence.

"Well, I just thought you'd like to know," Louise said trying to reign herself in a little, "Hopefully, we can all get back to normal soon. I'll let you go, you must be tired."

The tossed mass of curls on his head, ruddy hand mark on his cheek and the puffy eyelids had not gone unnoticed. She'd quickly realised she'd woken him from sleep.

"Yeah, grand, thanks."

"Night then," she said.

Louise stepped back and as she did so he closed the door, simultaneously switching off the porch light, leaving her standing in the darkness.

Louise's eyes were slow to adjust to the sudden lack of light as she gingerly made her way along the uneven path back towards the pavement and her car. Inside, a slight hint of vanilla had replaced the wet dog smell from earlier. *Money well spent*, she thought. Sitting in her seat she pushed herself as far into the upholstery as possible. It felt good, warm and comfortable. At last she was on her way home to her own house. Her hunger pangs returned as she started the car and a few moments later, her mobile rang in her bag.

"Hi Louise, JJ here." He didn't wait for a response. "Thank God Harry's OK. I just left them there now.

Niamh said there was no point in us both waiting. He looks fine though, doesn't he?" Again, he didn't wait for a response. "Niamh's so relieved. Well done you for finding them. All's well with the world again, hey?"

Louise sat upright, immediately on her guard. What did JJ want? He never phoned her and he could have thanked her before she left the hospital if he wanted to.

"Ah, yeah, JJ. This is a surprise. Is there anything wrong?"

She doubted there was as he had a fairly flippant tone.

"No, no, nothing wrong, all's well."

She felt her skin crawl, as though dozens of microscopic insects were suddenly scattering over her body.

"OK, well I'm driving now JJ. Yeah, really delighted Harry's back safe and sound. You'll all sleep well tonight. Talk to you soon, eh?"

She hoped that would be it. Perhaps he needed to let off a bit of steam and had no one to talk to, but why her?

"Sure… actually I was wondering if I could have a chat?"

Her stomach sank. Squirming, she re-adjusted her position in her seat, trying to maintain her concentration on the road while her head was whirling.

"Chat?" she said, "About what?"

"There's something I need to talk to you about but Niamh mustn't know."

"Hmm… a surprise?" Louise said hopefully, grasping at straws.

"Not exactly."

"Ah, JJ, I don't know. Niamh is my boss as well as my friend."

"It's nothing to worry about," he said with determination, "Can we meet?"

She didn't know what to say; the feeling of insects scurrying over her skin intensified. Anxiously she rubbed her face. Silence hung between them.

Louise barely followed the rest of the conversation, but by the time she hung up, she was aware that JJ was expecting a visit from her the following evening.

"Drive safely now," she heard before the dial tone indicated he'd gone.

After the call, Louise went into automatic pilot. Her body completed the tasks of driving for her, while her brain partially shut down. When she got home, she vaguely remembered intermittently seeing pedestrians and other cars on route but only as though she were a casual observer not the person in charge of her car.

She couldn't recall if she'd stopped at the crossroads and looked left and right or if she'd taken the long or short route home, yet somehow, ten minutes later, she'd safely arrived in her driveway with a sinking feeling in her gut.

Quickly going inside, she locked the door behind her. *Why am I so paranoid?* Though her mind was unable to register any danger in his actual words, she felt a real sense of fear.

Once more, her hunger pangs were forgotten, a shower her new priority. Standing under the running water Louise regretted that she'd not suggested meeting straightaway – now an entire night and day of worry lay ahead.

After showering, feeling cleaner but still uneasy, she headed for the fridge and the leftover macaroni cheese. Putting it in the microwave, she stood staring at it circling through the little window until the *ping* pronounced her food was ready to eat. It smelt good but the aroma she'd been anticipating and looking forward to for so many hours didn't revive her appetite. Her stomach churned. *What does JJ want?* she wondered while playing with the food on her plate.

A locked door in her brain began to open, taking her back in time; back to her last contact with JJ, more than forty years ago.

It had been in a supermarket carpark in Dublin. Louise was eighteen years old and hadn't seen or heard from Jonnie (JJ), who had been nineteen years old at the time, for more than a week. She'd known him for almost a year. Not hearing from him was nothing new but she was getting sick of it and was finally beginning to realise that he was just using her for sex after a good night out. They only ever met at parties and when he spotted her he'd make sure she knew he wanted her, but then afterwards he'd cut all ties until their next chance meeting.

This, her first sexual relationship, had been at a time in her life when she was regularly drunk and vulnerable. Jonnie had not helped; he'd only added to her woes by facilitating her further descent into alcohol and drug abuse. It was not a period Louise ever enjoyed looking back on.

The week before the carpark meeting, he'd not even bothered to make sure that she'd returned home safely after a party; he'd left her by the bins in an alleyway near her home. Louise had awoken the next morning feeling confused, ashamed and afraid. It was a turning point for her.

She continued to push the macaroni cheese around her plate as she reminisced. *God, why was I so desperate for his attention?*

That day he'd looked hungover when she spotted him in the supermarket carpark; she'd immediately noted the sunken eyes and gaunt face. Yet back then she'd thought him attractive, even with a hangover. There'd been so many times since then that she wished she'd been able to see past her youthful lust for him; it would have saved her a lot of heartache.

The young Louise had been so cross that day, and had intended to give him a piece of her mind; to insist he treat her with more respect. She'd marched right up to him and he'd seemed to take a moment to recognise her.

"Hey Fairy," he'd said, looking down at her.

Their height difference forced her to crane her neck to look up at him. As a teenager, Louise had been petite and fairylike; her nickname an apt one. Envisioning her youthful figure, she briefly grieved her slim, young frame which had over the years, from her point of view, somehow mutated into a solid square block. She was very square these days, she thought.

Louise remembered being determined to find out if he was serious about her. How naïve she had been to even ask! He'd looked at her as though she were completely stupid.

"No," he'd said in the most exaggerated and sarcastic tone she had ever heard, elongating the word unnecessarily. "I'm not into that Fairy."

"What do you mean?" she'd retorted.

"Look Fairy, if you're not into just havin' a bit of fun, let's forget about it. I'm a sex-only kind of guy." He'd smiled down at her, amused by her little outburst.

Even now, sitting at her kitchen table as a mature woman, Louise could feel the mortification, and the heat of shame rose to her face yet again as she recalled how foolish she had been.

Back then, unable to stop her lip from quivering, she'd been acutely aware that she was close to tears. She'd felt her watery eyes stinging and was so conscious of blushing, knowing her body's responses were giving her away and that he could see how embarrassed she was.

It had felt like he could read her inner thoughts; that he knew how much she enjoyed the attention he gave her – when he decided to. How much she loved him… yet he was laughing at her; at being able to manipulate her – such a foolish little girl. How easily she'd been duped by his charms.

"Fuck you!" had been the best she could muster before turning to walk away.

Louise recalled the sudden sharp pain. How his fingers had dug into her skin as she turned, grabbing deep into her upper arm. The weightless sensation as he'd yanked her backwards with such force she had lost her footing and ended up half-standing, half-kneeling, suspended in his grip. Subconsciously, she rubbed her arm. His grip had been so tight it had left a purple, yellow and green reminder that had lasted for over a week; a bruise with all five of his digits engraved in her skin.

"Don't you disrespect me you little tart," he'd growled down at her, "Doesn't take much to get you to spread your legs. You're a dirty fucking little bitch. Just a handy hole at the end of the day."

She'd been terrified. Louise remembered scanning the carpark, hoping nobody could hear his vile words but also praying somebody could see them in case he hit her and she needed help.

Then, just as suddenly, he'd let go and she'd dropped to the ground like a squeezed-out teabag. Louise pictured the young Fairy bracing herself for a kick but JJ had walked off, throwing both hands up in the air and giving her the middle finger as he left. He hadn't turned around to see how quickly she'd scrambled to her feet once the danger had passed; she had been grateful to be spared that humiliation.

Louise never saw him again after that day, not until she'd started to work for Niamh.

When she moved to the area and applied for her job she had no idea who Niamh was or who she was married to. Jonnie was nowhere in her thoughts and she certainly wouldn't have put them together. After all, Niamh was significantly younger than him.

It was shortly after she'd started her new job when she met him again. Still shoving her macaroni around her plate, she remembered that day too. Harry was only a toddler at the time and JJ had dropped by the surgery to pick him up. It was a Wednesday and Niamh and Louise had been about to start their mid-week late evening clinic.

She hadn't been entirely positive it was him at first, despite the sudden electric charge which surged through her when she saw a man entering the clinic who resembled Jonnie. He'd quickly disappeared into the surgery to collect his child and she'd remained in the reception area, welcoming the first few appointments through the door.

A quarter of an hour later, when JJ was about to leave the clinic, Niamh had taken the opportunity to introduce him to her. Busy trying to disentangle Harry's car seat from the nappy changing bag that he held in his hand – that same hand that had gripped her in it's vice all those years ago – he'd not taken much notice of her, more concerned at that moment with the entanglement. It had given Louise the opportunity to examine his features in more detail.

His scar identified him to her. It ran three inches along the side of his cheek to his ear, barely visible but unmistakable nonetheless. She'd known then for certain that he was Jonnie, and the realisation had taken her breath away. The fright caused her to splutter and cough. She'd had to leave the room to get a glass of water and regain some of her composure and when she'd returned he'd already gone. Niamh had apologised to her for his lack of interest and told her about his bad day at the office.

For months Louise tortured herself, wondering if he knew her. She'd changed so much physically and so had he. Even his accent and voice had changed. She didn't want him to recognise her. She had too much to lose.

After meeting him a few more times she became more confident that he didn't seem to remember her at all… That was for the best. Already very fond of Niamh, who was an easy boss to work for, she loved her job, new house and the area.

In fact, Louise had almost everything she'd ever wanted in her life and had no intention of moving again. Thinking it would all be ruined if her past with Jonnie was disclosed, she decided to say nothing about their past encounters.

Occasionally, she wondered if JJ recognised her at some point over the years but had also chosen to say nothing. Perhaps, like her, embarrassed by his younger self? She sometimes thought she caught him looking at her from a distance, but always managed to convince herself it was just her imagination. And as time went on with no definite indication that he recognised her, she allowed herself to relax, apart from the odd occasion when her conscience pricked at her for her pretence.

Louise had been shocked that JJ and Niamh were a couple and wondered what Niamh had seen in him? Was it the same traits he'd used to easily impress her? He was still attractive and possessed the same magnetic charm and charisma (when it suited him). Yet when she'd known him he had such a low opinion of women, of her at least anyway. Could he have changed that much?

She was sure Niamh wouldn't put up with a disrespectful husband. Niamh was accomplished, sophisticated and financially independent. She had certainly never given any indication she was being treated poorly at home. There had been a few days when she'd seemed particularly distracted in the clinic and hinted at the occasional row but that was it. It had to be different with Niamh. And Louise concluded over time that the problem with her and Jonnie must have been the drinking and drugs.

As Louise and Niamh's friendship grew there were days when she really wanted to divulge her story. It felt wrong to withhold such a truth, but it had never been the right time, and then too much time elapsed. There could be no breaking the secret now. There were too many complications. She could live with her regrets and her guilt for keeping her secret from Niamh. She had managed to keep secrets for years and anyway, Louise told herself, *I've no right to change other peoples' lives in order to ease my own conscience.*

Her skin began to crawl again. Why did he want to meet her?

Three very different Sundays

Niamh woke feeling like she'd run a marathon and then been hit by a bus. Every muscle ached. Stretching out her arms and legs she yawned loudly as she rolled over to stroke Patrick who was waiting by her bed, his tail thumping back and forth in expectation of going outside. It was six a.m. and the sun was yet to fully rise.

Today was going to be a glorious day. Life wasn't back to normal but it was close enough. Pulling on a pair of woolly socks, Niamh brought Patrick downstairs and let him out into the back garden. Like the previous days, it was a frosty, foggy morning. She breathed in the icy air, enjoying the cool shock to her system while she watched a robin hop from bush to bush, its feathers puffed up to keep warm.

Ordinarily she'd be flicking through her phone messages unaware of the garden beyond, but today she noticed the ice crystals on the leaves and the tiny drizzle particles that made up the fog. She noticed the coldness of the patio beneath her outstretched foot, which she was using to hold the door open, and even noticed the musty dewy scent of the early morning air. Today Niamh was fully alive – not just existing – and she was able to smile again.

The Gardai were due to visit at nine a.m. but didn't arrive until ten a.m. Harry was settled in front of the television watching his cartoons, a sure way to keep him amused while visitors were in the house. Patrick lay on his bed nearby with his head between his paws, raising it occasionally, inquisitively tilting it from side to side when Harry moved about on his beanbag or shouted out at the television. All was calm this Sunday morning.

"We won't detain you for long," one of the Gardai said, "Just need to follow up from yesterday."

Again there was a male and female Garda. They looked very young to Niamh but then, more and more people were starting to look young to her.

Surely it wasn't that long ago when these two young bastions of the law completed their schooling, she thought.

They asked if she'd had a quiet night and briefly filled her in on their enquiries so far. They also wanted to check if she had any more information. Had Harry disclosed anything?

Niamh remained diplomatic but she was irate. Over the years she'd become very good at hiding her frustration with others' ignorance. She was well aware that need begets knowledge and only too conscious of the fact that, if she were not Harry's mother, she'd be pretty ignorant too. Her life's circumstances had dictated her education, so it was with sarcasm rather than anger that she replied,

"Harry's not going to be able to help with yer enquiries."

They seemed embarrassed by their ignorance, but she didn't feel sorry for them. It was a life lesson they needed to learn. They'd clearly not fully informed themselves of the details of the case. 'Non-verbal' and 'autism' must have been in the file somewhere.

Twenty minutes later, they were gone. She was glad when they left as it gave her a few hours with Harry on her own; a normal Sunday before the weekdays began. Returning to the kitchen, she made herself a cup of tea.

There'd been lots of cups of tea over the last few days. *It's been like a death in the family, the lead up to a funeral*, and that thought evoked an image of Harry in a little white coffin. Her back muscles tightened and she arched her spine to relieve the spasm.

Niamh could see Harry through the open French doors connected to the living room and watched him swaying, humming and shouting while she sipped her tea.

The calm in Niamh's home was not reflective of the situation elsewhere. Elsewhere, trouble was brewing that Sunday morning.

Finn, distressed from his most recent bout of

questioning by the Gardai, had a very restless night. He was angry that JJ had pointed a finger of suspicion in his direction and was banging around the house for much of the morning, taking his frustration out on his furniture and fittings; unable to shift the idea that he needed to let JJ know what he thought of him.

JJ had barged into Finn's life without any invitation and he wanted him out of it. It was bad enough that he had accidentally run over and killed Twitch last July, but suggesting to the Gardai that he had kidnapped Harry as an act of revenge, well, that was a step too far. Finn knew his job at the school would be jeopardised because of JJ's accusations. He was enjoying his new role helping Harry with his Makaton signs; that was probably all ruined now. The principal wouldn't be able to let him return to work any time soon; he would have to put him on extended leave until the Gardai had cleared his name. Finn had no idea how long that would take. Worse still, all this attention was going to remind people of his past crime and no doubt he'd have to put up with rumours for years to come. He already knew what that was like. No smoke without fire, or so they said… and this time, it was all because of JJ.

Needing to ease his agitation and clear his head, he put on his coat and headed out for a walk, wishing he had Twitch to accompany him. As he marched along, he tried to decide what he was going to do about the predicament he found himself in. He wasn't going to let

JJ get away with this.

Like Finn, Louise was also very anxious about JJ's sudden involvement in her life. She'd been awake since five thirty a.m. unable to sleep. By nine thirty a.m. she decided she couldn't wait any longer and with a shaky hand picked up the phone to dial JJ's number. Misdialling on the first attempt, she tried again.

"Hello JJ."

"Mornin'," he said, "Or is it afternoon? Ha, ha. I had a bit of a lie-in so I've lost track, ha, ha. Just heading for a coffee to wake me up. What's up?"

JJ was lying. He'd also had a sleepless night despite the numerous glasses of whiskey he'd drunk. He too was worried about his meeting with Louise and, in the early hours of the morning, had sat up going over the different ways he might approach the subject he wanted to discuss with her. Casual, threatening or blunt and to the point? He remained undecided.

"I was wondering JJ, could we meet this morning instead of tonight?"

Fucking great, he thought, *she's keen to get it over with too*.

"Sure, I'm not far from ya now, I can drop by. Will you give me a coffee?"

He sounds so casual and at ease, she thought, *such a contrast to me.*

"Now? Well, erm…"

"Only fifteen minutes away," he said.

"Erm…" *Just do it,* she said to herself, *get it over with.* "OK then, see you in a few minutes."

Louise dropped the phone and, regretting her lifelong relaxed approach to housework, flew into a tidy-up tizzy. JJ had never been inside her house before; even on the rare occasions when he'd collected Niamh from there he had always texted from the car and Niamh had gone out to him. This suited Louise. She hadn't wanted him in her home; it was enough to deal with seeing him out and about.

Everywhere she looked there was stuff: a tea towel flung across the table, cereal bowls in the sink and a full bin bag left on the kitchen floor ready to be taken out to the roadside bin for collection on Monday morning. Various magazines and papers were on the table and chairs. Even the vacuum cleaner had been abandoned in the corner since last week, though at least it was easily accessible so she could suck up the breadcrumbs from under the table.

First, she dragged the bin bag outside the back door, not wanting to risk getting caught putting it out the front. She shoved things into drawers and under chairs and cushions, cursing and swearing as she did so, and a few minutes later the place was looking a bit tidier. Lastly, to gather her breath and calm herself down, she folded the checked rug on her armchair so the little frills lined up perfectly, and then draped it over the back of the seat.

Louise wasn't going to allow JJ to look down on her

for her lack of homemaking skills. She knew very well that would be an easy target and she needed to feel confident.

Looking at her flushed reflection in the hall mirror, she tidied her hair by putting it back behind her ears. She'd been in such a rush to tidy up she hadn't even thought about her appearance. *A tiny bit of foundation would've helped*, she thought, but there was no time. He'd be here any minute.

She was filling the kettle when the doorbell rang, still a bit breathless and flustered. The sound made her jump and she spilt some of the water across the countertop. Wiping it away with a tea towel, she threw the wet cloth into the sink with the cereal bowls, and taking a deep breath, she walked towards the door. His silhouette was visible through the glass. She let her breath go and opened the door.

JJ stood sideways, as though he were looking about to see if anyone could see him. No sloppy t-shirt and jeans for him today; instead a smart polo shirt and grey cord trousers completed his attire. He had a formidable air about him.

"Hi, come in," she said as casually as she could.

He clapped and rubbed his hands together, blowing some warmth into them.

You'd swear he'd been standing out in the cold for ages, thought Louise.

"Cold out there today," he said, as he stepped inside.

She turned and he followed her down the narrow hallway.

"The kettle's on," she announced as she entered the kitchen, trying to sound confident, "I'll get you that coffee. Instant OK?"

There was some introductory chat about Harry and Niamh and how glad they both were for his safe return, but it wasn't long before Louise couldn't cope with the suspense any longer and rather inappropriately blurted out,

"So JJ, what's the big deal?"

That feisty tone instantly reminded him of Fairy, the cheeky disrespectful madam she'd been when she was younger. Buttons duly pressed, his tactics were decided there and then, his old emotions getting the better of him.

She saw his face change as she asked the question. He lost his breezy casual look. His eyes seemed to harden and his face muscles tensed. She kept a firm hold of her mug and waited.

"Well Louise, you never did like beating about the bush, did you?"

Louise was paralysed; he seemed to be referring to the past. Did he know?

He continued on, "It's like this – I know me and Niamh have our differences but I don't want to worry or upset her anymore. She's been through enough. Don't you agree?"

"Yes, absolutely."

"So I decided I'd better have a word with you; clear a few things up so we can decide how to best manage the fallout if Niamh finds out."

Louise tried to tighten her jaw which had grown slack with shock.

"I don't understand JJ. What are you talking about?"

The only thing keeping her connected to reality right then was the heat from the coffee mug clasped in her hand. Her sole thought was, *please don't say you know who I am.*

"Do you remember me saying last night that the person who was blackmailing me was someone I knew years ago?"

"Yeah, I do JJ. What did you say his name was again?"

He didn't respond.

"Well Fairy, that person has a connection with me *and* you."

Fairy – so he knew. Louise started to panic. What should she say? How long had he known? Should she deny it? She couldn't speak.

He sat examining her across the table, searching her face for a reaction and watched as the blood drained from her cheeks. She avoided eye contact and lowered her head, frantically trying to put words together in reply. *He's known all along. He's always known.*

JJ recognised that he had the upper hand when his

words silenced Louise and decided to take a more gentle approach.

"Look, I expect you recognised me at some point just as I recognised you. It's been a long time and a lot of water's run under the bridge, hey?"

Louise still wasn't able to respond and continued to sit with her head lowered, heart thumping, staring into her coffee as though suspended in time.

He continued, "When I realised, I decided to say nothing. You hadn't said anything and... well, we didn't part on good terms so I thought we should let bygones be bygones. I expect you thought the same."

Louise just couldn't find her voice, her thoughts continuing to silence her. *He's known all along.* She couldn't believe it. She felt like she was eighteen years old again, catapulted back to a time when she had felt powerless and at the mercy of those around her.

"Hey, Fairy, are you all right there?"

JJ needed some kind of a response to make sure she had understood. This was important.

"I wanted to forget the past," she blurted, "Why are you doing this now? Could you not have just let it be?"

She wasn't confident. Her voice broke and she sounded defeated; keeping her head down, she was unable to look at him.

"Look Fairy," he said.

The repeated use of her old nickname finally spurred her on to retaliate.

"Stop it! Please stop calling me that. I'm not Fairy now and haven't been for a long time."

The brief retaliation felt better than the despair which was engulfing her.

"Sorry, Louise then. I'd rather not be having this discussion either. Just bear with me for a minute and you'll understand why."

"OK," she mumbled and waited again.

JJ gathered his thoughts. He wasn't sure how best to proceed. *It's strange*, he thought, *no matter how many times you rehearse a speech, it never quite seems to work out the way you planned.*

"OK, so can we start by agreeing that if Niamh found out we were… intimate, shall I say, with each other years ago and we'd kept that secret from her all this time, well, it would be distressing for her. Yeah?"

What is he getting at?

"JJ, I could lose my job as well as my best friend. You and Niamh are already going your separate ways. What do you want?"

"Hear me out, will you. Remember when we were a thing and that guy Williams from the youth club and me were suspects in the disappearance of that young lad, Eoin, from the youth centre… and we were exonerated."

Louise nodded. She remembered clearly. It was one of the most humiliating experiences of her life; the shame of it all.

"Yes, I remember."

The look of disgust on her parents' faces flashed before her. The Gardai had never had reason to come to their door before, unlike many of the neighbours, yet it was their eldest daughter Louise who'd prompted their visit; instantaneously they'd become no better than the rest of the residents.

She remembered how embarrassed she'd been when the Gardai had asked her if she'd spent the night with Jonnie, and how she'd wished she could tell them that she couldn't remember where she was that night. Of course they would have asked why, and she'd been afraid Jonnie might tell them exactly how drunk she had been, and worse still, what else she'd taken. Anyway, he'd already told her she had spent the night with him, so she must have. She'd felt ashamed for being unable to remember being with him.

If she had denied it, that would have saved further embarrassment for herself and her family, but she couldn't have done that to Jonnie. She was in love with him, or at least she had thought she was.

So Louise had to say, "Yes."

And she'd endured the Gardai dismantling her character with their expressions and accepted the rage and disappointment in her father's eyes. So yes, she remembered it well.

"Fairy," JJ broke into her thoughts, "He's the bloke who's been blackmailing me."

"Who? Williams or the young lad? I still don't get it

JJ."

"Williams," he said, "Long John," as though that should be obvious to her. "Look, they'll be going into his history to find out why he might want to blackmail me. I'm part of that history and so are you. I hope it doesn't come up but, just in case, you were with me that night, you were my alibi and they might want to clarify that with you again, if they trace you to here."

Without thinking and still traumatised, Louise responded.

"Jesus JJ, I won't be able to remember! Sure, I didn't know where I was that night. You told me I was with you, so I said I was, but I really don't know. Was I really with you? Is that what this is about?"

His expression changed again.

"Listen Fairy, you were with me. For fucks sake, why would you say anything else at this stage? You were with me all night. Jesus that's the last thing I need now – you changing your statement. What the fuck are you talking about?"

He was clearly on edge. He'd hoped after today's visit that he would leave reassured that she'd be ready for any questions from the Gardai and that she'd stick to her story. Now he wasn't so sure, and he needed to be. Leaning across the table and locking her into an intense stare, he put his hands over hers, pressing them into her mug.

Louise wanted to recoil but she was afraid to. He was

angry. He took on a gentle but determined tone while keeping a firm, uncomfortable grip on her hands.

"I'm sorry, I'm stressed. Louise, look, I came here to give you the heads up, to give you a chance to get your head around this and not be taken by surprise if they do follow you up. I hope they don't and if they don't then neither of us need disclose anything about our past, but if they do, I'm sure the Gardai won't have to tell Niamh about every detail of their enquiries, especially, you know, in these circumstances. I'm sure they'll be sensitive about the situation when they realise Niamh doesn't know about our past relationship. It'll all pass over quick enough… unless you start doubting the truth and change your story."

He paused for a moment, then holding his stare, he pressed her hands even harder and with great emphasis said,

"You were with me Louise. Niamh need never know. I don't know about you, but if I was Niamh, I'd worry we'd kept the old flame burning and that's why we were so secretive, only coming out into the open when we had to. Stick to your story Louise. The Gardai can be very discrete."

With that, he pulled his hands away and got up, knowing he'd made his point.

Louise knew a threat when she heard one.

Louise

Louise felt wretched. JJ's veiled threat to disclose her past was tormenting her. Knowingly or not he'd catapulted her back to one of the most painful periods in her life. Her saddest moments were no longer at a distance from her; the healing effect of time had evaporated. She was a teenager again, shrouded in a sense of shame, fear, rejection and inadequacy. Mentally and physically weakened by JJ's threat, her memories all came rushing back.

Louise was the oldest of four children. Her parents worked hard but making ends meet had been difficult. They endured long hours in low-paid jobs, and to reward themselves drank heavily in their leisure time, just like their neighbours.

The family lived on the south side of Dublin, not by the manicured streets and park areas facing out to the sea, nor those places people liked to go to for a meander around the shops at the weekend. They lived in a small council estate comprised of four, low-rise blocks of flats; each block two storeys high, hidden away from the pretty seaside facades. 'Prison block H' they'd bitterly called it.

It had been just like a prison with its long grey corridors and evenly spaced doors that signalled the entrance to each residence. The corridors carried sounds like an echo chamber and funnelled the coldest winds in winter.

Louise had hated the dark and dank stairway that led to their second floor flat. The smell of stale beer and urine always indicated that she was nearly home, and as she got older she'd often held her breath going up those stairs.

Their door was halfway along the upper corridor. When it was first painted, it had been bright yellow but by the time Louise was in secondary school the paint had peeled and faded. Black kick marks near the bottom and dirty finger marks around the doorknob were the most predominant features by then. It was generally ajar when she got home from school so that Mrs Nichols, their next-door neighbour, could hear if trouble was brewing with her younger siblings. They got home from school by four p.m. and her mother left for work at four-thirty p.m. Louise didn't arrive home until five p.m. Mrs. Nichols covered the half an hour gap Monday to Friday in return for some of her mother's good will when she needed a small loan of money. There'd never been a dinner waiting for Louise, nor a welcoming hello from her parents.

She'd shout, "I'm home, Mrs Nichols," as she walked by her neighbour's open door, closing it as she passed by.

In the musty-smelling interior of her own home, her two sisters and brother would be sitting in front of the television in the corner of the room, cereal bowls in hand, watching children's afternoon TV.

On the rare occasion her mother was home when she arrived in from school, she'd be rushing about in a flap late for work. Generally, Louise only saw her at breakfast time when she was always tired and irritable after her night shift, needing to sleep and eager to get her children out the door to school as quickly as possible. It had never been a pleasant start to the day.

Louise knew deep down her parents loved them all; it hadn't been a home without love, yet they had struggled to express it. When she was younger it appeared to her as though they'd not the time nor energy to display it, making ends meet their main concern. Then, as she'd got older, from her viewpoint, they became more concerned about how much she (as the eldest) could do to help them out at home, devoting more time to chastisement and criticism than tenderness.

Her favourite memories were from birthdays; they were never forgotten and the children were always made a fuss of. The few hours on Christmas morning were also a joy, full of love and laughter until the effects of cider consumption took hold of her parents. After that the siblings left them to it, scattering to their rooms or out into the cold to join the other festive orphans of alcohol abuse.

At six p.m. every evening her father arrived home from work. He was a short and slightly built man; the parent Louise most resembled when she was a young girl. He lived in a dream world of better things to come and would be constantly planning one thing or another to improve their situation. Sadly, for one reason or another, his ideas failed to materialise and nothing had ever changed.

Louise's mother generally prepared the raw ingredients for dinner before she left for work and Louise cooked them when she got home from school. She always had the meal ready on the table for her father's return and he'd devour his food like a vacuum, not speaking until his stomach was full. After his dinner, he'd have a bit of fun with her younger siblings, even if that fun involved teasing them, then he'd fall back into his chair and doze.

Later in the evenings, their neighbours – her father's drinking buddies – visited and Louise and her siblings retreated to their bedrooms to complete their homework. Louise shared her bedroom with her two sisters, with the sole boy enjoying a bedroom to himself.

If it hadn't been for the nice nun who'd encouraged Louise at school, she wouldn't have bothered doing her homework at all. In the living room the noise of chat and laughter over the sound of the television made it very difficult to concentrate. Even in the confines of her room there had been constant in and out traffic, the door opening and banging closed each time her sisters came and went, be it arguing or playing. Their neighbours had joined in with the distractions too. They'd stop by to say,

"Great girl."

"Aren't you the little scholar."

But these comments had nearly always been followed by a request or a question,

"Has your mother any more of that lovely boiled cake?"

"Would you be a good girl and run to the shop and get…"

At times, it had all felt like a conspiracy engineered to make her fail at school. Such unforgiving distractions she could have done without in her early teens, but she remained keen to show the nun who believed in her just how good she was.

In the girls' room, there'd been two bunk beds, one on either side, with just enough space in the middle for a chest of drawers which overflowed with clothes. This was centred under a window that faced onto another similar block of flats behind them. The musty smell was strongest in the girls' room, where black mildew spots stained the net curtain; a curtain that was often stuck to the windowpane by the condensation which trickled down behind it.

Her mother occasionally took the net curtain down and put it into a bucket of bleach to get rid of the mould spots, always hanging it up again the same day, dry or damp, to stop the neighbours from looking in. As a child, Louise had been fascinated by how speedily the mildew redeveloped. Like regularly watered cress seeds scattered on top of damp cotton wool, the mildew always sprouted again without fail, its growth accelerating during the winter months when there was more moisture in the air.

The family were respected in the area and had a good reputation. None of the children got into much trouble, unlike many of the neighbours' offspring, and Louise's parents had been very proud of that fact. But by her mid-teens, Louise had tired of the drudgery. She was tired of being good and responsible. Her friends were out having all the fun and she was ready to stretch her wings.

Weekends, the time when her parents 'de-stressed' after their long working week, also became the time Louise wanted to unwind. Combining school with part-time housekeeping and childminding had been hard work for her. Just like her parents, who spent much of their weekend drinking at home with friends or in the local pub, when they could afford to, she also began to 'socialise'. Being the eldest child the expectation had been that she'd babysit when her parents went out, but Louise had other plans.

Her 'Irish twin' sister Rose, only eleven months younger than her, was quieter, shyer and a bit of a home bird. She'd no strong desire to spread *her* wings, and Louise had no difficulty persuading her to cover for her while she went out. She had no money but her friends shared their cider and cheap hand-rolled cigarettes with her. It had been enough until she was sixteen years old.

Not long after that birthday, the well-meaning nun at her school happened to spot her out 'socialising' one day and decided a weekend job might be just the incentive she needed to keep her on the straight and narrow. She arranged a few hours of work for Louise at a local café on Saturday mornings. Louise was delighted! With money in her pocket, her drinking began to flourish.

All the same, despite the distractions and alcohol consumption, by the time Louise was seventeen-and-a-half years old she had somehow managed to complete her secondary school education with a presentable Leaving Certificate; the first in her family's history. It had been a proud moment for them all.

After leaving school, she continued to work at the café and they increased her hours. As an earning member of the family, she was now expected to contribute to the family's income, so at the end of each week she gave half of her wages to her parents for her upkeep. Louise had begrudged doing this as the extra cash hadn't resulted in better circumstances at home, just an increase in her parents' drinking.

Simultaneously, her own drinking habit began to escalate which made it much harder for her to keep her job. By the time she'd turned eighteen, she'd become what her friends called, "A bit of an alci."

Despite their own alcohol abuse, her parents worried about her rapid decline. Blind to the fact that their own drinking habits were a problem, they'd been powerless as they tried to curtail her activities – as far as they'd been concerned, they were able to function 'normally', unlike their daughter, who didn't seem to be able to manage her drink at all. At their wits end, the only meaningful threat they had was that she'd be kicked out of home if she lost her job. Louise made sure not to lose it.

Around this time, she met Jonnie at a party and fell for him immediately, seduced by his flattering advances. He became her first love. They began to meet regularly at parties and he quickly introduced her to recreational drugs.

Louise's friends had warned her that he was trouble, and just using her for sex, but she'd thought she was in love. She hadn't wanted to lose him. He'd been the only person saying sweet things to her at a time when everyone else seemed to be finding fault. She had daydreamed endlessly about him when they weren't together and built their relationship up into something much more than it was.

With her social life almost out of control, she was often dazed and distracted, and had been put on a second warning at work. Her parents couldn't understand what was going on with her and were angry and disappointed. They'd felt they had been supportive parents. They'd never risen a hand to their children as their parents had to them and they had given Louise opportunity; she had a decent education and privileges they'd never had. Why was she wasting it?

The situation grew worse and Louise started to experience blackouts. Often she couldn't remember the events of the night before, grateful to wake up in her own bed the following morning.

Then the Gardai came to the family home to ask Louise where she had been on the night Eoin went missing. Jonnie had been one of the last people to be seen with him, they'd told her.

That day, Louise had been suffering from a merciless headache and felt sick to her stomach. She'd been forewarned by Jonnie that the Gardai might visit and thankfully her parents had been out when he'd stopped by. They hadn't known about him and she'd wanted to keep it that way. If they'd known she had a boyfriend there would've been repeated warnings about not getting pregnant. Having a child out of wedlock was one of the worst things you could do in her parents' eyes.

Society and the church made them turn their backs on such mothers.

Jonnie had said to her, "Thank God I was with you all night or I'd be in right trouble."

She'd no choice but to believe him because she couldn't remember where she had been that night.

She'd waited petrified, hoping the Gardai would come and go before her parents got home. She hadn't wanted them to hear her confess that she had spent the night with Jonnie. Unfortunately for her, it ended up being her father who answered the door. He'd been shocked to see the Gardai standing on his doorstep and initially thought Louise's mother or one of her other siblings had been involved in an accident. His relief was short lived when they'd asked to speak to Louise. The Gardai asked their questions and Louise gave her answers, including that she had spent the night with Jonnie. Then they'd left.

Her father reacted badly; he'd been furious. It was the first and last time he ever slapped her. She could remember that slap to this day; the scalding heat of it across her cheek. As much as it had hurt, even worse was the shame she had brought to her parents.

It was her penultimate fall from grace. She'd never forgotten that either.

Soon after the interview with the Gardai, her job at the café was lost; so too her relationship with Jonnie. Louise had not known that day in the carpark, the last day she thought she'd ever speak to Jonnie, that she was pregnant.

Shame on you

Louise tried to conceal her pregnancy for as long as she could, but she had awful morning sickness and by her tenth week her mother had discovered the truth.

In those early weeks, her parents' responses were confusing. Her mother fluctuated between complete condemnation of her and overwhelming empathy, while her father kept his distance and barely spoke to her. He hadn't even been able to look her in the eye. One thing, however, was made abundantly clear: her pregnancy had to remain a secret as it would bring great shame to her and her family.

With no idea what to do, Louise had spent most of her time curled up on her bunk bed crying into her pillow until her mother decided to take control of the situation to protect her reputation. Her solution came in the form of Angela, a third cousin on her father's side whom Louise had never heard of. She was an older lady and she and her husband lived outside of Dublin further down the country. Louise hadn't been told where; it was felt it was better she didn't know.

It never crossed her mind to question her mother, she'd been too overcome with anxiety, but years later, in hindsight, she would see that these 'relatives' were really complete strangers; a convenient extended family connection that made her problem disappear.

"They've tried for a child for many years but aren't able to conceive," her mother told her. "They are desperate to have a child; if you agreed to give them your baby, they'll fund a university course for you in return. It'll have a better life with them. You simply have to give the baby up. It's the morally right thing to do. They're good people. If you don't give it away, it'll ruin your life."

Each day the rhetoric had been repeated to her. She was terrified of being shunned by her family and the wider community. It couldn't have been made more abundantly clear to her that sex before marriage was a sin, and she saw no way out other than to do as her mother suggested. She couldn't keep her baby. It would be a bastard forever more.

"Do you really want to give your child that label for life?" her mother had said. "If you really want what's best for your baby, you'll do what's right and give it a proper family."

There had been a very strict stipulation in this arrangement of convenience, and that was that Louise would never make contact with her third cousin. She would never enquire about Angela's surname or mention the child again. By then, Louise had been totally convinced that she didn't want the baby anyway – there was too much shame attached to being an unmarried mother – so that arrangement was fine by her. She had stopped thinking about her child, she had only felt relief that things would be 'fixed'.

Resigned to doing the 'morally' right thing, in order to protect her own and her family's reputation, her mind had been immobilised by shame and threats of abandonment. Jonnie wasn't given a second thought. How quickly Louise's love had turned to hate.

Louise was sent to stay with her cousin Maeve, who lived in England, until the baby was born. Maeve was a nurse in her early thirties. She too had fallen pregnant some years earlier and had given her baby up for adoption.

"Everyone will come out a winner," her mother had said to her as they hugged goodbye at the Holyhead ferry terminal.

Inevitably, the birth day eventually arrived. That day, Louise had second thoughts. It was a sunny day but her room was darkened by the drawn curtains. Only Louise and Maeve were present, although from time to time Louise thought she could hear voices downstairs. She had liked and trusted Maeve who had been kind to her during the months they'd spent together, but Maeve hadn't said who the voices belonged to so she hadn't asked; neither of them really wanting to think about Angela and her husband expectantly waiting downstairs.

There were no pain killers available and Louise was conscious of having to be quiet.

"The walls are thin, shush, shush," Maeve had implored, "It'll be over soon."

Louise grunted, grinded, squirmed and sweated for hours, at times thinking she was going to die. The pressure, the pain and then the extraordinary relief at the point of delivery.

He hadn't cried like she'd thought he would but she heard him take his first breath and had felt a sudden urge to hold him, just for a moment, to see what he looked like. That's when the knocking on the door started, gently at first but quickly increasing with urgency. Maeve had tried to quiet Angela on the far side of the door, but she'd been desperate to see her new son, anxious to take him away, afraid there might be a change of mind.

The intensified knocking gave Louise the opportunity to take a quick glimpse of her baby boy. Maeve had to lie him down on the seat beside her to unlock the bedroom door.

"Shush, I'm coming. Have a bit of patience would ya?"

A brief glimpse was all that she got. It had been futile

trying to commit his features to memory, but she'd tried anyway. She watched him as he scrunched up his face and stretched his arms and legs beneath the white sheet that swaddled him, his little fingers escaping and peeping over the edge. He'd such tiny fingernails. A quick smell of him as she'd reached across for a touch of his silky hair. Then she'd had to pull her hand away; Maeve had returned to pick him up. Turning towards the door with the child in her arms, Maeve blocked Louise's view of her son… Just like that he had disappeared; gone; taken into the light that streamed through the open door. He had been handed into the arms of another more worthy mother. Louise had wanted to shout,

"Wait, just wait! I'm not sure. Give me a minute, just a minute."

But with the exchange done, she'd stayed silent… Her baby was gone.

Afterwards, Louise watched her cousin busily dispose of the bloodied sheets containing the placenta. She'd been horrified by the sight of so much blood and her sudden fear of dying momentarily outweighed the loss of her child. It took her cousin some time to reassure her that all was well. She'd told her how good she'd been, and how it was all for the best. Then pulling back the curtains to let more light in, Maeve had left Louise on her own to rest.

That was when Louise first noticed the small piece of caul from her child's forehead adhering to her fingertips. She had sat for a long time, crying and staring in disbelief at that little piece of caul stuck to her fingers, and when the sunshine streaming through the window highlighted the tiny dust particles floating in the air, she had covered it over with a tissue to protect it.

Overwhelmed with emotion Louise's heart broke that day and it never fully recovered. Back then she had felt she'd made a huge mistake and the thought that, *I should have kept him*, was a thought that had never left her. Over the years she regularly lay awake late at night wishing she could turn back the clock. Wishing she could right the wrong she thought she had made in letting someone else take her baby. *If they'd only given me a few minutes with him then maybe it would've been easier*, she often thought. She'd felt so connected to her little boy… but he was gone.

Louise stayed in England after the birth, moving into a bedsit courtesy of her new benefactors, and started her chosen course in veterinary nursing. She had always loved animals and this was the next best thing to her dream job. To be a veterinarian required top grades and that was beyond her reach. They'd said she could do anything she wanted to, so she had chosen this.

Many, many tears were shed in those first few weeks after the birth. Maeve tried to help, reassuring her that her emotions would pass, yet she'd cried even more months later when she was no longer certain she could recall her baby's face.

As months turned into years, her acute distress receded, but it never went away. She never forgot her baby boy, but she did move on; Louise had no real choice, convinced by all those who loved her that it was the best decision she could have made for her and her child.

She threw herself into her studies and did very well. There'd been no more fall back onto alcohol and drugs. Louise was determined to do better. She wanted a better life. After the course finished, unable to face returning home, she'd stayed in England, working in various veterinary practices for the next ten years.

When she eventually return to Ireland, she was the star of the family, the eldest daughter who'd done well for herself; the one who had escaped 'Prison block H.' Louise of course never felt this way about her achievements. She never forgave her teenage self for being so weak; she hated herself for allowing her life to be dictated by others. She hated herself for giving her child to strangers. She hated herself for still feeling ashamed all these years later. Her sense of being a fake, of not being worthy of respect and admiration, ran deep. Her success in life was a constant reminder of her failures too.

JJ's revelation brought back many memories and she took recourse to re-opening the envelope she rarely opened anymore, lodged at the back of her bedside table.

Sliding her finger underneath the barely adhered flap, she carefully bent it back. Inside she could see the tissue paper and took it out, gently teasing it apart. It held the tiny piece of her child's caul, the bit that had adhered to her fingers on the day of his birth. She'd kept this sliver of skin-like material safe all these years as an everlasting reminder of her son; a son his biological father knew nothing of.

The office

JJ was back at work, sitting in his office, observing the comings and goings from his window. Today was the day Bellingham & Company were finalising their latest project: the re-development of Dominic's Park. In a few weeks, the site would be levelled and groundworks begun.

He was painfully aware that he wasn't the most popular member of his team right now, having spent the last few weeks slowing progress with his dissention, and was keen to put everyone straight on the reason why.

News had travelled throughout the building about Harry going missing on Friday and being found again on Saturday evening. JJ had already received several claps on the back with comments such as, "You shouldn't be at work today," and "You should be home celebrating with your family," but his well-meaning colleagues weren't aware that he found being at work much easier than being with his family.

At 9.50 a.m. he got up from his desk and walked through the open-plan office across to the large conference room at the far side of the building. He opened the door, looked around and headed for the coffee machine. He was the first to arrive for the ten o'clock team meeting, and keen to get going. Taking a shortbread biscuit to accompany his coffee he took his seat. One by one the remaining five members of the team arrived.

His boss Sandra, a portly middle-aged woman who was always on her mobile, was the last to enter. She was still engaged in conversation on the phone when she took her seat. A colleague put a mug of coffee on the table in front of her and she acknowledged the gesture with a nod of her head. JJ wasn't that fond of Sandra; he'd always felt he could do a better job than her, given half a chance. Likewise, Sandra wasn't too fond of JJ.

After finishing her telephone call, she started by acknowledging Harry's safe return and wished JJ and his family well. JJ waited until she was finished; until he was sure she was about to start the meeting proper, before pushing his chair back and standing up. He cleared his throat and said,

"I'm sorry Sandra, but before we start, there's something I need you all to know."

He could see the strain on her face, the taught lip, the slight narrowing of her eyes. She'd just about had enough of JJ these last few weeks; so much so that she

118

was actually considering a period of enforced leave with a view to terminating his post.

"I need you to know why I've been trying to dissuade you from going ahead with this development. I'm very aware you must have found my change in stance frustrating, and I appreciate how patient you've all been with me these past few weeks."

JJ glanced around. He had the attention of all his colleagues. He cleared his throat again.

"I want you to know that I've been blackmailed. The blackmailer wanted me to stop this project from going ahead. Harry didn't just go missing, he was kidnapped."

Someone gasped a little, then silence. Everyone was fixated on him, astounded, waiting for him to continue.

"It's been going on for a number of months, cumulating in Harry's abduction. I want you to know I've never been against this development. It's a great project," he stressed, "and I'm delighted we can now get going."

Sandra intervened,

"Wow JJ, how awful! You poor thing. How horrendous." She was genuinely taken aback. "Did the Gardai know?"

"No, Sandra I told no one. The blackmailer had been threatening to hurt or kidnap Harry or Niamh, and I couldn't risk it. They know now of course. They asked to call here today; they want phone records. I hope that's OK?"

119

"Yes, of course, JJ, that's not a problem."

Sandra would have liked to sympathise more, but she was keen to find out why JJ's blackmailer wanted to stop their redevelopment. She knew it was going to sound more inquisitive than concerned but she had to ask.

"Why did they want the project stopped JJ?"

"That's what the Gardai want to know too. That's what I've asked myself over and over again, but he didn't give me a reason, not at any time, not once throughout the whole thing. He said the reason didn't matter, I just had to get it stopped."

JJ took a breath.

"There's another thing," he said.

"This is like somethin' out of a movie," one of his younger colleagues muttered, regretting his rather rash comment almost immediately as he noticed the disapproving looks from his colleagues.

"I knew the guy from years ago. He was the coordinator of a youth project I attended as a young lad. I stayed in his house for a while when I was at university. He lived in Dominic's Park."

Sandra looked visibly shocked.

"You never said you lived there," she said, trying to process this new piece of information about him. *I would never have associated you with such a deprived area*, she thought to herself.

"No, it was a long time ago," he said before he

quickly moved the conversation along, "So once again, I apologise and hope you understand I had no choice."

That was enough information to give them. He wasn't about to delve into his childhood; not in a conference room full of middle and upper-class people who had no idea about the kind of life he had left behind. He'd said his piece and now just wanted to get on with the meeting. Yet suddenly everybody wanted to know more details. *Jesus, this is as bad as the interview at the station on Saturday night. Question after question – you'd think they could solve the mystery on their own*, he thought.

After what seemed like an eternity to him, Sandra eventually interjected, "Well, perhaps we should leave things to the Gardai. Time is marching on. We really do need to get this project rubber-stamped so we can proceed. The contractors are ready and keen to begin. Thank you for filling us in JJ, and again my sincere best wishes to you and your family. I'm so glad we don't have to thrash out any more of those grievances and concerns today. What a relief," she said with a sigh.

"Yes, yes," replied an embarrassed JJ, "I'm so sorry about all that."

"Well done you for hanging in there," one colleague said.

"Hurrah for Harry's safe return!" came the response from the younger member of the team, who had just redeemed himself.

It's done, JJ thought to himself, *I can relax.* There was nothing more for him to do. The Gardai would investigate and he could get back to his job. Yet he was feeling jittery, like he'd won a big prize and needed to celebrate.

Without a constant dissenting voice from JJ, it didn't take long to wrap up the plans, but once back in his office, he found it hard to settle.

The arrival of the Gardai later in the morning to retrieve his phone records did not help. They checked if there'd been any further contact from Long John.

"No," was the short answer, before he rapidly passed them on to his secretary to sort the phone records.

He didn't like being the focus of office gossip and was very aware that the Gardai's presence was drawing attention to him. Like Sandra, looking on from her office. He willed them to be quick and was relieved when they left.

He watched their blue and white car exit the carpark and smiled at the way it made heads turn, people wondering what they were doing at Bellingham & Company. Then he turned back to his desk and again tried to concentrate on his work.

By lunchtime it was clear he was wasting his time. He needed a drink and space to relax. Setting back off across the open-plan floor to Sandra's office, he tapped the window gently with the back of his knuckle. She was at her desk engaged on the phone as usual and motioned for him to enter. JJ stood waiting for her to finish. This always made him feel inferior, like a child in school waiting for the headmaster's attention. "Talk to you soon," he heard her say and then she made eye contact.

"Sorry to disturb Sandra, I was thinking I might take the rest of the day off, if that's OK with you? I've been working on adrenaline and now, well, it must be because it's all over, but I just feel whacked."

"Sure, sure, of course."

She was actually quite glad that he'd be out of the office. Perhaps then everyone's focus would return to their work instead of gossip.

"Take the rest of the day off. See how you are tomorrow. No worries if you need more time off. See how you go. It's been a traumatic time for you all."

Sandra was careful not to mention Niamh by name as she didn't want to get involved in his personal affairs.

"Thanks Sandra," he said, "I'll be fine, just need to rest up a bit. Perhaps have a drink or two," he added with a grin.

She looked up again.

"I suppose one or two wouldn't do any harm."

The smile she gave him was forced. Her smiles rarely ever reached her eyes. JJ could count on one hand the number of times that he'd seen her genuinely smile. As far as he was able to ascertain, it was reserved only for the achievement of large profits; it was elusive to colleagues and underlings.

Feeling childishly giddy at getting some time off, he bounded down the back stairwell, the wind pushing against the door as he left the building to cross the carpark.

Walking towards his car he glanced across the road to the bus stop at the far side. He often kept track of the people at the bus stop, and over the years had begun to recognise most of the regular figures who waited there. It was his idling office activity.

Today, as he peered through the boundary fence, he recognised a face that was not normally there. It startled him. Finn stood across the road, and he was staring straight at him. He'd never been there before.

Not one to be intimidated, JJ stared right back. He maintained eye contact as he clicked his car keys, all the while wondering what Finn was doing there.

Still angry about the accusations JJ had made about him, Finn stood his ground. When he was sure JJ recognised him, he slowly raised his hand and lifted his middle finger. *That should send a clear signal*, he thought. *I'm no pushover. He'd better play with more caution when it comes to messing me about.*

An elderly couple who were standing at the bus stop were oblivious of the cat-and-mouse game taking place right beside them.

JJ didn't hold his stare for long. Once he saw Finn's crude gesture he got into his car and started the engine. Reversing from his space, he looked behind to check his exit was clear. When he turned back, Finn was nowhere to be seen.

The elderly couple were still there so he knew the bus had yet to arrive. He didn't want to be too obvious in his intentions but he couldn't resist the urge to look about him, half expecting Finn to land on the bonnet of his car or jump up beside him. JJ made a hasty exit, furious that Finn had managed to unnerve him.

I'm not going to let him get away with this. Does he honestly think he can intimidate me? The waster!

Once he got out onto the road, he phoned the Gardai.

"Hello? Hello, it's JJ Hennessy, here. Can I speak to someone dealing with my blackmail case?"

He was put on hold and thirty seconds later continued the conversation,

"I wanted to let you know that Finn was across the road at the bus stop from my work just now."

He went on to describe the incident.

"I know this sounds mad but well, you know, because you brought him in for questioning on Saturday, and because of that incident with his dog, I'm a bit worried he might be losing it. You know the reputation he has, what he's capable of. Anyway, I wanted to let you know in case he turns up again."

That should do it, JJ thought.

After he hung up, feeling rather smug, he began to pick up speed and as he did so he noticed a tugging on his steering wheel. Slowing down and loosening his grip it became evident that the car was definitely pulling to the left. JJ had no choice but to pull over onto the hard shoulder. Feeling very uneasy, he got out to check his tyres and sure enough his back left was flat. He looked around to check if Finn was in the immediate vicinity and then got back into his car.

"Hello, it's JJ Hennessy here again," he said when the Garda answered the phone.

Within fifteen minutes a patrol car was at his side. JJ was rattled. Finn fighting back was an unexpected turn of events… maybe dragging him into this had been a mistake. But the wild goose chase had given him the time and space he needed. He hoped he'd not underestimated Finn.

The breakdown service arrived to fix his wheel and the man advised him it was most likely he'd picked up the large nail they found in his tyre on the road. JJ suspected not. He suspected Finn had something to do with it, but not wanting to look paranoid in front of the Gardai he decided to keep his suspicions to himself.

When he got home, he poured himself a whiskey. This wasn't the afternoon he'd planned, and he was mad – raging to be more precise.

Fucking Finn, the bastard. He'd better stay away if he knows what's good for him. I don't want any more complications to deal with, he thought.

After a second whiskey, he had calmed down a little and gave the scenario more thought.

126

I'm probably overthinking the whole Finn thing, he said to himself. *Finn just needs to cool down. I might even try and have a chat with him in a few weeks, after the court case. Clear the air. The less enemies the better. He'll understand that I couldn't tell the Gardai about the blackmail, once he calms down, and anyway it wasn't me that pointed the finger in the first place. It was one of them who asked if I was the person who had run over his dog a while back. Technically, they jumped to the revenge motive themselves, with only a little encouragement from me.*

He was about to help himself to another whiskey but decided against it, thinking it better that he stay vigilant. He wasn't sure if Finn was a threat but it was clear he had become a complication.

A small victory

It was getting dark when Finn got home, flush from his little victory.

Not long after JJ'd pulled over with the puncture, Finn had cycled right by. Well-disguised by his cycling attire; his helmet and scarf pulled over his face and a full rain cover concealing both him and his bike, Finn had been confident no one would be able to make out any features at all, least of all realise it was him.

He was also confident that he hadn't been seen earlier when he'd left a potato with a nail embedded in it under JJ's back wheel in the carpark.

That morning just after JJ had arrived at work, Finn dropped his little 'present' under the back wheel of his car while JJ was crossing the car park to the front entrance.

Finn headed off for a coffee afterwards. It was a forty-five-minute cycle ride either way the coffee shop but it had helped him pass some of the morning before he returned to the bus stop at lunchtime. He expected JJ went out for his lunch and, sure enough, he had emerged from his big posh offices. Having removed his cycling attire by then, so that he was easily recognisable, he'd stood there, hoping JJ would notice him. Thinking back over his middle-fingered gesture, and how nervous JJ had looked as he watched him drive away, he enjoyed re-living the rush of gratification he had felt. *I was brazen out*, he thought to himself, *one for you Twitch. Worth the risk*.

Twitch's lead still hung on the wall by the backdoor, Finn unable to discard it, even though it was late last summer when he had died. Looking at it now, he could visualise him jumping up and down, popping into view over the half window, now boarded up.

His little happy jack-in-the-box, circling around his feet every time he came into the kitchen waiting for him to reach down to pet him. How he would welcome all that again.

Finn had been with Twitch when he died, and he wished he could get rid of the excruciating and detailed images he held in his memory from that day. *JJ truly deserved his little scare today,* he thought.

That day last summer, Twitch was due his annual shots. They'd walked to the clinic, Finn dragging Twitch along when he became too interested in a smell or wanted to take off after another dog.

His little Jack Russell had no qualms about the

129

veterinary surgery. He'd loved the affection lavished on him by Louise and Niamh, and over the years Finn had also warmed to them, they in turn becoming more comfortable with him. Visits were always a pleasant experience, a chance to catch up on little Twitch and how he was doing.

Leaving the clinic that day, his bill paid in full, he'd picked up two bags of dried dog food. Finn had been very strict with Twitch's diet on account of an allergy to grain and rarely gave him scraps from the table. That day, Niamh and Louise commented on how good Twitch's teeth were because of his care.

He remembered opening the door onto the main street, holding Twitch's lead lightly in one hand and the bags of dog food in the other. He remembered the heat from the sun; it had been a scorcher of a day. He'd looked to his right and was looking left when he stepped out onto the road with Twitch a few feet ahead on the end of his lead.

The jeep had come at speed out of nowhere. Twitch had no chance. Being that couple of feet further ahead, he'd taken the full force of the hit.

Brakes had screeched as he watched his poor Twitch's body go under the jeep, disappearing below the front bumper then reappearing as he rolled along underneath the length of the vehicle.

Twitch made several attempts to scramble back to his feet in those seconds, but then the lower back bumper had caught him a second time. He'd lain strewn on his back, paws writhing in the air, initially silent then a whimper, before he'd fallen silent again. The jeep came to a halt but it was too late. The damage had been done.

Dog food was scattered across the ground. Twitch's blood was spotted on the road. Finn remembered it as if it was happening again before his eyes. He could see himself, crouched at the side of the road, almost fearful to reach out and touch his dear friend who was by then motionless.

Behind him he'd heard the voices of Louise and Niamh and felt a hand pulling at his shoulder, trying to move him away. He'd watched Niamh pick Twitch up and take him inside. Twitch's head had flopped loosely. Louise had stopped a passer-by to help Finn into the waiting room and she'd raced inside to assist Niamh. Leaving him on a chair, the passer-by had given some comforting words akin to,

"It will be OK."

Only it hadn't been OK. Just a few minutes later, Niamh and Louise emerged, both ashen faced.

"Finn I'm so sorry," Niamh had said, "I couldn't save him, his injuries were too extensive. He didn't suffer, he died almost instantly."

Not able to take her words in, and through a fog of confusion and grief, Finn had noticed JJ was sitting opposite him, apologising, saying he hadn't seen them, that the sun was in his eyes.

"What?" he'd heard himself ask repeatedly. Was Twitch dead?

"I'm sorry mate, it was an accident. I'm sorry."

Finn had wanted to leap up and punch this man, tackle him to the ground and beat the living daylights out of him, but he couldn't move. He'd been paralysed by grief. Was Twitch really dead?

Louise had given Finn a glass of water and he'd swallowed a sip. It helped him to regain some of his composure. Then she'd taken him in to see Twitch in the consulting room, reassuring him he'd died instantly, but he'd known different; Louise hadn't seen Twitch struggle to find his feet under the jeep. He had. He hadn't corrected her though, it wasn't her fault after all, and he'd allowed her to console him with her kind words.

They'd wrapped Twitch in a blanket, leaving only his head exposed. Crusts of dried blood remained evident on his ears and muzzle despite their attempts to clean him up as best they could; the hair on his head was still wet from their efforts.

Finn remembered thinking about the dead people he'd seen in his life, who looked like they were sleeping in their ornate coffins with the silk surround. They always looked at peace, ready to move on to wherever, resting while their friends said goodbye. His Twitch hadn't looked like he'd been sleeping. He'd looked very dead and he would never forget that.

Aware of raised voices in the waiting room, Louise had said something to him; he could never remember what. Then she'd left him alone with Twitch. Gently, he'd touched the little dog's head and stroked the blanket that covered him. He'd rubbed the little pointy canine tooth that was exposed, then pulled his lip down to cover it. Running his hand over the blanket again, feeling Twitch's mangled body underneath, he'd bent to kiss Twitch and then fled from the surgery.

As Finn opened the door to run out into the street, sounds reached him as if he were underwater. Niamh and Louise called after him, but he couldn't hear their words and hadn't stop. Looking like a man possessed, he'd stumbled as he ran home. Only parts of that journey back remained with him, including the sudden jerk after his shoulder collided with Mr O'Neill; the surprised look on his face and the jab of a stone wall that had grazed his arm as he'd swept by.

It had been hard to get his key in the front door, his hand wouldn't stop shaking, and once inside, he'd roared and shouted, cursed JJ and wept for his companion. Over and over he'd re-played the scene in his mind, wishing he had delayed his exit from the surgery just a few seconds more, allowing the jeep to pass by without incident. But wishing hadn't brought Twitch back, and nothing would.

Later that afternoon, Louise had phoned and visited him but got no response. Finally, both Louise and

Niamh grew so worried they called the Gardai, apparently much to JJ's annoyance. He had claimed it was an accident and hadn't wanted their involvement. He'd been driving too fast and knew it.

The formal voices of the Gardai asking if he was all right as one of them peered through his window, accompanied by the loud knocking on his front door, forced Finn to emerge from his shocked state that afternoon.

"Are you OK in there?" the voices had asked.

"Yes, yes," he'd said as he opened the door.

He remembered their expressions as he emerged with swollen eyes and a blotchy, reddened face.

"Can we come in for a moment Mr O'Sullivan?" one of them said, and he'd let them in.

Finn had been taken aback when they spoke with compassion. As the accused, his previous experience of the Gardai had been very different. He almost began to weep again.

"Can you tell us what happened?"

That's when he'd felt anger rise within him, anger caused by his loss. Oh yes, he could tell them. His poor Twitch; it hadn't been his fault he'd died. He told them everything in great detail; that JJ had been driving much too fast and that there were probably skid marks in the road to prove it. Finn reminded them of the thirty-kilometre speed limit imposed in that area. They'd asked if he wanted to press charges. He most definitely had.

Those charges were still to come to court, but he'd have his day in court with JJ and JJ would pay for Twitch's death and the loss of his companion.

Later that evening, Louise and Niamh had waited for him at the clinic to pick up Twitch's body. There had been more condolences and he recalled Louise cried. They'd put Twitch in a little box, still wrapped in the same blanket as earlier, and insisted on driving him home. He'd sat in the back of the car looking down at the box on his knee, still in disbelief, and he'd stroked the lid gently with the palm of his hand.

Finn watched them drive out of sight before he brought Twitch inside to the kitchen where he should have been jumping up and down like a jack-in-the box, twirling around his feet waiting for his pat on the head.

Taking the lid off the box he'd carried him around the whole house one last time – the sitting room, the hall, the bathroom, the bedroom and then back down to the kitchen again – all the while chatting to him as though he was still alive. He'd even thought about keeping him by his bed overnight, but he'd known he shouldn't as that would just be weird, and he was weird enough already...

Finally, when he'd been able to bear it, he had put the lid back on the box and brought Twitch out into the garden. Even though it had been dark by then, the heat of the day was still present. Putting the box on the ground beside him, he'd slowly and methodically dug a hole in the soil, which had been hardened by the recent heat. When he'd finished, he laid the little box in the ground and again ran his hand over the lid.

"You're a good boy Twitch, the best."

As gently as he could so as not to damage the cardboard coffin, he'd covered the box with soil, then stood quietly for a while looking down at the grave. Afterwards, he went back into the house and had a very long shower.

It was months before the mound of soil in the backyard began to level. Each morning when he saw it, he felt as though his heart was being torn out. He was grateful when it reduced in size and the grass's re-growth covered the bare patch of earth once more.

Finn re-visited the clinic once after Twitch's death, touched by Niamh and Louise's care, he gave them flowers as a thank you.

Now, sitting on his couch, he wasn't sure how he felt. He'd planned to teach JJ a lesson today and wanted to feel satisfied. Although re-living his earlier encounter had given him some pleasure, inevitably crossing paths again had also brought with it the vivid memories he wished would fade. He was annoyed that he also felt sad.

In his ignorance and despite his sadness, he decided his revengeful act had been worth it. But Finn had no idea who he was up against with Mr JJ Hennessy.

JJ

Right now, JJ hated the world and everyone in it. Life had put another obstacle in his way but he wasn't going to be defeated. He always won in the end, even if that meant others had to experience a bit of 'discomfort' on the way. It was just the way it had to be, his logic being they didn't know how good their lives were in the first place, so a few hitches here and there would make them more appreciative of what they had.

He was driving by Finn's house the evening after his encounter with him at work when he noticed the Garda car parked outside. The distinctive blue and white paint work was instantly recognisable. Slowing down he smiled. The car would be a beacon for neighbouring gossips. *Serves him right*, he thought, *he won't mess with me again,* and the image of Finn sweating while the Gardai made their enquiries about where he was the day before boosted his endorphins.

There were many times as a youngster when JJ

arrived home to see the same blue and white car parked outside his parents' house. Both drug addicts, they were well-known to the Gardai. He'd lost contact with them years ago and had no idea if they were still alive. Nor did he care. They'd never had any interest in his wellbeing; too absorbed in their own highs and lows.

JJ, like Louise, had lived on the south side of Dublin, but in a different school district to her. He'd also lived behind the wealthy properties, not in a flat complex, but in an old council estate with semi-detached homes, much like Dominic's Park. He had a sister, May, who was three years older than him. They'd not got along as siblings and when he was ten years old, she'd suddenly died.

As a young boy, Jonnie had watched May being targeted by the local bullies and he'd often joined in the bullying himself, not knowing any better. Unable to stand up for herself, May had become an easy target and he hated her for it because it meant he could never decline a dare. The bullies taunted him with the words "Sissy May" and threatened to beat him. He'd learnt quickly how to hide his vulnerability by presenting a hard and brave front, not wanting to end up like his sister May.

Poor May's life ended very abruptly when she was only thirteen years old. Her death changed something, deep within Jonnie, forever. Unable to understand how he felt, he'd struggled to manage his emotions. There'd been so many of them: guilt, anger, relief, fear, sadness and loneliness. They had just kept coming, and he'd not known what to do with any of them.

At ten years of age Jonnie thought he might lose his mind, but then he discovered he could suppress the emotions he didn't wanted to feel. He found his 'off switch', and once he had, he practiced using it as much as he could. It wasn't a perfect solution but it was better than nothing.

In his late teens and early twenties Jonnie struggled to keep control of his 'off switch' – his emotions resurfaced and it almost caused his demise – but he managed to adapt and for the most part his 'off switch' continued to serve him well.

It frustrated him that he couldn't completely suppress his emotions; he viewed them as a weakness within himself, and he wished he didn't sometimes feel like he was drowning under a tsunami of them behind closed doors. It was then that he'd seek out solace in the whiskey bottle.

May died after drinking a bottle of vodka. Neighbours had heard her shouting about how she could fly and seconds before she jumped from her bedroom window, one of them had been walking across the street to complain to her parents. Her parents hadn't known what was going on upstairs as they had been downstairs, unconscious on the settee.

The image of her twisted body on the concrete below

139

was hideously vivid for JJ.

Her hair splayed out in a circle around her head, and beyond it her wine-red blood flowed, filling the nearby cracks in the concrete yard; her arms still outstretched as though she were flying.

Months later, he found faded blood splatters soaked into the wooden stick that held up the washing line, strung across the middle of the yard. As younger children, that stick had been used to delineate their separate playing areas so as to avoid the inevitable rows between them. His father had beat him that day he found her blood, for breaking it in two.

Jonnie's was a completely dysfunctional family. After his sister's death, he'd spent a short period in a children's home and hated it. Not used to rules or a regular routine, he'd found it overwhelming. He hadn't had to stay there long though as, surprisingly, his parents managed to comply with a period of rehabilitation, and once they'd convinced the social services they were reformed, he'd been happy to be allowed back home. It took less than a year for 'normality' to return, and at twelve years of age he could do as he pleased, so long as he stayed on the right side of the right people.

School was a disaster. Jonnie had no interest in learning. His teachers knew he was a bright child but they'd been unable to engage him, and after his third expulsion, he'd been introduced to one of Dublin's new alternative schools.

The city's alternative schools were set up to provide education and stability for children and teens like him, who were floundering in the mainstream system; children who found conventional schooling too far removed from the world in which they lived.

They were inspirational places – places of hope. His future mentor, nicknamed Long John Silver or Long John for short, had been one of their staunchest supporters. A spokesperson for Dublin's less privileged youth, his nickname given to him by the teens he worked with because of his unkempt, greying, shoulder-length hair.

Jonnie had thought he was cool, unlike the middleclass headmasters and teachers he'd met before. Long John seemed to be in touch with real life, and Jonnie had wanted to impress him. He'd engaged with his teaching philosophy, and in this new and nurturing environment he began to flourish.

Life, it seemed, had taken a turn for the better. Jonnie became the poster boy for the school and local area. That of course had its problems, as being smart wasn't 'cool', but Jonnie was tough, and Long John always had his back. He constantly worked hard to maintain Jonnie's respect and adulation, and he was genuinely delighted when Jonnie effortlessly passed his Leaving Certificate.

Although there'd been no improvements in his home

life, Jonnie could see a way out for himself, and with Long John's support, he successfully applied for a place in university to study business.

By this time Long John was more than a father-figure whom he respected and admired: he'd become someone Jonnie idolised. It had been an obvious step to accept his offer of a room, rent free, in his home. His house was closer to the centre of town and to the university than Jonnie's parents' house, and Long John offered a more stable, quieter environment in which to complete his studies. Of course he'd said yes, this was his chance to get away from his past and begin his journey to a better future.

Yet just a few months into his university course, Jonnie noticed changes in Long John, or rather, noticed things he hadn't had the opportunity to see before. His life was taking another turn, but this time, for the worse.

Things turn sour

Back then, when Jonnie was about to start university, Long John lived at number fifteen Dominic's Park, and Jonnie had been completely unaware of the environment he was about to move into.

He'd only interacted with Long John in the alternative school surroundings, and although he hadn't expected anything to be plush about his new abode, he had expected something different to his own sparsely furnished family home. To his surprise, Long John's house had been far from homely.

He'd immediately noticed the regular pattern of people who came and went. It reminded him of his parents' home. He was no fool – he'd seen this all before – there were too many people coming and going and too many hushed and angry conversations taking place downstairs. It hadn't taken long for Jonnie to begin to question if he had made a big mistake.

The first time he'd witnessed Long John injecting

himself, he'd been shocked. Drug use and dealing was something that Long John had publicly rallied against for years. Realising what was happening, he had silently backed out of the kitchen without being noticed and had spent a sleepless night trying to decide what to do.

He'd worshipped Long John. Could it really be true that he was just like the rest – a wheeler-dealer, out for what he could get. If he couldn't trust Long John, who could he trust?

The realisation that his mentor was a fake had devastated Jonnie, but he hadn't been defeated. He'd been so sure he was succeeding in his attempts to forge a better life for himself, and he had still hoped he could. Realising he'd probably already witnessed too much, knowing who frequented the house, he rebuffed himself for being so easily duped. What a fool he'd been.

Jonnie had known he should leave and find a place of his own; he couldn't risk staying with Long John anymore. Still confident his mentor had a genuine interest in him doing well, he began to hint at spreading his wings, but this had not been well received.

Like any fledgling learning to fly, Jonnie had landed on the ground not far from the nest from which he'd flown, and like many young chicks he'd found himself in grave danger. Yet there were no parents to rescue him from his predator, Long John.

Jonnie's disappointment would have been surmountable had it not been for the fact that Long John and his associates had other plans for him. They needed him and were not going to let him go that easily.

He had tried to rebel, as a teenage son might against his father, but it had been futile. Jonnie was intended to become part of a drug-smuggling ring. His intelligence and blemish-free Gardai record made him valuable to the gang. They weren't going to let him go and Long John's job was to persuade him, the easy or hard way, that this was his preferred destiny. Like it or not, Jonnie's fate had been sealed by the time he was eighteen years old.

He had persevered with trying to persuade Long John to let him leave for some time, but Long John eventually tired of his whinging. He started to use coercion over charm to get Jonnie to comply. Jonnie's life changed for the worse and threats of severe beatings and even death became a constant.

Eoin, the teenager who went missing from the youth centre, had been the final nail in Jonnie's coffin. Long John deliberately put him in the frame. He made sure he and Jonnie were seen picking Eoin up from the youth centre that day, supposedly to give him a lift into the city centre. Jonnie had innocently got out of the car at the entrance to Dominic's Park and left the two alone to continue the rest of their journey without him.

Eoin was beaten to death for his father's misdemeanours, his son paying the ultimate price for his disloyalty.

Long John had given him all the details of Eoin's murder and reminded him that he was one of the last people to be seen with him. Jonnie had been terrified the blame would rest with him. He just had to hope that Long John's martyr-like reputation would protect him from suspicion.

In Jonnie's eyes, Long John had become a monster. He had no idea how desperate he was; having been told in no uncertain terms to bring young Jonnie into line. He hadn't been aware this was Long John's last-ditch attempt to protect them both from physical harm.

A search warrant allowed the Gardai to dig up the newly laid foundations of the conservatory at Long John's house during their investigations. Nothing was found.

Months later, Jonnie arrived home from university to be met by Long John and an accomplice, a neighbour who Jonnie had seen around.

The pair of them had dug a hole in the foundations where the Gardai had previously searched. When Jonnie walked in, he heard them laughing at a joke they'd shared, and when he'd looked down to where they were digging, he saw what appeared to be a frozen body. It had been wrapped tightly in black polythene and looked solid and wet as though it was starting to defrost. They'd already partially covered it with soil. He'd been grabbed and pushed forward and he'd tried to pull back.

"Come on you little shit, come on and help, after all

I've done for you."

Long John was high, higher than Jonnie had ever seen him.

"Here," he said as he threw him a spade, "Put your back into it. We need to be quick."

"I can't," Jonnie had whimpered.

They'd grabbed him, one on either side and pushed him onto his knees, over to the hole containing the defrosting body.

"Do you want to be on top?" Long John had spat, pushing Jonnie's head down into the hole.

The combination of the awful stench and the force of the men's hold had made it hard for him to breathe. He'd tried to push himself up and had managed to take a gasp of air when his survival instincts kicked in.

"No!" Jonnie had shouted back at Long John, struggling to free himself from their grip. "Let me up."

That was it – he'd known from that moment that there was no going back. He was involved as deeply as he could be. He could either get on with it or die. He hadn't wanted to die.

The following day, in the supermarket carpark, he'd seen Fairy for what he thought was going to be the last time. Knowing then that he would never be able to have a normal relationship with her or anyone else, whether he liked them or not, he had done what he had to do – he'd located his emotional switch and turned it off.

Over the years, Jonnie gained his associates trust and

because he was intended to be 'the clean face' of the organisation, his role in the drug-smuggling ring became more and more business-like. He'd not been required to get involved at the sharp end any longer and could almost pretend it wasn't happening at all. He began to wonder why he'd ever bothered to fight back against his fate. Regular society was not for the likes of him, and as his mentor frequently pointed out, he'd had it good. He was able to own a big house and have a flashy car without suspicion. He should be grateful.

Jonnie was fairly content with his lot until, in his early forties, an unexpected opportunity arose that made him think again about the possibility of living a normal life, and he grabbed it with both hands.

The gang he'd been embroiled with began to decline. It started to disintegrate under pressure from a younger and even more ruthless group. He saw his chance to 'retire' and had approached Long John to negotiate an exit. To his surprise, a compromise had been agreed and he was finally set free. It was all going very well until now. He had been enjoying his new life as a legitimate member of society – well, almost legitimate. He was never going to part with all of his ill-gotten gains. He genuinely thought he deserved them.

If the re-development of Dominic's Park hadn't been approved, he'd be getting along with life just fine. He wouldn't be having to defend his safety and revert to fight mode.

JJ wasn't going to risk being returned to the underworld he'd left behind. He was intent on protecting himself first and foremost. And he certainly wasn't going to let anyone, especially someone like Finn, pose a threat to him.

He was ready to do whatever he needed to do to survive. He'd done it before and he knew he could do it again.

Sometimes it's hard to change

Finn's mood shifted when he saw the Garda car outside. He hadn't even considered that JJ might contact them. His mistake – assuming JJ thought like him.

As usual, there were two Gardai, one of them was about Finn's height, five foot eight. The other was taller.

"Can we come in?" the taller of the two said, his authoritative tone indicating to Finn that he wouldn't be seeing the caring side of the Gardai today.

"Yes, come in. Is there a problem?"

He directed them into the sitting room, much like his parents would have done with the parish priest in the past. The sitting room was the 'good room'.

As they'd grown older, the priest had visited Finn's parents every week, and he'd always sat in the sitting room on the same chair; that chair forever referred to as the Priest's Chair by Finn. The sitting room was the place for the Gardai too, and he'd sit in the Priest's Chair for good luck.

"Can you tell us where you were yesterday at around one p.m.?"

Finn flinched.

"Ah… let me think… I was here," he said, wishing now he'd been less bullish.

"Are you sure of that, Mr O'Sullivan? We have been informed by Mr Hennessy that you were at his place of work yesterday afternoon."

Finn looked at the floor. He was sitting with his feet apart and his hands on his knees, trying to maintain a confident stance. He raised his head, looked them straight in the eye and lied.

"I wasn't there Gards. I don't know what he's talking about. He clearly has it in for me. Can I make a complaint? Surely this is harassment?"

The Gardai looked at each other, then the shorter one said,

"Was there anyone here with you?"

"No, I was watching TV alone."

"OK, fair enough, but we must warn you that if you approach Mr Hennessy it will be viewed, as you said yourself, as harassment. Is that understood?"

"I don't want to have anything to do with that guy," he said, being careful to watch his language, "I just want my day in court with him for dangerous driving. He killed my dog and now he's telling ye I'm a kidnapper and a stalker. He seems to be the one harassing me. I should be the one making the complaint."

They both stood up, knowing they had no solid evidence to prove any wrongdoing. The purpose of their visit was to caution Finn following JJ's complaint and they had done that.

"Thanks for your help," they said, "But bear in mind what we've said."

Then they left and he shut the door behind them. Finn was trembling. Returning to the sitting room, he sat for a while in the Priest's Chair until it passed.

Finn feared that JJ's accusations were putting him in danger of a return to prison. *None of this is my fault. I was just trying to stand up for myself. Why am I always seen to be in the wrong? At least this time mam and dad aren't alive to suffer the consequences.*

Back in his late teens, when he was previously convicted, it had almost killed them; they couldn't believe what their only son had done. He had been a promising Gaelic football player and was on the county team. Avid fans, his parents never missed a match. They cheered and roared their way through every game from the side-lines, and afterwards at home there'd be a full evening of entertainment as they dissected the players' performances. It had always been a vigorous discussion and the one thing they'd all equally enjoyed.

As an only child and the apple of his parents' eye, Finn had been used to getting his own way at home. He could do no wrong, and he had little patience with those who thought differently. At school, his temper created problems with other children. He wasn't much liked by their parents either who considered him to be over-indulged.

Encouraged to play 'Gaelic' from an early age, his parents hoped the team element of the sport would teach him how to get along with others. In some ways it had helped him, in so much as he'd been a talented player and became a wanted and important member of the team. Without his teammates, he'd likely have been very alone growing up.

Always a dangerous opponent in matches, Finn hadn't been afraid to take a chance, and he'd often scored a goal worth three points or a kick over the bar worth one point to ensure a win for his team just before the final whistle blew. He revelled in being the hero in the changing rooms afterwards and because of his talent, his temper had been to a certain extent tolerated by his coaches and teammates; passed off as an excess of passion for the sport.

They all lectured him about his short fuse, and he'd control it for a while afterwards, but he always reverted to type. His predictable moods were like Groundhog Day, and unlike his talent, his fiery reputation had not been an asset to the team. It became a weakness the opposition took advantage of as often as they could.

During one particular match, a season final, Stephen – the young player who was marking Finn – tried his best to take advantage of Finn's short temper. He'd been ruthlessly agitating him in an effort to provoke a punch, keen to get Finn sent off for misconduct so his own team would benefit from being one man up.

The match was extremely close. Finn did well to keep his temper under such provocation but unfortunately by the end he'd been unable to produce any of his last-minute magic. His team lost and they were crestfallen in defeat. It was the closest they had come to winning the final in years. They'd all thought they'd do it that season; their pre-match hopes had been high.

Stephen of course was delighted with his team's victory, and when the end of match whistle blew, he pushed Finn and made a mocking remark; sixty minutes of unrelenting agitation apparently not enough for him.

Enough was enough. The match over, Finn threw a punch but swung wide. Stephen laughed and Finn was on top of him in an instant. A brawl broke out on the pitch; it was an unsportsmanlike display.

The newspapers were not kind to the team. *A disgraceful display* was one headline. *Bad sportsmanship* another. Finn was highlighted as the instigator, and he and his team were rightly shamed for their behaviour. The worthy battle they'd fought against the opposition had been overshadowed by five minutes of unruly madness. A goal scored by Finn from a tight angle which had given them the early lead was barely mentioned; neither was the amazing save in the second half by goalkeeper James.

Feeling aggrieved, and in spite of a warning from their coach, the team decided to drown their sorrows that weekend. They were despondent, headstrong young men who were in no mood to listen to good advice.

"Fuck it, sure we're off till next season now anyway," had been the prevailing attitude.

That Saturday, Finn had to work late, so he told his teammates he would meet them in town at eight p.m. By the time he'd joined them, the others were already inebriated and in high spirits. Finn generally avoided drinking shorts, well aware that he became a bad-tempered drunk, but being way behind the others, he'd accepted a concoction in a pint glass so that he could catch up fast; then he'd continued with his usual pints.

He couldn't remember exactly what had happened later that night. Others remembered clearly though.

In court months later, witnesses described how Stephen and his teammates entered the pub where Finn's group were drinking. They were also very drunk, celebrating their win against their rivals. Insults were thrown, initially believed to just be competitive banter. Then apparently, Finn had launched himself across the bar, knocking others out of his way as he did so. James, the goalkeeper, had tried to stop him but couldn't and Finn, described as being out of control, aggressively propelled himself towards Stephen.

Stephen was laughing at him again, mocking him.

Finn remembered that detail. He punched Stephen hard on the jaw and the force sent the pint Steven was holding up into the air. Unable to halt his forward momentum, Finn then fell on top of Stephen as he fell to the floor and the pint glass shattered about them.

Stephen had dropped like a sack of potatoes, the weight of two bodies falling together increasing the impact. He banged his head on the metal footrest of the bar with great force and never regained consciousness, dying in hospital a week later.

On his day in court, Finn's solicitor spoke about his restraint in the match under severe provocation and how sport had taught him to channel his aggression, seeking to highlight the level of harassment that had taken place beforehand.

Stephen's solicitor had counter-argued that Finn had indeed learned to 'channel' well – channelling every bit of rage within his body into a punch that killed a young man in the prime of his life; a young man engaged to be married.

The court case went on for weeks, but in a nutshell, it was concluded that Finn was a danger to society.

He could have been sentenced to as much as twenty years in prison so he was very lucky to get a five-year sentence for manslaughter. In the end, he only served three years with the remainder spent on parole.

He could never forget those thirty-six months of prison life; thirty-six months of abject fear. The sense of claustrophobia each evening when the cell door closed had never left him, nor the nightmares about the concrete wall he faced each morning when he awoke. On sleepless nights, he could still hear the sounds that echoed everywhere in the darkness – shouts, banging and sometimes crying – all so hollow and bleak.

There were stories that his victim's friends had made threats. They knew people inside who would seek revenge. He'd had to remain constantly vigilant and every day he'd lived in fear.

As part of his rehabilitation, Finn wrote to Stephen's family from prison to apologise. He'd felt sure it wasn't going to help them, but he'd hoped it might. He was completely sincere in his regret about the punch that had led to their son's death. It sat heavily on his conscience, but he also retained a sense of being a victim. Excusing his behaviour in this way helped him to stop thinking of himself as a killer. He told himself that there were lots of extenuating circumstances in his case – so many ifs and buts. He constantly reassured himself it had been a terrible accident.

His parole officer used to say, "Finn you have to take responsibility for your actions. You can't keep throwing the blame elsewhere."

"I didn't start the altercation. I wouldn't have started anything. My teammates tanked me up. I don't drink much usually. It was an unfortunate accident, only one punch. I was very, very drunk."

All the excuses hadn't change the fact that Stephen died by his hand. It had been his decision to throw a punch, drunk or not, and this Finn found hard to own.

By writing his letter to the victim's parents, he'd also hoped it might ease his own conscience; that it might make him feel slightly better to say how sorry he was. Yet it hadn't and nor had anything else, not even the confessional visits with the prison's priest.

He became deeply depressed and was told he needed to forgive himself, but if it had been totally his fault that Stephen had died, how could he forgive himself? Believing he was the victim of circumstance, even in the tiniest measure, helped him more.

There were tears every time his parents visited him in prison, and over the three years he was there he'd witnessed their physical deterioration. His father became stooped and his mother seemed to halve in weight. They'd looked drawn and tired. It had hurt him greatly that he, their only son – their pride and joy – had become the cause of their distress and was now incarcerated in 'The Joy', Mountjoy Prison.

The immediate happiness following his release was short-lived. Walking through his own front door, feeling the embrace of his parents, and staying up until midnight just because he could, had all been great. Yet there had been no getting away from the fact that he would forever be an outcast in the community. He now had a reputation as a dangerous man; a vicious and spoilt bastard.

His parents suffered too, perhaps even more so than him. They'd tried putting themselves in the shoes of Stephen's parents: what if Finn had died? Could they ever forgive Stephen? But their son Finn wasn't a bad person though, it'd been an accident, and they'd cried for him, so too for Stephen's family. They wanted to defend their son but when they had tried, they'd been told they were callous.

By the time Finn was released from prison, his parents had already distanced themselves from the community. Ashamed and not knowing what to say or do, they were all too conscious of the whispers,

"They were awful parents. That boy was never told no…"

The accusations and gossip were relentless.

He was banned from playing Gaelic football but that made little difference to him as many of his teammates had moved on in life, completed their university degrees and/or got jobs and moved away. Those who remained were uncomfortable being seen with him in public. He hadn't wanted to go out anyway. The shame was too deep.

In their new reality, the outside world became too harsh a place to navigate for the O'Sullivan family. They kept to themselves and other than close relatives, the priest became their most regular visitor. Pride and joy in their son had been replaced by sadness and loss.

After his release, Finn's probation officer helped him secure some work in a garage out of town, but as a non-driver and with no interest in cars, the job hadn't lasted for long.

For a while he'd worked as a night-time security guard closer to home. He'd been able to walk there, and thankfully saw no one at night.

A few years later his fortunes took a turn for the better after the local GAA (Gaelic Football Association's) chairman passed away, and James, Finn's teammate who had tried to intervene the night Stephen died, took over as Chair. James wanted to modernise the club and high on his agenda had been to hire a part-time caretaker. He instantly thought of Finn.

"Finn deserves a second chance," he'd said to the board, always having felt sorry for him having been involved in a few bar brawls himself in his youth without suffering such severe consequences.

There was controversy of course, but overall the board agreed Finn should be allowed to regain a connection with the club. He had been a law-abiding citizen for many years since his conviction.

Ecstatic with the offer, Finn jumped at the chance. To him it meant he was finally being accepted by the wider community; perhaps even forgiven?

Seeing his return to the club, even if only in a caretaking role, had helped his parents too. They also thought it signalled that Finn was being allowed to move on from his youthful mistake. Stephen was dead – that sword would never leave their hearts – but maybe their son still had a chance to move on from his past?

Finn's parents died within a year of each other. His father had a heart attack shortly after Finn got his caretaker job with the GAA. His mother died from stomach cancer six months later. They would have been so proud five years ago to see him get his present caretaking job at St. Therese's school.

Locals said the couple succumbed to death once they felt their son was going to be all right.

Finn took their deaths hard. He hadn't wanted to be the son he'd turned out to be; he wished he had still been their pride and joy. He hadn't felt he'd fully atoned for the pain he'd caused them, and now he never could. He'd wanted more time to show them he was a good person but it was all too late.

He withdrew from society after his mother's death and came close to losing his job at the GAA club, but they had rallied around him and that show of support helped him to keep going at a time when he might have given up completely. Twitch, his scrawny little terrier, also made a significant difference to his life in those days. Twitch was his constant loyal companion, helping him to heal.

Sitting now in the Priest's Chair after the Gardai's visit, he contemplated how his life was again descending into chaos, and once more he heard the voice

161

of 'Finn the victim' telling him it wasn't his fault. He was partly right, but he wasn't helping matters either. Sometimes it's hard to change.

The clinic

The clinic had re-opened and life was returning to some kind of normality. It was early April; even the weather had improved. Harry was back in school and Niamh and Louise were busy at work.

The morning passed quickly with a backlog of visits to get through, and there was a lot of upbeat conversation about Harry's return. It almost felt like the lead-up to Christmas with so much goodwill in the air.

Louise tried but failed to shift her sense of doom. She had hoped work would take her mind off her worries, but she still felt anxious.

It wasn't yet lunch break, but she was already eating a sandwich from her lunch box. Louise knew comfort eating contributed greatly to her middle-aged spread but she hadn't the resistance to fight back, at least not this week anyway.

As she ate, she overheard a conversation between Niamh and JJ – something about Finn following him.

She only caught part of it but it was enough to stop her eating and return the sandwich to its box.

Niamh's habit of repeating everything said to her on the phone, as if she needed to process the information aloud in order to understand it, normally irritated Louise, but today she was grateful for the insight. There was something about Finn at a bus stop, and JJ's car. The Gardai were mentioned too.

There was no need for her to subtly ask about the call. Niamh was keen to recount it as soon as it ended.

"I don't know what's up with JJ and his God damn obsession with Finn! I mean, for God's sake, he killed the guy's dog and then said he might be behind Harry's disappearance. Now he's imagining he's seeing him at bus stops, and he thinks he's put a nail in his tyre. He even put the Gardai back on to him."

She flung her mobile to the side in disgust.

"If he doesn't let it go Louise, he'll drive Finn insane. Jesus, he could resort to old form. The poor guy, I mean, give him a chance. JJ just doesn't want to go to court. He doesn't want to admit he was driving dangerously fast." Then haughtily she added, "I don't think Finn will be withdrawing his statement now if that's what he's angling for."

There it is, Louise thought, *more impending doom and gloom. I should have guessed JJ would be the cause of it all.* She felt the piece of sandwich in her stomach curl into a lead-like, tight ball and wished she'd brought her antacid tablets with her. These last few days she'd been eating them like sweets. *Fuck JJ,* was what she was thinking, but instead she said, "Poor Finn. Have you heard what's happening with his job at the school?"

Louise expected Niamh might have been in contact with the principal on account of Finn's involvement in Harry's education at school. She knew Finn had become involved in encouraging Harry to use his sign language.

"No. They said he's suspended with full pay until the investigation is complete. It sucks. I think Harry misses him in the playground. You know what buddies they've become."

"Do you remember the first day we met him? I'd never have thought you'd end up letting him and Harry be buddies then," Louise said with a smile.

"Jeez yeah, I know," Niamh replied, thinking back, "He had Twitch in that box under his arm. I didn't realise who he was till I saw him. Gave me a bit of a start. I was scared of him. I remember thinking, why'd you have to pick us? He'd such a bad reputation, didn't he?"

Louise raised an eyebrow in agreement and Niamh continued.

"God, I was careful with my words that day I can tell you… You, on the other hand, Miss I'm-so-lovable," Niamh smiled at the memory, "You were all gushy. I've never seen you so keen to win a new client over!"

Louise laughed, "I felt sorry for the guy, and when I

saw that shivering little pup, well, even a heart of stone would warm. Suppose that's why I was so upset when Twitch died."

Niamh could picture Finn coming towards her, his wavy hair in need of a wash, neatly slicked back over his ears. He had said nothing to her as he passed her by, heading straight for the consulting room. Head lowered, he'd carried the box under his arm before firmly planting it down on the shiny metal examination table. Still not a word spoken, he had carefully removed the lid, putting one hand inside to stop the squirming little puppy from escaping.

Twitch had been no more than a few months old, tiny and quaking. He'd been a scraggy little puppy with dark eyes that flitted about nervously, but his perfectly even half-brown, half-white face had been adorable. He'd looked even smaller than he physically was in the large hands of Finn. After lifting the puppy out, Niamh remembered Finn saying, "This lad arrived in my garden a couple of days ago. I'll keep him if no one claims him."

"Hey Louise," Niamh said teasingly, "Wasn't that the first day I ever had words with you about over-stepping the mark?"

"I didn't though! You were just overly careful that day. I've never seen you so 'professional'," she quipped in reply.

Normally, Louise let Niamh lead the conversation

with clients, but that day, it was she who had responded to Finn's suggestion that he keep the puppy if no one claimed him.

"Well, there's been no reports of a missing puppy so I think you're fairly safe there. He's very cute, isn't he? Yeah, I'd say you're safe enough. I'm sure if a local lost a small pup like him we'd have heard by now, there'd be notices up. Poor little thing was probably dumped."

Niamh had glared at Louise, wondering what on earth had gotten into her and had asserted her authority.

"I do have to let you know, Mr O'Sullivan, regardless of ownership, you'll have to pay for today's check-up if we continue. Or would you prefer to wait a few days and see if he's claimed?"

Finn had been happy to pay.

"I thought you'd frighten him away!" Louise said, smiling broadly and then added, "Do you remember when you inserted the thermometer into Twitch's rectum? Finn literally squirmed! I nearly started laughing. You'd swear he was the one on the table. I knew then he was an aul softie at heart."

"Still, I was careful for a long time to be respectful – not that I'm not normally – but I mean careful not to engage in banter. It was a good few years before I risked that. I was so afraid he might misconstrue something I said and take offence. Suppose I was afraid of an outburst."

"Just as well you employed 'Miss Lovable' then isn't

167

it?" Louise joked.

Niamh laughed in agreement.

"God it's horrible though isn't it, I mean, I know he killed that guy, but it wasn't like he planned it and well… Oh, I don't know… Anyway, he actually turned out to be OK, didn't he?"

Niamh seemed to be trying to convince herself that she'd made the right decision in allowing Finn and Harry to become so friendly at school. Some seeds of doubt and wariness remained, and probably always would.

Over the years, even though Finn wasn't one for showing his softer emotions, she had warmed to him and often wondered why he wouldn't let others see his gentler side. He was extremely good at hiding it. That was why, when the school nervously approached her about Harry taking a liking to Finn in the playground, she had not been alarmed, and when they'd suggested they use their friendship as a way to expand Harry's learning experience, she had happily agreed.

It wasn't surprising that Harry recognised and latterly gravitated towards Finn in the schoolyard. Niamh's appointments regularly overran so she often worked later into the evening than she'd planned. Her childminder, Anna, dropped Harry at the clinic on those days, as it was on her way home.

Twitch had a few setbacks as a young dog; he'd developed chronic dermatitis as a result of his allergies to the grain in his dog food and he also had a couple of ear infections. Those conditions along with being neutered meant he'd been a regular visitor to the surgery for a period of time, and as Finn usually took the latest appointment, Harry was often sitting on his chair in the corner of the room on his iPad. Finn always smiled and gave him a little wave upon entering and leaving the room and sometimes Harry would jump down from his chair to pet Twitch before they left.

One day at school, at the end of his lunch break, Harry had been having a particularly hard time, and his teachers were struggling to get him to co-operate. He hadn't wanted to return to his classroom and had run across the yard in Finn's direction. Standing behind Finn, he'd jumped from side to side each time the teachers tried to take his hand. In the end, it was Finn who returned Harry to his classroom, and from that day on, they seemed to develop a connection with each other.

In an attempt to communicate, Harry started to go to Finn in the playground, trying out the new Makaton signs he'd been learning in the classroom. That was when the principal approached Niamh with the suggestion that it might be a good idea to get Finn involved as a way of encouraging Harry to generalise his learning. Finn had readily agreed to learn basic Makaton signs so he could understand and respond to Harry, and it became a regular break time activity for the two to exchange signs. The day Harry's teachers saw him sign the word for friend to Finn in the yard, everyone was reduced to tears.

It had been a great success story and Finn was really enjoying the experience, but then Harry had vanished and Finn was taken in for questioning. Now everyone was wondering about the prudence of their decision.

The next client arrived. Niamh and Louise stopped reminiscing and reverted to their professional roles.

It was a long afternoon and Louise was finding it hard to concentrate. *JJ is such a prick*, she kept thinking. *Why would the Gardai want to talk to me about the alibi statement anyway, even if it was that guy who'd blackmailed him? It was years ago… Imagine*, she thought, *he knew who I was all along but he's waited until now to threaten me. What game is he playing?*

"Louise! Come on, you're on another planet today," Niamh commented.

Louise tried to refocus but it wasn't long before her thoughts wandered again. She was holding a dog's paw for Niamh to stitch. Holding the dog reminded her of the day she'd dropped Twitch over Finn's front wall. It was shortly after she'd moved to the area. She'd heard lots of stories about him and his circumstances after her arrival in the town and had known he was struggling following his parents' deaths.

Someone had left a puppy at her front door the evening before. It wasn't the first time it'd happened.

170

People always assumed that she, in her role of veterinary nurse, would find a good home for an unwanted animal. It was a professional hazard; a problem solved for the 'giver' and a problem created for her.

Privately, Louise had been thinking pet ownership might help Finn, given the positive psychological impact she knew it could have. She took it as a sign when the puppy was abandoned to her care and decided it was worth a try – the little fella had needed a home after all.

Dropping the puppy over Finn's wall had taken every bit of courage she possessed. She'd been afraid she'd be caught, knowing she risked losing her nice new job if she was spotted.

After depositing him in Finn's front garden, Louise had waited nearby and been very disappointed half an hour later to see Finn emerge from his house, pick up the scrawny little puppy and put him back out onto the street.

When the coast was clear, she had snatched the puppy up and taken him home. At home, she'd festered for a few hours and then decided to try again. She dropped him back over the wall while she casually walked by and opened Finn's gate slightly to make it look like the puppy had found a way back in.

Then while she waited patiently in her car, parked as far down the street as she could go without losing sight of Finn's front garden, she'd worried afresh about how furious Niamh would be if she found out. Finn passed right by her on his return from a walk, and Louise had to stop herself from conspicuously sliding down into her seat to hide.

After he'd spotted the puppy back in his garden, he'd looked around rather suspiciously, and Louise had watched as he picked the scruffy little bundle up to examine him. A few minutes later, he'd disappeared around the back with the puppy in his hand, and she had waited and waited some more until she was confident he wasn't going to put him back out on the street. Then she'd returned home happy, hoping they'd get along with each other.

Two days later, Finn phoned the clinic to make an appointment for a check-up and vaccinations. Louise had spent that morning of his visit worrying he'd seen her leave the puppy; afraid he'd already tired of it and was going to give it back to her. Well aware Niamh would be livid if she discovered she'd involved the local veterinary clinic in a dog dropping incident, she'd realised how irresponsible she had been and had convinced herself that she would be getting the sack. As she'd anxiously awaited the appointment time, the apprehension building inside her had nearly made her throw up.

Thank God it all worked out so well and I was never discovered, she was thinking when Niamh interrupted her thoughts.

Towards the end of the day, it was Niamh who was contemplative.

"You know that fidget spinner Harry used to love, the one he had the day you found him?"

"Yeah."

"Where in the hell do you think he found it? It's been bugging me. He's not had it for months."

"Maybe it was in the garden?"

Niamh wasn't seeking an answer, she was thinking aloud again.

"JJ's offered to take Harry this weekend, you know. Don't say anything to anyone about this Louise, but I hate it when he gets him at the weekend. He always comes home out of routine. I'm supposed to be the one getting a break, but I end up having to do twice the work for half the following week to get him back on track. Thank God he doesn't volunteer very often. I was thinking I might suggest it'd be better if Harry stayed with me for a few more weeks before we moved him about again. You know, with the trauma he's been through?"

"Well for what it's worth, I think it's better you take a break. No offence, but you look exhausted."

"Yeah, but JJ could seriously mess things up if he doesn't follow the behavioural plan. He's not good at following the rules, Louise. He just doesn't listen to anyone else. I swear he thinks all these therapists are trying to make things worse, not better. It's been hard enough as it is. Harry's regressed a lot since he went missing. It's no picnic at home at the minute. It's been bloody hard, and I don't want to make it any worse. I'll have to think about it."

"Just make sure he knows he has to follow the plan, Niamh. Tell him how hard it's been. Surely he'll understand? It's not like he's a stranger. Harry's his responsibility too you know, it's not all up to you."

Niamh wondered why she'd said anything at all. *How could Louise understand? She doesn't know that I'd prefer it was all left up to me. Louise doesn't know JJ or what he's like; she doesn't know that he won't be told anything, regardless of the consequences. He always thinks he's right.*

Louise noticed Niamh seemed distant. She suspected she'd said something wrong but didn't know what.

"You're tired Niamh, don't let him get away scotfree. Take the break, you need it."

The little bell at the front desk rang and they moved on to deal with the last client of the day – Mrs Hollander and Dizzy, the one-eyed and rather vicious cat whom her owner adored. They were going to have to impart bad news to her shortly.

"I'll see," Niamh said. "Don't you just hate this bit of the job? Have you got the tissues there, Louise?"

Sleepover

Later that night, having settled Harry in bed after another difficult evening, Niamh was exhausted. It was the first time she'd ever seriously considered the social worker's offer of respite. She'd not felt this tired in years. Not since the day a very concerned early services team suggested to her that she needed to take more care of herself. That day, they'd used an analogy about her needing to put on her own oxygen mask before putting on Harry's and Niamh had been so stressed and tired, she'd thought they were recommending oxygen therapy for Harry.

"I heard something about that somewhere," she'd told them before she had noticed how bemused they'd looked.

"The oxygen is for you Niamh," one of them had replied.

Niamh had got better at lifting her head for some oxygen since those early days. She understood the need to have some personal space so that she could function better, and she knew this was definitely one of those times.

Even though it often seemed to create more work, getting Harry back on track after his visits with JJ, she still felt he was better off with his father than in the care of strangers. No matter how many times she was told the 'strangers' wouldn't stay strangers once she got to know them, she just hadn't been able to contemplate using respite as a support to date.

This evening she was trying hard to convince herself to listen to the advice about taking care of herself. *If Harry went to the respite house, I'd at least be guaranteed follow-through on his behavioural plans. I'd get a break without any fall-out consequences. I'm definitely going to look into setting it up,* she told herself.

There was no regular access agreement between JJ and Niamh. He visited a few times a week but mostly only stayed for ten or fifteen minutes; a quick visit to check all was well. He didn't normally volunteer to take Harry unless Niamh requested it. This disturbed her. It was as though JJ didn't want too much time with his son, so she only asked him when she desperately needed some sleep. His suggestion to give her a break this time had come as a surprise and without thinking it through, she'd agreed. Now she was having second thoughts. *I'll test the waters over the phone again,* she thought. *If he sounds anyway noncommittal, I'm definitely going to arrange a visit to see the respite house.*

Reluctantly, she picked up the phone and dialled JJ's number.

"Hi JJ," she said, "I was phoning about this weekend."

"Sure," he said.

"Well, I just wanted to warn you, it's not going to be an easy weekend. He's regressed quite a bit – some of his old behaviours have returned."

"OK," he said, "Like what?"

"Well, the obsession with the old spinner for starters, and the kicking and biting. We've just adjusted his behavioural plan. If you want to wait for another weekend that's fine with me, JJ."

Niamh continued to stress the extent of Harry's regressions, trying to gauge if JJ sounded like he was up to the task.

"Right then," he said, "Sounds bad all right, you must be knackered. Let him come, you need to have a break."

"It's really important that we both follow the plan. They said we have to be very strict about it, JJ."

He responded as though he were the more responsible parent of the pair. Of course he'd follow the plan. Didn't he always? JJ might have sounded flippant to Niamh but at the other end of the phone he was listening intently. *This isn't good*, he thought, *that fucking spinner*.

"The psychologist's come up with some suggestions," Niamh said, "I'll fill you in when you come to collect him. Please JJ, can you promise you'll stick to the plan?"

JJ knew what Niamh was like about new behavioural plans. He felt she was too inflexible with them himself, but feeling guilty about the difficult time she was having, he decided not to start an argument about her lack of conviction in him. He promised to be compliant.

"Thanks, JJ," she said and hung up.

Niamh wasn't sure if she was happy but she did need a break and Harry would be with his father after all. Her considerations about using the respite service were on hold once again.

Friday evening arrived. JJ was at the door and Harry's weekend bag was packed. Patrick didn't need anything as he had a bowl and bed ready at JJ's house. Niamh went over the new behavioural plan three times. *Jesus*, JJ thought, *does she think I'm thick?*

Harry took his father by the hand and all three headed off to the car. Niamh watched them until she couldn't see the car anymore. She felt the imaginary string attaching her heart to Harry elongate as the car moved away into the distance. When they disappeared out of sight entirely, it was as though it had snapped. She was awash with emotion and wanted to run after them.

"Come back! I'm fine. Leave Harry here with me."

She felt like he'd gone missing again and it was too

much for her to bear; it evoked both the recent memory and the physical sensations that accompanied it. Shutting the door, she felt weak and her tears flowed yet again. Trying to stop herself from crying, she told herself, *for God's sake, he's only down the road,* as she tried to get a grip on her emotions. *This must be what post-traumatic stress is like. I just have to relax, breathe deeply and run a bath,* she reasoned. Bathing was one of her favourite ways to relax; its medicinal benefits working wonders.

After the bath, she lay on her bed. Moments later, she was asleep, and didn't wake again until nine p.m. Feeling groggy, she got up and rang JJ to check how Harry was.

"Jesus Niamh, it's only nine o'clock," he said. "He's fine, stop worrying for fucks sake or I'll bring him back."

Dinner was a takeaway with a bottle of wine – a whole bottle for herself – and crisps too. She was back in bed by eleven p.m. and by eleven-thirty p.m. she was fast asleep, not waking until eleven a.m. the next day.

Niamh did nothing that weekend other than eat, rest, sleep, and phone to check on Harry.

JJ brought Harry and Patrick home on Sunday afternoon. Harry seemed quite subdued.

"He didn't sleep that well last night," JJ said.

"It's all gone backwards, hasn't it?" she replied.

"You know, you don't need to phone a few times a

day, every day, when he's with me. He's only down the road. I'll tell you if I need you, Niamh."

Niamh could hear the irritation in his voice.

JJ wanted to make a point. Niamh always called to check how Harry was but this weekend the number of calls she'd made were ridiculous. He didn't understand why she had to call at all.

"Sorry JJ. I know."

"So it's a deal then?" he said, hoping to take advantage of the situation to get her to stop ringing, "The next time no phone calls?"

"No phone calls," she said unconvincingly.

He didn't stay; he said he needed to meet a colleague in town. There was always some excuse to get away quickly and once he'd handed over Harry and Patrick, he was gone. He was happy his good deed was done and he was free for another few weeks.

Niamh didn't want to stay in for the afternoon; her head was aching from the wine she'd consumed over the weekend. She rarely drank anymore so anything more than a glass or two had this consequence.

"Let's get out for some fresh air. Patrick!" she called.

With his harness on and attached to Harry he was ready for work and off they went, the fresh air clearing her head. She was so happy. All she'd needed was a little sleep. *Me and Harry will get through the next few weeks. He'll regain his losses and make more gains. He's a bright boy*, she thought as she swung his hand in hers. She felt light and airy; life was good.

It was only then that she realised he didn't have his fidget spinner but he seemed fine without it so she said nothing. *How did JJ managed to get it away from him? The psychologist said it would probably take longer this time.*

When they got back home, Niamh looked through Harry's bag for his spinner but it wasn't there. She couldn't find it anywhere. A feeling of dread rippled through her. What if he needed it later? If so, there'd be a 'meltdown' to deal with. She only had the newer versions in the cupboard which were much less flashy.

Reticently, she picked up the phone.

"Oh yeah," JJ said, "I binned it. Took it from him after he went to sleep on Friday. He threw a complete wobbler when he woke up Saturday morning. I let him wear himself out and then gave him some chocolate which helped to end it. He got it back at bedtime last night so he'd go to sleep, and I took it away again after. Put it in the bin this morning. Thought it'd be better for him to go back to using the new one. It's less flashy, isn't it? Sorry, I completely forgot to say. Anyway, I pulled off the band-aid for ya, problem solved, weeks ahead of schedule."

Niamh listened in disbelief, anger surging through her body, but what was the point in arguing with him? She should've known explaining the behavioural plan was a waste of time. Wasn't that exactly why Harry had

181

been making more progress since JJ left?

She wondered what else he'd changed in the plan over the weekend. Had he followed any of it? It was only a matter of time before she'd have to deal with the consequences. She knew JJ didn't care; as far as he was concerned the problem was dealt with, and she should be grateful.

Niamh hung up and began to rummage in the cupboard for the newer spinner, keeping her fingers firmly crossed that Harry would accept it. If she was really lucky, he'd only start to look for it at bedtime.

The rocking began at six p.m. and was quickly followed by the screaming. There was no consoling Harry. He wanted the old spinner. When he started to bite himself, Niamh wrapped his weighted blanket around his shoulders and played his favourite music tape in an attempt to soothe him. It worked and eventually he began to calm down, then thankfully he accepted the newer spinner. They were both tired by then and she just wanted to put him to bed, but not wanting to disrupt his routine again she decided it would be better to run his bath as usual.

Harry loved his bath time; he loved the bubbles and it was the only time he easily accepted her touch. His touch responses puzzled Niamh as they varied so much. Soft or strong strokes with a sponge in the bath were generally good but yet he often pulled away from her soothing hand at other times. She could never be sure how he was going to respond.

In the bath, Niamh put soap onto a rough sponge and started his occupational therapy. She began with strokes to his legs and arms then moved to his back. As she did so, she noticed tiny pinch marks. *Oh no*, she thought as she continued to rub him with the sponge, *he's pinching himself again. JJ and his cavalier approach to getting rid of that old spinner has re-started the night-time pinching. How many more regressions am I going to have to deal with*?

Harry was happy splashing about in his bath with as much water on the floor as in the tub so Niamh took the opportunity to look more closely and noticed there were a lot of pinch marks. As well as those on his arms and legs, there were also a number on his back, even in between his shoulder blades. She wondered how he could reach there and was taken aback by the total number of little bruises she found – counting twenty in total.

In the past, pinching had been a nocturnal occurrence, usually when Harry appeared particularly tense. On those nights he had woken regularly, and Niamh and JJ had often argued about whose turn it was to get up to settle him. Allowing Harry access to the spinner in bed had enabled him to comfort himself without resorting to pulling at his skin in frustration, and being able to calm himself had meant they were less often disturbed at night. After the tension in the house reduced following JJ and Niamh's separation, the pinching had all but disappeared.

She was rinsing the soap from his back when she started to become suspicious. *JJ always said I was too soft. The pinch marks have dramatically reduced since he left. There are pinches between his shoulder blades – has JJ done this? Is this his way of punishing him or is Harry just stressed by the loss of his spinner and the weekend away from home?*

She ran her fingers over the marks. She couldn't be sure and so couldn't start making accusations. Oh God, poor Harry, how she wished he could talk.

Pulling the plug out, they both watched as the water disappeared down the drain *glug, glug, glug*. Harry swept the last bubbles away with his hands and sucked the suds off his fingertips one at a time.

She took another look at the myriad of little bruises as she dried him and counted them again. Surely she was being foolish? Little bruises did appear on Harry's skin occasionally. Her head was racing. Was that after visits with JJ? She just didn't know.

Niamh got her phone and took pictures while he played with his toothbrush at the bathroom sink. In the morning she'd check to see if there were more. She put on his shorts then tucked him into his bed – a surgical tucking in, all the way around, the way he liked it – and he got his spinner to twirl.

"Night night darling," she said as she moved out of

the room to sit outside the door until he was fully asleep.

The key to getting Harry to sleep quickly was to stay close by so you could tuck the blanket back in if he kicked it off. Tonight, he didn't; he was tired and in no time at all had fallen asleep.

Niamh didn't get up straight away. She sat in the corridor, with an arm across Patrick's back. She pulled her fingers through his thick hairy coat whilst holding the phone in her other hand, flicking through the pictures of the pinch marks.

In her head she methodically went over again and again all the information she had about this pattern of behaviour. The pinch marks had become less frequent after he was allowed the spinner in bed and had radically reduced since JJ had moved out. They'd both put this improvement down to there being less tension in the house, but was it her or JJ who'd first suggested that? She didn't know. Harry still had pinch marks sometimes but was that only after visits to his dad's? Oh God, she really couldn't say.

All she could say for certain was that it had been happening less and less, and JJ had been spending less and less time with Harry. Was JJ capable of hurting his son? Had she been completely blind? He'd never hurt her. They'd had some monumental arguments, but he'd never hit her.

There was the odd occasion when he'd gripped her too tightly, but he was always so apologetic when that happened.

Oh God! Her thoughts were racing now. *What about the time he threw the chopping board at the wall in temper?* He'd lost control completely that evening and she'd been terrified.

The longer she sat and thought about it the more occasions she recounted when perhaps he had shown that he was capable of hurting his own child. How had she not seen this before? Why had she thought of them as one-off incidences? Why was she so stupid?

She berated herself for being so self-absorbed and self-pitying. *I sent my son away for a weekend of abuse at the hands of his father while I sat drinking wine and sleeping like a baby.* Then she questioned her thoughts. *Am I being a bitch, thinking the worst of JJ because I'm mad at him? Has Harry just started to pinch himself again and I want someone to blame?*

Niamh, ordinarily a confident and resilient woman, now felt real self-doubt, doubting her abilities as a mother, her role as her son's protector and her understanding of the marriage she'd had with JJ.

She sat there on the landing, questioning if she'd been blinkered, if she'd subconsciously overlooked the truth because she did not want to face it.

There was one thing for certain though – JJ hadn't offered to take Harry again and she'd not be asking him to. She was determined to find out the truth.

Justification

On Monday, JJ took the day off work. 'Recovery time' he called it. He was thinking about his weekend with Harry and was starting to feel nicely drunk as he sat comfortably on his leather-studded settee, nursing another whiskey to console his guilty conscience.

It was a cruel but necessary thing I did, he thought to himself. *Niamh should thank me really; it's going to save her weeks of extra frustration grappling with Harry trying to reduce his dependency on that spinner. I always have to be the bad guy. She's way too soft, and those bloody psychologists! Well, they just need to justify their existence. If we all got on with life, they'd be out of business wouldn't they?*

He briefly stopped his train of thought to acknowledge exactly how ignorant Niamh was about the situation and allowed her a little compassion. *Maybe I would have taken the slow route this time if I had the time?*

JJ didn't enjoy hurting Harry; he believed he was only doing what was necessary to keep them 'all' safe. There was too much at stake. He was good at convincing himself he was doing the right thing even when he wasn't.

Experience had taught him the importance of tying up loose ends and Harry's old spinner was a loose end that he needed to get rid of. Once it was gone, it'd be forgotten.

"What's the name for it?" he said aloud, "Ah yes, Aversion Therapy."

It's worked well for centuries, he thought, *weren't most of us raised on it? All this positive stuff – what a heap of shit; months of pandering to get the same result. Short, sharp pain and it's over. Yes, Niamh should be grateful to me for pulling off the band-aid and getting it over with. He'll have forgotten about it by now anyway, poor kid.*

JJ had been surprised by the extent of Harry's regression; he hadn't realised it was quite so bad, but he couldn't tell Niamh why, she wouldn't understand and he needed things to get back to the way they were before suspicions were aroused. *Typical*, he thought, *that the one person who can't say anything might be the very person who could undo everything.*

His thoughts wandered as he continued to drink and he began to think about what a gifted life Niamh had, coming from her perfect well-heeled family. In his mind's eye, he pictured a ladder and placed her near the top. He begrudgingly thought,

On the ladder of life, she's never stood on the lower rungs and there isn't any risk of her sliding down one or two either – not with her family around her. She might keep them at arm's length, but their arm will nonetheless pull her right back up whenever she needs it to. Haven't they already had to bail her out because of her idealistic ideas about her perfect clinic? She'd have to have a tougher business head on her if she was to rely on her income alone. She'd never have got that clinic off the ground in the first place.

He often thought about peoples' positions on the ladder of life and about how this affected their opportunities and choices. He'd remind himself that the world was not a level playing field and that once a person's ability to make a choice was lost – as it commonly was for those at the bottom of the ladder – then it was all about survival. In nature, only the strongest survived. This attitude helped JJ keep his conscience clear.

I've had to be self-centred and single-minded to survive, other people haven't – lucky for them. I can't go back and change the life that created me, the man I am today.

"I am who I am," he'd say, "I may be damaged, but I won't be beaten."

Niamh gets through life bouncing up and down on a

safety net; I go through life walking on a tightrope, getting blasted from either side with nothing below me. How could she ever understand what it's like to be me? She has no idea how lucky she is. I didn't choose my situation in life but I have to live with it. It's not onwards and upwards for all of us.

The whiskey was definitely taking effect; he was feeling maudlin. Left alone with his thoughts and his bottle of whiskey, some might describe him as self-pitying while others would say philosophical. Either way, sitting further back into his couch he continued to navel-gaze at his life, watching as it circled in his mind and reaching in to grab at the memories and thoughts that helped him reconcile his conscience with his actions.

I have no family to help me. They've been lost to me for years and won't be there to push me back up the ladder. If I fall, I'll fall to my death, just like May. I have no choice other than to do whatever needs to be done to keep myself safe. No pain, no gain, he told himself.

He gulped more whiskey, unable to stop himself from seeking solace in the drink even though it never really seemed to work for him.

There was no legitimate way out for me but I found my own way out, he thought, *I have to look out for myself, no one else will. Even Long John, who was employed by the state and paid a wage to help me, used and abused me. Not even Niamh, the woman I thought*

190

loved me, stayed. No, she's too busy looking out for Harry. He's the most important person to her.

With half the bottle now empty JJ continued justifying his actions. *I'm just fighting back – isn't that what you're expected to do? Don't give in, fight back? I put my faith in the system – a system that brought Long John to me and look what happened! If you can't win then join in. It's taken me most of my life to get to here. It mightn't be perfect, but I sure as hell ain't going back. No one's going to mess with me anymore.*

And as the evening wore on, sprawled across his settee, JJ's sub-conscious mind began to throw out snippets of his past, like movie trailers; movies he hated, but had no ability to edit the script of in his current semi-conscious state.

They always began with the various headlines in the newspapers, then re-played what had actually occurred. He found it strange that he knew the exact details behind the headlines.

The movies that played in his head that evening were based on the headlines: 'Another heist in Dublin. A security guard is shot dead' and 'Gardai seeking information on local missing teen.'

Jonnie hadn't asked to be involved in the heist; he hadn't even known where he was going that day. He had been told to give the lads a lift, so he had. Told he'd have to wait for them, so he would. It was only as he had parked the car on the street that he'd realised what they were about to do, but it was too late to pull out by then. Anyway if he'd run away they'd have killed him. Too afraid to think, he'd continued to do what he was told.

In his mind the movie began to play.

The security guard is chasing after his accomplices as they race towards the car screaming at him to, "Go, go, go!"

They get in, and Jonnie turns to check they are all inside. As he does so, he sees Mick raise his gun and shoot the security guard in the chest, just as he reaches the car. They are all screaming at him.

"Drive! Drive!"

Shock and fear render him immobile. It's only a split second but long enough for him to see the expression of horror and despair in the man's eyes as he falls onto the car window, clinging to his last few seconds of life. He can see that the security guard knows he's made a mistake and is about to die but it's too late for him. There is more shouting and Jonnie feels thumping on the back of his seat.

"Go, fucking go!"

His foot hits the accelerator and in his wing mirror he sees the security guard slide off the car and onto the ground as they speed away.

All the newspaper headlines that week reported the story of the murdered man – what a great person he had been and how much he'd loved his young family. At the time, Jonnie had wished he hadn't read any of the articles; he'd wished they'd hurry up and bury him so it would all stop. He'd told himself that it was the security guard's own fault – no job was worth that – he should have known better than to try and stop them.

The next headline... the next movie: 'Gardai seeking information on local missing teen', often plagued JJ's memory in all its minute details.

The dull thud of fists and boots meeting flesh; the weight of their impact on a body; the crack as a head hits a door frame; the blood on their fists; the gruesome site of an unresponsive body as it flays about on the ground; it's relentlessly kicked about on the bloodied grass.

A movie about one of the first beatings Jonnie had witnessed in the early days. It involved a young man called Kevin. The beating always stood out in his memory.

Kevin owed money to the gang and his beating was intended to be a lesson to Jonnie; a warning as to what would happen to him if he was ever disloyal. They put on a good show but in their enthusiasm the lesson had gone too far, and Kevin had died.

He had been a known drug addict with a long list of convictions for petty crime. Locals knew he was in trouble, so at first it was assumed he'd gone into hiding. It took some time before he was reported as a missing person. His body was never found and he never came back of course. Yet his story only made headlines in the local press. Only Jonnie and the tall fir trees had been witness to the brutality of his death.

He didn't know the exact whereabouts of Kevin's body, but he knew it was buried somewhere in the Wicklow mountains.

The nightmare usually ended with him waking up in the dark, sweating and gasping for breath, surrounded by his soft pillows and clean white sheets.

This time, in his drunken stupor as he lay on his couch, the movie began before the fatal assault.

Kevin is crying and begging for mercy on the way to Wicklow in the back of the car. Jonnie is thinking that Kevin would have been in school if he were further up life's ladder, sitting behind a desk leaning on his elbow in boredom. Instead, he is in the back of their car, red-eyed and snotty-nosed, about to be given a severe beating in the middle of nowhere.

JJ was roused from his slumber. He felt sick. Was it the result of the movies in his mind or the whiskey? He lifted his head but it was too much effort to move so he lay back down. He was back in the car on the way to Wicklow.

Jonnie is feeling the fear, both Kevin's and his own. Kevin has fallen silent in the back seat between his two captors, realising the futility of his tears. Jonnie doesn't turn around; he doesn't want to see his face and stays focused on the road ahead.

They arrive in a wooded area and park the car. Kevin is dragged out. He doesn't even try one last attempt to plead for mercy. Mick punches him in the stomach and Kevin falls back against the side of the car. Jonnie hears Kevin let out a groan.

"Jonnie get out. Watch and learn," Mick shouts.

Kevin receives several more blows from Mick, then the other two join in with repeated punches. They take turns to hold Kevin up against the side of the car when he is no longer able to support his own weight.

Jonnie prays he can't feel the blows; that he is not conscious enough to feel the pain. There are short, gasping breaths after the first few strikes and for a very brief moment, Kevin's frightened eyes plead for them to stop.

Jonnie observes how crumpled Kevin's clothes begin to look when he becomes limp, as though they don't fit him. His t-shirt rips at the shoulder seam as they hold him aloft, his jeans sag around his hips, and Jonnie sees a chain on his neck with a pendant. He wonders if it is a gift from a loved one. All the while the sound of thud, thud, thud continues.

He is afraid to look away so he tries, as much as possible, without being noticed, to focus further afield, behind Kevin, into the dark shadows of the trees beyond. Kevin and the beating become a blur. He can't bear the lesson; he's not able to cope with this.

It's not long before Kevin's eyes glaze over and his attackers tire of holding him up but they continue to kick him on the ground. Kevin is unconscious or maybe even already dead so what's the point of continuing? Surely he's learnt his lesson by now?

They are done, and take a moment to stand to admire their handiwork while they catch their breath. Mick looks back at Jonnie to make sure he is still paying attention and nods down at Kevin. He wipes some sweat from his forehead, leaving in it's place a streak of Kevin's blood.

"See what he made us do to him?" he says. "Don't make us do that to you."

Jonnie had been forced to help put the body in the boot of the car. It was the first time he'd experienced what a dead weight felt like. There'd been no remorse for their excess.

It later became clear to him that a beating was an odds game – it depended on the mood of the attacker whether a person survived or not.

Kevin's broken and bloodied body was disposed of in a pre-dug shallow grave.

Jonnie can hear the sound of a stream nearby and feel the soft, undulating forest floor under his feet as they carry Kevin's body to his grave. Such a contrast to the harshness of what he just witnessed. He wonders how many pre-dug graves exist for such occurrences and if there is a grave set aside for him somewhere too – just waiting for him.

They are monsters, he thinks.

Young Jonnie received his first beating on the way back to Dublin that day. But he was saved from the replay of that movie by a violent coughing fit. Unsteadily, JJ pulled himself upright.

Pouring himself another glass he questioned whether he'd ever had the choice or opportunity to get out when he was younger, and as always concluded he had not.

His thoughts returned to his favourite ladder analogy. *Did I start at the bottom rung or was there an even lower one where Kevin started? Is that why Kevin is dead and I'm still alive?*

Louise, he thought, *how did she do so well for herself on her ladder of life? We are kindred spirits – both starting low – but she's done very well.* He wondered if she harboured the same kind of secrets he did. Was she haunted by her past or was she a good example of that which the state had denied him? Did she meet a better Long John who helped her one step at a time? *The sex was good*, he thought, *I wonder? Ah, who cares. She'd better stick to her alibi story, or she'll be sliding back down her ladder.*

As he lost consciousness his glass slipped gently from his hand to the floor, wobbling from side to side but staying upright, keeping the last dregs of whiskey intact.

Lain there on his comfy couch, in his comfy living room with all his modern conveniences around him, he couldn't escape the nightmares that circled in his brain. As the night set in, there was no end to the violence and despair in his dreams. The moivies replayed again and again.

With his head flung back in a deep state of sleep, a single tear rolled down the side of his face and ran along the groove of his scar. There was no one to see it, not even JJ.

Game-changer

Twelve months earlier, shortly before JJ and Niamh separated, it had been another normal day at Bellingham & Co., until Sandra announced during the team meeting:

"Dominic's Park is to be our newest acquisition for re-development. Today we'll be exploring our options."

Dominic's Park. JJ had looked up at Sandra and then at the sheets of paper being passed around the table. There it was again. *Dominic's Park* in print. Sandra's voice had disappeared into the distance; he'd no longer been able to hear what she was saying. Straightening the pages of the document in front of him he'd glanced around at his colleagues before looking down to re-read. *Dominic's Park.*

Oh Christ, Dominic's Park.

Stunned, sitting and staring at the paper, not moving an inch for a few more moments, JJ had suddenly found it hard to breathe. Unable to sit still in his chair, he'd felt clammy and dizzy like someone was squeezing him very tightly around his chest. Standing up, he'd excused himself before leaving the room.

With his vision blurred he made his way to his office and there he fell backwards into his chair, still clutching the piece of paper in his hand. Every part of his body had begun to shake. He couldn't stop it. The more he'd tried to take control the tenser he'd become and the shaking had only got worse, until he'd been shaking so violently it had made his chair rock.

Standing up and stretching momentarily brought him some relief, but as soon as he sat back down the shaking had returned. It felt like it always had, as if he were about to have a heart attack, but he'd not called for help. Instead, he'd reached for the glass of water on his desk and took a sip. Then he'd taken steadying breaths in and out, tellling himself to slow the breaths down as he tried to relax into the shaking.

"Let it go," he'd said to himself, "Let the shaking do its thing."

After what had felt like an eternity, his breathing regulated itself back to normal, and slowly the shaking subsided.

This was not the first time JJ had experienced a panic attack. He'd had many over the years – the first on the day he'd witnessed the fatal assault on Kevin. That day, on the way back to Dublin in the car, the others had started arguing about where they wanted to stop to get some food, and the normality of that conversation sparked a sensation of panic within him. He hadn't known what he was experiencing back then, and had genuinely thought he was going to die.

Feeling unable to breathe and needing air he'd opened the car window, but the others had told him to close it. They'd said they were getting cold, yet he couldn't breathe.

He'd started to fidget uncontrollably, undoing his jacket and holding his jumper away from his throat. When they'd wanted to know what was up with him, he'd started to gasp and beg to get out. He'd felt so sick and dizzy; his heart had been pounding so much he thought it might pound right out of his chest.

Infuriated with him, they'd turned off the main road and pulled in on a side road. He'd stumbled out and bent over, with his hands on his knees. He'd tried to get oxygen, but he still couldn't breathe.

In this position, something had appeared below his face. With no time to react to the booted foot, he'd been knocked back against the car. The blunt pain of the boot below his chin returning him to reality. Unable to focus and in shock, he'd become the new punch bag.

They'd shouted abuse at him as they repeatedly punched him.

"Pull your fucking self together!"

"You're a disgrace to manhood!"

"Sissy!"

T*hud*, *thud*, *thud*, just the same as they had administered to Kevin earlier. Jonnie was convinced that he too was about to die.

He took some consolation from that fact that he couldn't remember the whole ordeal, hoping Kevin also lost awareness of the ferocity of the blows he'd received before he died.

"Can you breathe now?" they'd laughed.

By then barely conscious, they'd picked him up and bundled him back into the car.

Later, back at Long John's house, he was dumped in his room, and it was there, after he'd fully regained consciousness, that he'd begun to realise the painful extent of his injuries. It had hurt – everywhere. Barely able to move, he'd wanted to call for help – but to whom? Not able to see past his swollen eyelids he hadn't even been sure where he was.

Gently he'd traced a long laceration running along the side of his face and wondered how badly he'd be disfigured. A short time later, he'd tried to sit up but a sharp pain in his ribs had forced him to lie back down. The broken little finger on his right hand had gone unnoticed until the following day, the pain masked by the difficulty he'd had trying to inhale, so painful were his ribs, back and stomach.

Jonnie had lain on his bed for hours that evening, waiting to die, wishing he'd not regained consciousness and praying to 'pass on' quickly.

At some point, the door opened and he'd heard Long John's voice telling him to drink. Feeling the jab of a straw as it was pushed into his mouth, he had sipped some water through it.

Those first few days went by in a haze. He'd felt fearful all the time – his greatest fears were of dying and of getting another beating, and each time the door opened his heart had jumped. Despite his severe injuries, he'd never complained, too afraid of that beating if he wasn't seen to be tough enough.

Each day in silence, he rallied against the pain to increase his flexibility, eager to show how strong he was in his recuperation, and slowly his physical wounds began to heal.

Although weeks passed by before he was seen outside again, Jonnie had been acutely aware that no-one had noticed his absence. It had been a hard lesson and one he'd never forgotten.

His assailants excuse for beating him to a pulp – 'to knock some toughness into him' – had of course not stopped the panic attacks. He quietly experienced them numerous times during the weeks that followed his savage beating – very painful ones while his wounds were still healing.

Over time, and with many hours spent privately researching on the internet, JJ became very adept at using coping mechanisms to manage their onset. Gaining an understanding of the bodily sensations he experienced, and realising that he could still function normally, had been a great help. The gang never saw what they considered a 'weakness' again.

The day Sandra announced the re-development of Dominic's Park as the company's new project, he'd been taken so off guard he'd had much more trouble than normal re-gaining his composure. Knowing he needed to get out of the office he'd told his secretary he was feeling unwell and had left before the others even finished their meeting.

Driving home in his car, he'd concentrated on changing the gears and had talked himself through all the physical things he was doing to keep himself calm – *I'm holding the steering wheel, I'm turning on the indicator, I'm looking in my mirror, I can feel the seat underneath me.* He'd reminded himself it was just a panic attack and would pass; he'd even invited the panic attack to do more as a way of diffusing the experience. He used every mechanism he knew of and it had helped as it always did.

Once home though, JJ had turned to a less helpful strategy. He'd poured himself a large glass of whiskey – his go-to medicine for that afternoon. With Niamh at work, Harry in school and Anna not due to arrive until three thirty p.m. he'd had plenty of time to 'calm' himself with the whiskey.

Not wanting to engage with Anna, he left a scribbled note on the table to say he was home and in bed with a migraine. Then he'd gone upstairs with his glass in his hand to think. Sitting on the bed and looking around his bedroom, he thought about the good life he had; things weren't that great between him and Niamh, but he had a job he enjoyed, two properties, two cars and an annual holiday. *There's no way Dominic's Park is going to ruin my life again.* He couldn't go back.

There must be some way out of this mess? he'd thought as he drank back the whiskey and then hurriedly returned downstairs to pour himself another final, larger one before Anna and Harry arrived home.

JJ had heard their movements downstairs a short time later; Harry had been shouting and crying about something that was upsetting him but he'd ignored it; he had more troubling things on his mind to deal with.

Turning on his computer, he'd clicked on the file relevant to that day's meeting to double-check. There was no mistaking it… it was the same Dominic's Park.

Gazing out across his perfectly manicured garden, which was nothing like the concrete backyard of his childhood home with its washing line divide, he'd wondered what on Earth he was going to do.

A journey back in time

Despite the whiskey, JJ had been unable to dull the sense of fear and panic brought on by Sandra's announcement.

In his room that afternoon, he hadn't been able to stop himself from thinking about the half-frozen body buried under the conservatory, the body of Eoin, the teenager who'd gone missing from the gym all those years ago. At least, he'd assumed it was Eoin's body and he'd wondered again, as he often had, how long Eoin had lived after he left him with Long John, heading into town.

Stroking the rim of his glass, he'd reflected some more about how his life had changed... how he'd worked so hard to build the life he had now and how he had no intention of losing it. Little by little that afternoon, his brain switched from shock and despair into combat mode.

Reluctantly, JJ had realised he was going to have to

make contact with Long John, the man who'd deprived him of the better life he could have had when he was younger, and the person who'd filled his head with violence and fear. Such a cruel twist of fate. He had always thought Long John might one day orchestrate his fall from grace.

This can't be my downfall, not now, not after all this time. I have to do something. The remains will have to be moved. Long John will have to remove them.

He had phoned work to say he'd be taking another day off sick, then he'd washed out the whiskey glass from which he'd been drinking. Niamh disapproved of his daytime 'tipples' and he had become used to hiding the evidence. After that, he had curled up to try and get some rest.

A few hours later, after he'd heard Niamh arrive home, JJ got up and somehow managed to get through the evening without igniting suspicion.

The next day, he'd left for work as normal, but when he reached the motorway, instead of turning left as usual, he turned right for Dublin. It had been a strange experience. Every mile he travelled towards his destination had felt as though he were driving backwards in time and the closer he'd got the more anxious he'd become, knowing full well his life hung in the balance.

Within the hour he had arrived outside Dominic's Park. *Tick, tick, tick,* the indicator sounded as he waited for the lights to turn green so he could cross the new dual carriageway. Not having been in the immediate area for years, it had looked very different to how he remembered.

JJ's only connection with the area since he'd moved on in his life had been through a charitable organisation that sourced summer jobs for a selection of local young teenagers. The youngsters spent a few weeks out of the city during the summer holidays, getting work experience in areas of interest to them, the summer holidays being a time when the absence of a structured day often led to an increase in youthful misdemeanours. It was an attempt to motivate them to do well at school and keep them out of trouble. The aim: to provide summer placements that would enable then to look beyond their immediate environment and strive to achieve better outcomes for themselves. JJ provided work experience opportunities at Bellingham & Co. It made him feel good to think he might help a youngster have a better future and the initiative had worked very well so far, providing good PR for him and the company.

His initial reaction to seeing Dominic's Park after so many years had been one of relief. He'd expected it to look very similar, but there'd been a grand new entrance with flower beds either side of it, and where houses had once stood there was a large parking area with a small playground beside.

Initially optimistic that it wasn't going to be the journey back in time he'd expected he might have to endure, he'd crossed the road and slowly driven further on into the estate, but in no time at all it had started to look much more familiar. The houses there hadn't changed; they looked exactly the same as the old corporation houses he remembered – rough, grey, pebble-dashed boxes. All identical except for a few which had been renovated with new exterior plasterwork and paint.

Driving down the once familiar streets, he had visualised the internal layout of all the houses, remembering his own box room at the back of number fifteen, only big enough for a single bed and a small bedside locker; his clothes always heaped in smelly bundles, dirty ones nearest the door, cleanest near his locker ready to be worn again. It had been a simple laundry system.

JJ recalled his open bedroom window, left unlatched to let in fresh air. It had looked out onto a small backyard. There'd been many times in the weeks after he'd moved there when he'd leaned close to the pulled curtains in the evenings, trying to hear some of the tetchy conversations taking place down below, wondering what they were about; hoping he was wrong about Long John.

He had continued driving, so slowly you'd think he was lost, but he'd known exactly where he was going, and as he got closer to number fifteen he passed Eugene's family home. Eugene had been one of the teenagers who'd been picked the previous summer for work experience at Bellingham & Co. JJ had got to know him quite well. He'd been a pleasant young man to have around the office but the general consensus had been that he needed to work on his attentiveness if he was serious about fulfilling his business career ambitions.

This was also the house Eugene's grandfather had lived in, and as he passed it, in his mind's eye, JJ had seen Eugene's grandfather clearly. He'd seen him laughing as he stood over the hole that he and Long John had dug in the conservatory floor, and he'd felt his hand on his back as he'd been pushed to the edge of the grave.

JJ had to turn away from the house that day, not wanting to distress himself any further.

On the next street, more of the homes had been boarded up, and the further on he'd travelled the more deserted the estate had become.

Rounding the last bend to the left, he'd seen Long John's house at the end of the terrace. *Please God let him be there*, he'd thought, feeling his stomach tighten, and he'd been almost alongside it before he'd realised that the house was completely boarded up. The overgrown garden indicated it had been vacant for some time and someone had daubed 'loser' in red paint across the front door; even that had faded and cracked.

Sat in his car looking across at the house, unable to decide what to do next, in his head he had again pictured the inside layout and visualised himself walking in for a look around. He saw Long John at the kitchen table with his cigarette and ashtray. He smelt the smoke and heard the voices of others in the conservatory beyond. He saw the dead body under the tiled floor and deciding he didn't want to venture in there, he turned instead to make his way up the narrow stairs, listening to the hollow sound of his shoes on the bare floorboards as he went. Looking up towards his little box room at the top, he left the voices behind him and stood for a moment outside his bedroom door before entering and shutting it closed. His safe space.

JJ had then begun to tremble.

"Shit."

Sitting in his car the day after Dominic's Park had come crashing back into his life, he had returned to the house he'd so foolishly wanted to live in after leaving school; the house from where he'd planned to launch himself into a different life. *If I could turn back the clock*, he had thought, *I'd never have crossed the threshold.*

It was the place and time that had effectively murdered what remained of his youthful prospects. Even as an empty shell, soon to be demolished, the house still threatened to annihilate his future. Hindsight was harsh.

Secrets

"What's up?" Niamh asked, "What's got into you? You've been acting so distant lately…"

Louise had been distracted since Harry's disappearance, but over the last few days she had become increasingly withdrawn. Niamh could see something was bothering her but Louise wasn't disclosing what it was.

"Oh nothing really, Niamh, just dopey this week, that's all." She couldn't tell Niamh about JJ's threat, she had to think of something else to discuss. "Actually I was just thinking about Finn."

"He's becoming a bit of an obsession!" Niamh smiled.

Louise ignored her.

"I saw him out walking this morning. He looked pretty down. It's so unfair the amount of attention he's been getting," she said as she pulled a grimace and rubbed her neck to relieve some of the tension it held.

"The gossips are loving it you know. His past is getting dredged up again. It's like they've forgotten all the years in between."

"I know," Niamh said, her smile now gone, "But that's the way it works, isn't it? You're guilty till proven innocent around here."

"Why didn't JJ say he was being blackmailed earlier, Niamh?"

"He just keeps saying it was too risky. I think he was a bloody fool. He put Harry's life in danger," she said forcefully, "I won't be forgiving him anytime soon."

Louise knew she'd touched a nerve and Niamh was about to react to it.

"He should've involved the Gardai from the get-go, and he sure as hell should have told me! For God's sake, I don't know what he was thinking. Still, isn't that why we've gone our separate ways."

She stopped for a moment, then rather unexpectedly added,

"He's changed Louise, he's not the man I used to know. Sometimes I wonder if I ever really knew him at all."

She was thinking of the little pinch marks on Harry's body but she didn't say this to Louise. Like always, as much as she loved Louise, she was careful with the information she imparted. She just said,

"Did it take Harry to show me the real man? You didn't know him before Harry came along. He was different then. When we were first married, he was funny, suave and confident. I think he really loved me. In fact, I'd go as far as to say at that time he was actually a godsend to me. He was the right man, in the right place, at the right time."

She looked pensive.

"Of course, after Harry arrived everything changed. I never said much back then, but we really struggled Louise. There was so little sleep. Harry just cried and cried. We were so tired and after a while, JJ just seemed to give up. He said it was my fault, he couldn't do anything right. We fought a lot. If not for the escape of work, I think I might have gone mad. I don't think he ever really got it, Louise. It's sad that my husband, the person I most want in this whole world to be in this with me, is the person who has the greatest problem with accepting Harry – him and my parents. Jesus, they don't get it either. They think he's plain bold half the time too."

Louise was shocked to hear Niamh sharing her personal life, it wasn't like her. *She must be struggling,* she thought.

"For a while, I thought he was coming around but he wasn't. He just started to say what I wanted to hear and then he'd do his own thing anyway. That was worse than the fighting in the end because there was no discussing anything. Sometimes I felt so alone Louise. I still feel alone. You know he says… He says I stopped loving him after Harry was born; that everything had to be my way and that he wasn't allowed an opinion. Once he even accused me of using him as a sperm donor." There was a slight pause, "I was thinking the other night, maybe he was actually glad when Harry went missing. How awful is that?"

Louise reached for her hand.

"I'm so sorry Niamh, I had no idea."

The touch of Louise's hand jolted Niamh. She realised her armour had slipped and she had to put it back on.

"How could you Louise? I've never let on. Honestly this whole kidnap experience – it's knocked me for six. I'm fine honestly, I'm fine. I've been fine. Just having one of those days myself. There's two of us in it, eh?"

Louise had never considered that Niamh might be more vulnerable than she appeared. Shame engulfed her. She'd no idea how hard Niamh had been trying to stay afloat. She always knew there were problems in her marriage, but thought her family were her rock. *I've been too engrossed in my own life and worries,* she guiltily thought.

Niamh attempted to withdraw her hand, but Louise didn't let her go.

"Honestly Niamh, if you ever want to talk, blow off some steam, I'm here. If you need a hand, please, you're not on your own. You'll never know how much I appreciate your friendship. A problem shared is a problem halved – isn't that what they say? Let's have each other's backs. No secrets."

Louise was thinking ahead – she was going to tell Niamh. *I am, I definitely am*, she told herself. Besides, she knew it was only a matter of time before the truth came out.

"Ha!" Niamh quipped, uncomfortable with the intenseness of the conversation, "You have secrets, do you? You must part with them soon then. Play fair madam."

To release herself from Louise's hand she playfully nudged her shoulder and pulled away.

Louise laughed.

"Sure Niamh, sure."

The little bell at the front desk rang once more and the pair set to work, but all afternoon Louise couldn't get JJ off her mind and she wished for once she could be brave and tell Niamh about everything.

The hours dragged for Louise. It was one of the rare days when she wasn't in the mood to work. She completed the tasks required of her more so by routine than conscious thought, her head a long way away from the clinic, lost in worry and regrets.

At home that evening, returning to the drawer in her bedside cabinet, she rummaged around for the white envelope. Louise hadn't looked at it this often in years. Rubbing her hand across the brown sticky tape stain, now dry and brittle, she was again catapulted back in time, recalling her grief, his soft velvety skin and the stream of light through the doorway as he was taken away.

Closing her eyes and freeing the tears already gathered, she cradled the envelope to her chest like a baby, the tiniest piece of him left behind. It was all she had but it had brought her some peace over the years, knowing a part of her son was still with her. Now though, that wasn't enough. It had to change. She had to take action.

The day Louise first set eyes on Finn she'd taken out the envelope, unable to reconcile the man she saw on the street with the tiny piece of caul and the child she had parted with over forty years ago. The man gesticulating at a group of teenage boys, shouting and swearing as they scattered in all directions, bore no comparison to the man she had pictured him growing up into in her mind.

Logically, she'd known they were the same person, that he was her son, but she'd struggled to accept the truth before her. He was nothing at all like she'd imagined.

Over the coming weeks, Louise had watched out for Finn everywhere, like a private detective observing him from a distance, and slowly she'd started to see resemblances – his chin, his eyes, his nose and her grandfather's auburn hair.

His hair colour had been a surprise. Louise had

expected him to be blonde; his hair had been so fair on the day of his birth. He had large hands – JJ's hands – like those which had hauled her off her feet that day in the carpark, large and rough, so unlike the hands that had seductively touched her body during the months before. *JJ must be to blame for Finn's aggressive streak.*

There were aspects of him Louise hadn't recognised; mannerisms she couldn't place. The way he shuffled along as though life had little interest in him and the way he held his hand to his face when he spoke, as if it were a shield to hide behind.

It took her a little time to come to terms with the fact that her son – for whom she'd come to this area to keep a motherly eye on – was this middle-aged man and not the person she'd imagined, yet Louise still so desperately wanted to embrace him.

In the end, it was her mother who had told her about Finn's circumstances and his whereabouts. Unbeknown to Louise, her mother had kept in contact with Angela on and off over the years, and as she neared her death, fearing eternal damnation for the part she had played in their separation, she had told Louise everything she knew about him; aware that Finn was now alone in the world.

Unlike her mother, Louise hadn't sought Finn out for fear of damnation. She simply felt compelled to know him in whatever way she could, and not wanting to further upset his life with revelations about his heritage, she had visions of being some kind of secret guardian angel. Back then, her plan seemed straight forward, but now in reality it was clear that it was never going to work out. Since getting to know Finn, it had become increasingly impossible to keep her distance.

After a few minutes, Louise returned the envelope to its hiding place at the back of the drawer. It was just like Finn – a secret kept close by but not publicly acknowledged. The time had come to tell the truth.

Going for a walk to try to settle herself and work through her thoughts, Louise passed by Finn's house. It was in darkness. *That's unusual, he's normally ensconced in front of the TV by now*. There it was again – the worrying. *If I told the truth, I'd be able to knock on the door and see for myself; check if he is home and how he's doing... that is if I'm not rejected.*

Walking on by the police station, she noted most of the windows were illuminated. *Is Finn in there being questioned again?* There was no way of knowing. She couldn't just walk in and ask. If she were known to be his mother, however, that would be a different story...

Louise had forgotten her gloves, and rubbing her hands together to warm them, she decided to keep going rather than return home to get them, knowing full well she'd not be able to sleep later if she didn't get a decent walk in before it got dark. After passing the last shop at the edge of town, she headed to the old road by the graveyard, and onto the new lakeside walk.

It was late afternoon; she had another hour of twilight before it would be fully dark and although this was an isolated spot, the familiarity of it made her feel safe.

The waters of the lake lapped gently below her to the left, while to her right, the conifer trees stood tall, casting long shadows across the screed-covered path, which was narrow and winding. Louise allowed the sounds underfoot and overhead to calm her mind as she walked.

Mr Rafters was walking his dog, Mac. He pulled the leash tighter to him as she approached. Mac was a bit of a nipper – one to watch out for when on the consulting table – and on cue he characteristically made a lunge for the oncoming threat. Mr Rafters was ready with a sharp tug on his lead, and the dog was abruptly brought back in line.

"Have a lovely walk," Mr Rafters said to Louise, "It's a beautiful evening."

"It is indeed," she said as she passed him by.

It was a two kilometres walk either way to the main road crossing. *There's plenty of time to get there and back before it's fully dark*, she was thinking, as she walked along the path which was now dipping down closer to the lake, parts of it laid with a boardwalk. The wood made it nice and springy underfoot but sometimes slippery in the wet weather. Louise had fallen here once before.

Just after coming off the boardwalk, at a point where

the path turned away from the rushes and back towards the woods, out of the corner of her eye she saw a man at the edge of the water. Thinking little of it, she assumed it was one of the many fishermen who came to fish, but when she looked again she couldn't see a rod.

Louise slowed her pace. It looked like Finn, but the distance was too far and the light was starting to fade. Not entirely sure, she kept walking.

Fifteen minutes later, after reaching the main road crossing and touching the post at the gateway, as she always did, Louise turned to walk back the way she had just come. It was getting dark faster than anticipated so she quickened her step. There was no point unnecessarily putting herself in harm's way by walking alone in the dark.

Away from the road and heading back towards the lakeshore, from the boardwalk, Louise could see the person was still standing at the water's edge and slowed down to give herself a clearer view.

It's Finn. What's he up to? she thought. *In all the years I've been here I've never heard that he likes to fish*. While trying to decide whether to approach him or just keep going, Louise saw Finn begin to move – not away from the water but straight towards it and that stopped her in her tracks.

Yes, he was definitely heading into the water. Instinctively she called out, "Finn!," watching all the time and willing him to stop. He didn't look back and kept walking into the lake, the water already up to his knees. Panic set in.

"Finn, stop! Stop! Please stop," she shouted.

There was too much distance between them and Louise's voice trailed away on the breeze. There was no way to get there in time if he was intent on killing himself. He'd be submerged in the lake's dark depths and there'd be nothing she could do. *Oh God, please let this not be happening.*

Off the path and trying to run, the water-laden reedbed underfoot slowed her pace, the marshland unmercifully boggy. The further towards the lake she went the more she sank. It was like quicksand, dragging her sodden feet to a halt.

"Finn, stop! Stop!"

Screaming now, her voice was hoarse, not used to being raised to shout at anyone let alone the distant figure of her son in the dimming light.

He kept moving, slowly and carefully, into the water as Louise continued to stumble towards him as fast as she could, out of breath but still trying to shout loudly.

"Stop! Please, just wait. Wait!"

Only having covered a quarter of the distance between them, Finn vanished behind the rushes. She couldn't see him anymore. Stopping and searching, hoping to see him re-emerge into her sight, Louise started to sob. Her son was going to drown himself and there was nothing she could do other than be a witness to the aftermath. Not a swimmer, she wouldn't be able to help him or even pull him out if he went too far. *Is this what's been in store for me all along? Punishment, not redemption?*

Soaking wet from falling into the soggy marsh, she set off again and stumbled once more, elbow-deep in the mud. Crying and trying to pull herself back upright Louise looked ahead, and there, standing back on the shores edge, she saw Finn.

"Thank God."

Motionless she watched, hoping he wouldn't move towards the watery depths again.

He still hadn't noticed her but she could now see he had something in his hand – a long-handled net and a fishing rod. Closer now and able to study the figure more carefully. Louise couldn't believe her eyes. *It's not Finn at all! It's a fisherman wading out to retrieve his rod and net. I must have missed the rod earlier. My fucking eyesight!*

Wet through to her skin, she suddenly registered how cold she felt. The brown sludgy mud from the reedbeds stuck to her from head to foot. Red-eyed, exhausted, completely out of breath and feeling quite weak, Louise watched the fisherman bend over to open a box intended for carrying home his catch.

She looked around to check if anyone had witnessed her foolishness, her relief rapidly being replaced by embarrassment, but thankfully she and the fisherman were alone and he still seemed oblivious to her presence.

With no other choice than to turn around and head back towards the boardwalk as quickly as possible, she set off, hoping to make it back before the fisherman was ready to return the same way. *He might have better eyesight than me and recognise the strange woman wading through the boggy land between us*, she thought. Her heart was pounding and her legs hurt. She felt like such a fool.

What had got into her? She was sure it was Finn.

Back on the boardwalk, Louise wasted no time, hoping to reach home without meeting anyone. It was almost dark and would be completely so by the time she got as far as the graveyard. Taking a short cut across the wasteland at the back of the cemetery would avoid the busier main street; from there it was only a short walk to her house, and with any luck she'd escape having to awkwardly explain her appearance.

As she walked, weighed down by her wet and dirty clothes, she thought about Finn and hoped he was home by now watching television and not out in the cold like her.

Glad to make it back unseen, her teeth were chattering by the time she reached her front door, but she didn't care; she was grateful to have made it there undetected; lucky to evade being the butt of local jokes in the pubs that weekend.

The hot water of the shower felt good as it streamed

over her, the heat stinging her cold skin as she watched the mud slip away down the plughole. The smell of lavender eclipsed the earthiness of the dirt, and standing there, she thought about how it had felt when she imagined Finn was going to drown. Louise knew for certain she wouldn't cope if she lost him again.

Wrapped in her warm dressing gown, she went to her bedroom to retrieve the white envelope. This time leaving it unopened, she put it on the bedside table and took a black pen from her pocket, writing on his name in capitals.

The time had come to disclose her secret and start telling the truth.

Telling the truth

Louise had made her decision and she was going to stick to it. She would be upfront with Finn, certain that keeping a discrete eye on him wasn't helpful to either of them anymore. She wanted to be a practical support to him. If he knew who she was, he would at least be in a position to decide whether he wanted to accept that support or not.

Lying on her bed the previous night, after she had put the envelope back in the drawer, Louise had visualised meeting him; every possible scenario ranging from Finn and her embracing to her being told to, "Get the fuck out of here!" She was so very afraid of the latter.

That morning, looking at her reflection in the bathroom mirror while she brushed her teeth, she told herself that today was as good a day as any to tell him the truth. The longer she prolonged the inevitable, the more anxious she would get. *Anyway*, she reasoned with herself, *he has a right to know. I should have done this years ago*.

By the afternoon, she was still stalling, finding reasons to delay leaving her home. *Come on Louise, you can't postpone this for another day,* she told herself as she picked up her coat and keys.

A few streets away, Finn had cooked his favourite meal – fried onions in gravy, steak, peas and mashed potatoes. It was one of the first meals his mother had taught him how to prepare, back when he had loved helping her in the kitchen and she'd thought he might become a chef one day. Never could she have foreseen her son being sent to prison just a few years later.

As he cut through his steak he thought, *I'm going to stay low, leave JJ alone. It's the safest thing to do*.

He heard knocking on his front door and contemplated not answering, but afraid it might be the Gardai again, he got up from his seat and left his dinner behind on the kitchen table. He opened the door and there stood Louise from the clinic.

Surprised to see her again, he politely said, "Hello."

She'd heard his footsteps getting closer as she waited for him to answer, her heart beating so fast she thought she might faint on his doorstep.

"Finn," she said in reply, "Would you mind if I had a word?"

"Amm…" Finn was taken aback, "Is something wrong?"

"No, no, I know this is strange, but please, could I

227

come in for a minute, there's something I need to tell you."

"I'm in the middle of me dinner," Finn replied, clearly confused by the urgency, but he liked Louise and didn't want to be rude.

"It won't take long, I'm sorry about the bad timing."

He stepped to the side and let her in. Louise headed towards the kitchen.

"I'm so sorry Finn, for disturbing your dinner."

Louise appeared tense and nervous; Finn guessed whatever she had to say to him was going to be important but he couldn't imagine what on Earth it would be. The atmosphere in the kitchen was already heavy with anticipation.

Without waiting for an invitation, Louise sat down at the kitchen table and Finn asked her if she wanted a cup of tea but she declined. Noticing how tired she looked he wondered if she had heard something bad about the investigation or his encounter with JJ? *What is she going to say?*

He felt very uncomfortable seated directly opposite her, a bit like a rabbit in headlights, he surmised.

I should have had that tea, she thought.

"Ah, maybe I will have a cup," she said, "I'll make it myself though Finn, you get on and eat, there's no point in letting your dinner go cold. Will I get you one too? I see the teabags here."

Finn nodded and she got up and began pouring water

into the kettle. Then she turned over a couple of mugs left on the draining board in readiness for making their tea, Finn watching her while he picked up his knife and fork.

She knew she was being overly casual in someone else's house. It would annoy her to have someone she barely knew poking about in her kitchen, but she didn't know what else to do. She tried to make some small talk about the clinic and about whether or not he was going to get another dog while the kettle boiled.

Finn wasn't going to be able to eat his dinner until he knew what she wanted to tell him; it all felt too awkward. He pushed his plate to one side, saying he'd finish it later just as she placed down the two mugs of tea between them.

Louise sat down and neatly folded her hands on top of the table behind her mug of tea. Swiftly becoming aware that the pose reminded her of the nuns in school when they were about to impart bad news, she took hold of her mug instead, thinking fleetingly, *what a ridiculous thing to think of.*

Finn was getting very anxious and could feel himself starting to sweat a little.

Would ya ever get on with telling me about whatever it is that's so important? God this is excruciating. Get it out woman, get it out! he was thinking… and likewise she was thinking, *Come on, Louise, spit it out*, but it was a difficult conversation to begin and she stuck with the

229

small talk,

"You've a lovely home, Finn."

"Thanks," he said, starting to flush a rosy red.

He was undeniably sweating by now and was trying to remember if he'd put on antiperspirant that morning. *Jesus, get on with it*, he thought again.

Louise bit the bullet.

"Finn, I've been wanting to say this to you for a long time but just couldn't find the right moment. I hope you won't hate me."

Shit, here it comes, he thought, looking at the steam rising from his mug much like the tension in the room.

"I'm just going to come straight out with it. Finn, I think I'm your mother, well, I mean, I am your mother."

He looked at her, and she looked at him, searching his face for a response. But there was none, no reaction at all, just momentary eye contact and silence. It was too much for Louise, she couldn't sit quietly waiting for him to respond.

"Finn, I know this must be a shock, I'm sorry to just blurt it out. Did you hear what I said?"

He let go of his mug and held on to the edge of the table with his hands as if to steady himself.

What the fuck is she saying? I've known her for years. I've a mother already. I don't want to hear this. Has she lost her marbles? How am I going to shut her up?

"Finn."

Louise's voice was choked with emotion. She could hear the crackle and knew she was about to cry. She'd imagined so many responses throughout the night, but not this – this lack of any response at all.

"Finn, are you OK?"

He pushed back from the table and stood up. Not saying a word he walked over to the sink with his mug in hand. Louise was suddenly frightened. He appeared angry. Was he going to hurt her? He began to pour his tea down the drain and she was ready to run.

As he dropped his mug into the basin, Finn was thinking back to the time, shortly before his mother's death, when she'd told him he was adopted. They'd both got so upset that day. He hadn't liked hearing the truth but she'd desperately wanted to tell him before she passed away, anxious to give him the opportunity to seek out his birth mother if he wanted to in the future. His birth certificate was a forgery, she'd told him.

He'd refused to let her give him much information so she hadn't been able to tell him about his mother Louise, or his grandmother who could be his point of contact. Reluctantly, she'd agreed to close the subject if he'd let her make one final comment, and he'd listened as she told him about how grateful she was to his birth mother for the gift she had given her. Then she had told him how much she loved him and soon after that she'd passed away.

Louise was still talking behind Finn, but he wasn't

listening. As far as he was concerned his adoptive parents were his mum and dad. He didn't want anyone else and certainly not the woman who had given him up. *I don't want to know. Why have you come to tell me this now*? Then he again recalled his mum saying how grateful she was to his mother for the gift she had given her… and Louise was this person.

Louise was in the middle of saying she'd leave and let him think when he interjected. Keeping his back to her he said,

"How long have you known?"

"I've known since just before I moved here. I found out after your parents passed on. I'm so sorry, I couldn't tell you, I often thought of it but—

"Why couldn't you tell me?" he interrupted again. *She's been spying on me for years. Known all this time but said nothing*, he thought.

For the first time, Louise really didn't understand why she hadn't told him. She couldn't placate him with excuses about it not being the right time. Those were the lies she'd told herself, unable to face her truth. This was her one chance to tell the truth.

"I was scared," she said, "Scared about your response, scared about what others would think of me. Scared of reclaiming my past—" she hadn't finished but Finn had heard enough.

"Right."

He still hadn't looked at her or moved from the sink,

and he was now starting to rinse out his mug.

"I'm so sorry," she blurted again, "It was a long time ago. I was young and foolish I'm sorry."

"Well, now you've got it off your chest you may as well tell me who my father is."

Louise was not prepared for that question. She'd not thought he'd ask so soon.

"What, your real dad?" she replied, sounding as startled as she felt.

"Yes, who's my biological father?"

He seemed so composed standing with his back to her, looking out across his small lawn to the wall where he used to kick a ball with his dad – his *real* dad.

Fuck, she thought, *I can't tell him. That's enough for today – the partial truth – the bit that might help him, not the other part that might destroy him.*

"I don't know Finn, I was only eighteen years old and you know, a bit wild. I was drinking a lot."

She felt so ashamed.

"Your mother was my distant cousin. I couldn't look after you and your parents really wanted a baby; they really wanted *you*. I knew you would be better off with them."

Continuing to talk to his back, Louise could sense his anger but she needed to say as much as she could before he told her to leave.

She remained standing, ready to go if he asked her to. Then she started to tell her story – of having her baby in England and giving him up because she felt she'd no choice. She told him about his birth and about keeping the little piece of caul. She told him she'd agreed to ask no questions after he was born. She told him about her own mother's pre-death wish to reunite them and how she'd told her where he was. She explained her decision to move to the area – to be there if he needed her – but how she'd never had the courage to tell him who she was. She was so sorry, so very sorry.

He listened with his head lowered, leaning his weight into the sink, and as the story emerged he began to turn towards her, occasionally glancing up to examine her features. He didn't stop her talking this time; he let her continue until she'd said everything she wanted to say.

When she finished her legs felt so weak it forced her to sit back down. There was silence again as she waited for Finn to respond. He went back to his seat, his cold half-eaten dinner and her mug of tea still on the table between them.

Finn was confused and unsure how to react. He didn't want to know about what he was hearing. He only wanted to be part of the family he'd had all his life. Yet listening to her story, and unable to deny his mother's gratitude to her, he felt some sense of compassion for the woman sitting across the table from him; a woman whom until today, he'd quite admired. What was he to think or feel now? He just didn't know.

"I loved my parents," he said. "They're always going

234

to be my mum and dad."

"Of course, of course, Finn, I don't want to replace them."

His words were like a dagger to her heart.

"Christ," he said, giving her an accusatory look across the table, "All those years, you were watching me, knowing what you know and saying nothing."

Louise felt mortified, as if she'd been caught snooping on someone, but it wasn't like that. She sniffed and wiped her eyes with a tissue from her bag, struggling to keep control of her tears.

"So you knew you were adopted?"

"Yeah, I knew," he said flatly, "But not until just before mum died. I can't believe it's you."

He didn't feel angry anymore, nor did he feel sadness or joy. He just felt numb, the same way he had the day he'd waited for the court's verdict. He was in shock and he knew from his previous experience that this wouldn't last. There would be a flood of emotion in the not-too-distant future.

"So you're my mother," he said impassively, "Does anyone else know?"

"God, no, Finn. No. Nobody. I've told nobody but you."

Then, realising this sounded like she was ashamed of him, she added quickly,

"I wanted to tell you and leave it to you to decide who knows what. I don't want to make trouble for you Finn.

It's completely up to you. It can be our secret or we can go public – as public as you like."

Louise spoke the words but she didn't mean them. Her true thoughts were, *I desperately want to be part of your life, but please don't ask me to publicly disclose this humongous secret about myself. I can't face that yet. Give me some more time.*

"Yeah," he said, "It's a lot to take in."

He used words he'd heard in films; an acceptable response in the absence of any words of his own.

He wanted her to leave now so he could think and consider the enormity of what he had just discovered, but Louise didn't seem to want to leave.

"I'm glad you finally know," she said.

Then, unable to contain her eagerness to help him, she added,

"Finn, is there any way I can help… You know, with your present situation?"

"What do you mean?"

Louise immediately regretted saying it, his tone indicating it was too much too soon, but it was too late to stop.

"Well, I know about the Garda investigation. Niamh's a friend, she tells me things. I'm sorry."

God, how many more times is she going to say sorry?

"I know about JJ reporting you too. Maybe I could be a character reference or something for you? Is there anything I can do?"

"No nothing, it's grand," he said. *Jesus, what the fuck*? he thought.

"I'd never hurt Harry. That bastard JJ's a prick you know, suggesting I was involved."

"I know," Louise said, "Anyway Finn, if you need anything, anything at all, let me know."

Realising it was probably time to let him process their conversation, she said,

"I suppose I better go and leave you alone. Sorry again about the timing. Can I leave you my personal phone number so you have it?"

From her pocket she produced a pre-handwritten note which she now slid across the table towards him.

Finn said, "OK," but left the piece of paper where it was, next to the sugar and butter.

"OK, I'll go." Louise stood up. "Thanks for the tea, and thanks for letting me tell you. Maybe we could meet up again soon? You're welcome to call over to my house one evening Finn."

He didn't respond and kept a bit of distance between them as she left.

At the front door he said, "Bye then."

Louise turned back to say, "Bye Finn," but as she did, he closed the door behind her.

Looking back and moving forward.

After she left, Finn returned to the remains of his half-eaten meal, chewing and swallowing but tasting nothing. His favourite dinner was wasted on him.

He stayed seated at the kitchen table for a long time, staring at the chair Louise had sat on before eventually getting up to scrape what was left of his onion gravy into the bin. Then he put his plate into the sink to soak. Normally, he washed up straight after his meals – he hated dealing with the floating layer of grease later on – but today the washing up was going to have to wait; he had a lot of thoughts to process. He headed to the Priest's Chair – his favourite spot to think in.

He thought again about Louise watching him from afar for all those years. It made him feel uneasy; it was creepy. He wondered what she'd thought of him, and he tried to remember if there were times he'd behaved poorly; times he, as her son, would have wished she'd not witnessed. He wondered what she thought about his conviction and prison sentence. She must know about it. Was that why she'd not come forward until now? Because she was ashamed?

Spying on him for so long… it was underhand.

He thought about the night she'd drunkenly sang karaoke in the pub, so out of tune. It had been hilarious and he'd had a good laugh about it at the time, mockingly mimicking her for weeks afterwards. Now the episode took on a whole new dimension. What an embarrassment, she was his mother! He wondered again about who his father was and felt sure she must know. He'd ask her further.

He remembered his birthdays as a child when his parents went over the top with their celebrations to ensure he had a great day. He wondered what Louise had done on his birthdays. Had she thought of him as he grew up? Had it been hard for her?

There were so many questions. *What would my life have been like if Louise had kept me? Would I have gone to college like her? I'd probably be living in Dublin now, not in a small town full of unforgiving gossips.* He also considered Louise's part in the trajectory of his life and questioned if she might share some of the blame for his downfall. *If I had been raised by her, would I have seen the inside of a prison? Does she feel bad about that?*

Instantly, he was swamped with guilt, not for his thoughts about Louise but because he felt his thoughts were disrespectful to his mum and dad. He reminded himself that he didn't deserve them and that they had been perfect. It was his adoptive parents, his real parents, who'd stood by him through the hard times when Louise was nowhere near; it was them he loved. They had loved him; Louise had discarded him, waiting until now to come forward.

Finn wished he could talk over his thoughts with his parents, like he had done in the past. They would have sifted through all the information with him, sitting side by side opposite him on the settee. They'd have helped him answer the questions prompted by Louise's visit.

Should I like Louise? Deep down he really wanted to. *Does she deserve a chance? Is she a victim of circumstance like me? Or is she more calculating than that?*

He wondered too what Louise was thinking. *Does she wish she could turn back time? How far back would she turn the clock? Would I exist at all if she could start again? I'd bring Stephen back to life if I could change the past but would she brush away my existence?*

He pondered the many fleeting moments in time, and how life-changing those moments could been. He remembered his mother saying, "What you do today, Finn, it affects your tomorrows son. 'Sorry' doesn't always work."

He wished he'd paid more attention to her.

At the end of the day, he knew he'd had good parents

who loved him, but he was uncertain about what to expect from Louise and wasn't fully sure he wanted to find out.

Tired of thinking, he flicked through an old photograph album for some consolation. Smiling faces looked out at him; happy memories, carrying with them all the love and care his parents had given him.

Louise on the other hand was in a very different mind space. Having unburdened herself of her secret, she felt freer than she could ever remember feeling. She had finally told the truth, and relief flooded through her. Right now that feeling even overpowered her concerns about Finn perhaps not accepting her – despite her desperately wanting to be part of his life.

She felt such relief that when she drove away from his house the self-doubting side of her worried she'd done this purely for herself and her own needs, not for Finn. Either way she was going to have to wait a while yet before she could truly determine whether she'd made the right decision about disclosing the truth to him after all this time.

Unlike Finn, who took solace in reminiscing that afternoon, Louise didn't have a memory bank in which to immerse herself. She didn't want to go home to an empty house to think and worry. She needed to talk, and unburden herself further, so after leaving Finn's house, Louise drove straight to Niamh's.

Niamh can keep a secret, she thought. *Anyway, Finn*

*might tell her or someone else before I get the chance.
I've no idea what he'll do with the information once he's
thought things through, and I sure as hell don't want
Niamh to hear it second-hand in the community – that
would be a real insult to her. I'm not betraying him, I'm
just covering my tracks.*

Niamh saw the car pull in as she was coming down
the stairs and opened the door before Louise rang the
bell.

"Hey you. What are you wanting? Come inside," she
said, already heading back into the kitchen and
expecting Louise to follow, "Long time no see
stranger," she laughed.

"Niamh," Louise said as they reached the kitchen.

The sound of her name and the anxious way it was
spoken was all it took to make Niamh pay attention. She
turned around to face Louise.

"What is it, Louise? Is something wrong?"

"No nothing's wrong Niamh, but I have to tell you
something. I should have told you a long time ago."

And then Louise was sobbing.

"OK, it's OK Louise, no problem, sit down," Niamh
said as she pulled out some chairs to sit on. She took
Louise's hand and squeezed it gently as Louise
continued to sob. "Here's a tissue," she said, pulling one
from her pocket. "What is it?"

"Niamh, this is going to shock you, and I hope you
can forgive me for keeping it a secret for so long. I'm

truly sorry about that. Believe it or not, it was Harry's disappearance which prompted it all. I've already spoken to Finn today. There's no easy way to say it."

"Finn?" Niamh repeated, wondering what on Earth she had to discuss with him.

"I'm Finn's mother," Louise said with passion and great resolve.

"What? Louise… are you serious?"

Louise certainly looked it.

Then, for a second time that day, Louise told the story of how Finn came to be adopted by her cousin and why she had sought the job with Niamh in the first place. Niamh sat in stunned silence.

"Well, that finally explains why such an over-qualified nurse wanted to work in my practice! You know, it must have been two years before I believed you really intended on staying."

Louise lifted her head and smiled.

Niamh continued, "Wow! I don't quite know what to say. You're a dark horse, aren't you Louise? So you've told Finn. How did he take it?"

Louise had regained some of her composure by now and repeated her conversation with Finn almost word for word.

"So you see, I don't know Niamh," Louise said, "Not bad, not good – he didn't really respond at all. It must have been a shock. I expect it's a normal enough reaction. I hope he's OK."

"I'm sure he's fine Louise. He just needs time to take it all in. It's bound to be a shock."

Revealing part of the truth to Finn and Niamh had been a great relief to Louise, yet she knew she had not fully unburdened herself. Not telling the whole truth to Finn hadn't been difficult, because she was sure that knowing the identity of his biological father would be too much for him. Yet for some reason she wished she could tell Niamh everything. It felt wrong keeping it from her.

"Finn's no idea I'm spilling my guts so soon Niamh. I promised I wouldn't, not until he decided what he wanted to do."

"Absolutely. No worries. I'll keep shtum," she said, "You let me know when the coast is clear. Honestly, I can't believe you've such a history Louise. I thought you were boring!"

They began to laugh and after chatting about it for a while longer, decided to open a bottle of wine in celebration. Two glasses later Niamh asked,

"Who was the father, Louise?"

Relaxed a little from the effects of the wine, Louise replied casually,

"That's a story for another time Niamh."

Niamh took the hint not to pry and Louise was thankful she didn't have to lie.

"I better head home. I'll leave the car here if that's OK?"

"Let me walk with you. Patrick needs a walk before bed and the fresh air and exercise might settle Harry quicker."

Niamh went to get her son's trainers, but they were still wet from an earlier outing on the sodden garden grass.

"One sec Louise, I'm just going upstairs to get Harry's other trainers."

The second pair were in the airing cupboard upstairs and had been there since the evening Harry was found. When Niamh returned with the trainers, Louise had already sat Harry on the chair she'd occupied during her confession and was putting on his coat.

"First foot Harry," Niamh said, bending to put on the trainer.

Harry took one look at the trainers and started to resist, wriggling about and trying to get down off the chair. Niamh ignored him, and Louise sat him back down. Niamh tried again but Harry kicked high, only just missing her nose. He wasn't going to give in easily.

"Welcome to motherhood," Niamh sarcastically said to Louise. "Please Harry, your other shoes are wet. Be a good boy. Let mammy put these on. Then we can go for a walk with Louise."

She took hold of his foot and once again tried to slip on his trainer but Harry reached down, pulled it from her hand and threw it across the room. It landed behind the television.

"Harry!" Niamh reprimanded.

He signed, "No."

Niamh signed, "Yes."

"No," he signed again.

"Please Harry," she implored as he wriggled free of Louise and jumped down from the chair.

Niamh was baffled.

"I'll get his wellies Louise, I don't have the patience just now. I don't know what's up with him. Hang on a sec."

She disappeared into the utility room to get his wellingtons from beside the back door. Harry had no problem putting them on and they were soon ready to head off.

Niamh didn't walk all the way with Louise. Louise didn't mind though; having unburdened herself, she was quite looking forward to a bit of time on her own to think. She'd a spring in her step, nothing could upset her this evening. Parting with a hug, Niamh turned to go back home.

Later that night, after Niamh put Harry to bed and poured herself another glass of wine, she noticed one of his trainers still lying by the chair. She examined it to see if there might be a reason why Harry hadn't wanted to put it on. Other than a small amount of olive-green paint on the sole there was nothing else wrong with it. Behind the television she found and retrieved the other trainer. Harry had a great aim. This other trainer also had paint on the sole.

Looking at the paint on both soles, she tried to remember the last time he had worn them. It was the day he was found. He had flicked them off after he arrived at the clinic, and Louise had put them in a plastic bag to bring home. They'd been soaked through and muddy. She had assumed that was why he wanted them off, but perhaps not…

Am I wrong? she questioned. *What did he wear going to the hospital? No, I'm right, he wore his clogs, the plastic clogs he always wears in the surgery. That was definitely the last day he wore these trainers.*

Turning the trainers over in her hands, Niamh tried to think of any place she'd been with him that had been freshly painted, but none came to mind. The only other option she could think of was school. She would check with the school tomorrow, just to make sure he hadn't picked it up there. She knew he hadn't spent any time with JJ that week, but she would phone him too just in case. If those telephone calls turned up nothing, she'd tell the Gardai – it might be a clue.

Later, as she lay in bed she thought, *the Gardai are going to think I'm foolish, but I don't care, I'm telling them. They can decide whether it's important or not. It's not worth risking missing a clue because of my pride.*

Whoever took Harry has to pay the price.

Twomey's pub

JJ answered his door and found the Gardai standing outside. They told him it was a courtesy call to let him know they were going to search number fifteen Dominic's Park – Long John's house. They wanted to identify possible indications as to why Long John didn't want the development to go ahead, though they soon revealed that they also wanted to ask JJ about the time Eoin went missing.

When they first interviewed JJ, he'd told them he had lived with Long John for a period of time in his youth, but since then they'd also discovered that he'd lived there at the time of Eoin's disappearance.

"Can we have a quick word?" one of the Garda at the door asked.

JJ let them in.

Both Garda gave him pleasant smiles, but JJ could detect their underlying determination to pick at loose threads and note inconsistencies, looking for a lead. He was under no illusion – he was being interrogated, albeit informally.

"You didn't mention the incident involving the missing young man – Eoin, wasn't it? – when you told us about your relationship with Mr Williams," one of them said.

"Did you not think there might be a connection with him and you being blackmailed?" the other added.

The question made him squirm, but he thought he did well to minimise Eoin's significance in his life. He passed it off as a distant memory, something he'd put out of his head. "… we were both cleared of any involvement anyway. No, it didn't cross my mind."

He told them Long John's aversion to the redevelopment probably had more to do with the residents having to move out of the area. Long John had always fought on behalf of the local community. Besides that, he really didn't have a clue.

They rightly looked unconvinced but, *so what,* he thought. It was their job to find the reason, not his.

JJ knew his connection with Eoin would be unveiled at some point, but he was still taken aback by their so called 'casual' questioning. Keen to take the focus off himself, he was glad when they gave him the chance to ask,

"Have you located Long John yet?" expecting them to say, "No." He was sure Long John was abroad and well out of the way. He'd tried all his old contacts and hadn't been able to find him. He actually hoped he was dead and gone, then there'd be no threat at all from him.

The most important thing now was to keep the focus off himself, especially when they eventually found Eoin's body. It was, after all, Long John who'd committed the crime. JJ's guilt only lay in not disclosing the murder. He was sticking to his plan and would maintain that he had been an ignorant young teen who knew nothing about any of it. A man who, after all this time, had consequently become an innocent victim of blackmail.

The Gardai stayed no more than half an hour, but the visit unnerved him. He was so nervous at one point that he considered telling them that Louise, his alibi, lived in the area, but his common sense prevailed. He was hoping he could keep her out of it anyway. Her involvement would only complicate his life further.

If she was identified, he reasoned it was going to be easy enough to deny he had ever recognised her. She didn't have any identifying marks, unlike him, and she had certainly changed. Forty years on, she was nothing like the old Fairy he had fancied.

He thought they might even consider her a suspect, as she could hardly pretend she'd not known *him* with his distinctive scar. In truth, he didn't care, so long as they left him alone.

JJ did, however, need to talk to her again. If the Gardai were interested in speaking to her and successful in finding her, it was likely they would be able to unnerve her the same way they had unnerved him. She might admit that she really couldn't remember where she had been that night.

As soon as the Gardai left, he texted her,

"Meet me at Twomey's tomorrow lunch. We need to talk."

Louise replied that she couldn't – it was too far away and she'd only an hour for lunch.

His return text read,

"BE THERE."

Reading his text, Louise sighed. She knew she had no choice but to meet him. She hated this: living her life at his beck and call. If only they could go back to pretending they didn't know each other... she wasn't willing to have any man, especially not JJ, calling the shots, and she'd take the opportunity to tell him so.

The pub was twelve kilometres away located in a remote spot mostly frequented by hillwalkers, and on the weekend by city dwelling Dubliners, seeking a place to relax.

Despite its remote location, Louise was uneasy, afraid that she might be seen. Knowing her luck, it would be the one day of the year when the local Tidy Towns Committee decided to have a walk and then lunch there afterwards.

She'd been to this pub before so it was easy for her to find again. It was located on the roadside, with the main entrance and parking around the back. She drove by the pub's gable wall and once in the parking area looked around for any familiar cars, almost missing JJ's, which was hidden in the far corner behind a skip full of old carpet. *He must be worried about being seen too*, she thought.

Looking in her mirror she combed back her hair with her fingers and scanned the carpark once more before hastily walking towards the pub.

Opening the heavy oak door briefly allowed light to flood into the dimly lit interior. The bar had changed since she had last been there. The large interior was no longer carpeted, as indicated by the full skip outside, a polished wooden floor now in its place. It had become the stylish rustic type of pub that could turn a decent profit under a competent publican.

Louise generally loved the smell of pubs; for her it signified the start of a carefree night out. However, today that same smell of stale beer spilt on soft furnishings turned her stomach.

She quickly scanned the main bar area for JJ but he wasn't sitting there – only two older gentlemen, who turned to see if their friend had entered. JJ wasn't occupying any of the open-plan seating areas either, but he was there somewhere, she'd seen his car.

All the walls were lined with snugs, small group seating areas with a central table. Each snug was enclosed by a dark wood surround, topped with colourful stained-glass windows that, when backlit, cast an array of colours across the wooden floor. Under normal circumstances, it would be a welcoming bar, but today it failed to comfort Louise.

She started to examine the snug's stained-glass windows for human shadows, and then she spotted him sitting in the furthest snug from the bar. He clearly wanted privacy. He had moved to the middle of the snug after he heard the door open and sat facing out so she could more easily see him from where she stood at the main door. Once he was sure she'd spotted him, he slid his whiskey glass to the side and shuffled back behind the wood and stained-glass surround, out of sight.

Louise was nervous but annoyed too. It felt very familiar to her, like the day she'd met him in the carpark as a teen, and she hoped this meeting wouldn't end as badly for her. She didn't want to be there. She wanted everything to go back to the way it was before, to when she thought he didn't know who she was.

She hurried straight across to the snug and, letting her emotions get the better of her, just as they had done in her teens, she said, "For fucks sake JJ, what would people think if they saw us together? Why did we have to meet? What's going on?"

She surprised herself with her forcefulness.

"I don't give a shit," he said, angered by her tone, "Now sit down."

Louise wanted to stand up to JJ but he still had the

253

power to frighten her, and the abruptness of his response ensured she complied. A bartender arrived to take her order and after he left, the pair sat in awkward silence for a few moments. JJ played with his whiskey glass and Louise closely examined her shoes under the table. Neither was sure how to restart the conversation but JJ managed to first,

"Sorry Louise but it's important, the Gardai paid me a visit. They'll be digging up Long John's house shortly."

"So, what about it?"

The adrenaline still racing through Louise prevented her from dropping her defiant air.

"So," he said in response, leaning across the small round table and lowering his voice, "They might or might not find a corpse."

Her body went rigid as the bartender arrived back with her drink. He put it on the table and left. Flummoxed, she replied in a more bewildered tone,

"What? I don't understand, what are you talking about JJ?"

"The lad, the lad who went missing, he was buried there," he replied.

"I still don't understand. Did you kill him?"

"No!"

Then JJ told her about the time when he had come home to find Long John and an associate burying the body; how they had forced him to assist. Louise sat

254

observing him, trying to take in what he was saying. He seemed genuine.

"I don't even know if it's him or not, it was fucking half-frozen, but I think it might have been Eoin."

"You told me I was with you that night he disappeared. Was I?"

"Yes, you fucking were! High as a kite and drunk as a skunk as always Fairy. Look I'd nothing to do with that kid's demise. They used him to keep me in line so I'd do as I was told. You know?"

"What do you mean, keep you in line? What was going on?"

"Doesn't matter, it was a long time ago. I've long since moved on and I don't want to go back. You need to be sure about your memory, OK? That is, if the Gardai come sniffing around asking you questions."

Louise didn't know what to think.

"Jesus JJ, did you murder that kid?" she said again, without meaning to.

"Have you not heard a fucking word I've said to you?" he retorted, visibly angry, "I had nothing to do with it. They used him to keep me in line. I knew stuff they didn't want passed on."

Louise looked at his reddened face and the pulsating veins in his neck and knew better than to ask more questions.

"Listen, if a body is found and it's him, then you need to stick to your story, whether you can remember or not.

Do you understand?"

Louise, struggling to make sense of what she was hearing, didn't answer. He gave the table a short, sharp bang and, realising he'd made too much noise, sinisterly lowered his voice.

"Fairy, do you hear me?"

She jumped as the table rocked, "Yes, I hear you."

"I've enough problems with that Finn bloke, I don't want problems with you too."

He looked across at her and added,

"By the way, what were you doing at his house the other day? I saw your car there. You were quite a while."

Louise was startled.

"Nothing. What, are you following me now? It's none of your business," she blustered, starting to blush like a child caught doing something they shouldn't be doing. She watched a sneer spread across his face.

"Jesus Louise, you're not having a fling with a toy boy, are you? Surely you could have done better than the local freak show?"

"Fuck off JJ. It's none of your business."

"Well, you're a racy auld one Fairy," he chuckled.

Louise was vexed and keen to regain the higher ground.

"Fuck off JJ," she said again.

JJ wouldn't stop.

"You know," he said, "That Finn's the spit of me

Uncle Jack. I used to wonder if there was a family connection somewhere. God forbid," he said, laughing in amusement.

Louise didn't know what to say or do. She tried to stand up but he grabbed her wrist.

"Sit down, what's the rush Fairy?"

"I've to get back to the clinic," she said, "I don't want to be late, we've a busy afternoon. I'll keep to my story, now let me go."

He was squeezing her wrist uncomfortably hard.

"Sit down Fairy," he said more forcefully.

So she sat. She tried to soften her voice, "JJ you have to stop calling me that, please."

"OK, Louise darling," he said patronisingly. "Since you're so friendly with that bastard, you can tell him to stay away from me. I've enough on my plate right now. Tell him to lay off."

He was rubbing the side of his face, thinking.

"Jesus, the sex must be good Louise, surely ye can't have anything to talk about other than that dead little rat of a dog he had?"

Louise felt a rage rising within her. *Why can't he just let it go*? Seething, she responded,

"Finn? Leave *you* alone? Listen here, he's a good guy. You killed his dog and implicated him in Harry's disappearance. You should lay off *him*. Just leave him alone JJ. I mean, what the fuck is wrong with you?"

JJ sat back to assess her body language for further

257

evidence of her feelings for Finn.

"Well, well, well. Who'd have thought? How many other toy boys do you have? You're a bit old for that now, aren't you?"

That was an insult too far and it provoked an unintended response from Louise.

"Oh for fucks sake, he's my son you imbecile!"

Her timing couldn't have been worse. *Shit*, she thought, *I've just said that out loud. And to JJ.* She couldn't take it back.

"Your son?" he said, looking perplexed, "But he had parents?"

She had no choice now other than to tell the truth.

"He was adopted by distant relatives of mine."

"Fuck me," he said, leaning back into his chair. "He's in his forties, isn't he?"

Louise could see him calculating dates in his head.

"Fuck me, who else were you messing about with back then?"

Louise couldn't think of how to respond to that accusation and he watched her examine her feet in silence, trying to think of a convincing response. Before she could come up with one...

"Oh Jesus, he's not mine is he? Please tell me the local freak show isn't mine?"

Louise continued to look at her feet. She could feel her face hot as a poker. Her eyes and ears pulsated with her heartbeat.

"Is that freak mine?"

He was gritting his teeth and leaning in towards her across the little table.

"Yes," she whispered.

Sitting back in his seat, he drank the rest of his whiskey in one gulp.

"I have to go," she said.

JJ let her go. He was dumbstruck. She ran to the door and out into the carpark, squinting in the brightness outside. What had she done? What would JJ do with the information? She'd told Finn she didn't know who his father was.

"Oh God," she whimpered.

Louise turned and re-entered the pub. JJ was still transfixed in the corner snug. She sat back down. He looked at her.

"Is he really?"

"Yes, but JJ please, I've only just told him. That's why I was at his house the other day. Please don't say anything to him. Please!" she pleaded.

"Does he know I'm his father?"

"No, I didn't tell him."

"Don't! You hear me? I mean it, don't. I want nothing to do with him. I've enough on my plate. I'm not taking on a lost cause. I can't believe he's mine, what's wrong with me? Sure I don't even know if you're telling the truth. You're some bitch either way."

He straightened himself up.

"Listen, keep him at bay and if the fucking Gardai find you, stick to your story and tell 'em nothing 'bout Finn understand? Nothing!"

"How would they know?" she said.

"You stupid, stupid bitch," he muttered, shaking his head as he stood up.

Louise remained seated as he pulled his coat from behind him. When he shuffled past her to exit the snug, he leant right down next to her face and snarled,

"You tell no one. No one. If I get an inkling... you hear me Fairy?"

Vomit-tasting bile surfaced in her mouth as she had flashbacks to her youth, of being dangled by an arm in a carpark. He stood upright and in a louder, more jovial tone said,

"Really Fairy, you're a prize tulip."

The two men at the bar looked across at him as he left. Louise watched him go too. She stayed sitting, not wanting to meet him in the carpark and needing a few extra minutes to process what had just taken place. She also needed a bit of time to allow her pulse to slow. The barman walked in her direction.

"Any lunch madam?"

"No thank you, I'm just going to head off."

Her phone rang while she was crossing the carpark. JJ's car was gone but it was his name that lit up her screen.

"Does Niamh know?"

"No."

"Don't tell her either," he said and then rang off.

What now? Was there a way to fix this, to make the problem disappear? Her life was being turned inside out and she seemed to have lost control over it. The only consolation she could cling to was the fact that JJ wasn't keen to reveal himself as Finn's father, but even that relief only lasted seconds; he'd always have his parentage of Finn to hold over her as blackmail whenever he wished.

As she got into her car, it was clearer than ever that she was going to have to tell Niamh about her relationship with JJ. She couldn't trust JJ to not change his mind. Telling Niamh the whole truth should be a relief, but she feared it would signal the end of both her professional career, and more importantly, their friendship.

As she slowly drove back to the clinic, she continued to mull over what to do, yet by the time she arrived and parked in her usual spot, she had no answers. She would have to mull it over some more and live with the worry in the meantime.

Telling a truth when she had something to gain felt very different from telling a truth that might lead to losing everything good in her life.

The unravel begins

JJ was in his car, on the return trip home after meeting with Louise in the pub, when his phone rang. He saw Niamh's name and disconnected. *Enough for one day*, he thought, *I don't need any more aggravation.*

In a state of disbelief about Louise's revelations, he was trying to visualise Finn's face while he was driving. He was adamant he'd have nothing to do with him; he'd make sure Louise didn't tell him, or anyone else for that matter, about him being his father. He looked nothing like him.

As Niamh's name disappeared from the screen, he noticed he was on the same stretch of road he'd brought her along the evening he had proposed. It was a beautiful strip of the lake drive which hugged the shore's edge. The gaps in the gorse hedgerow gave the same teasing glimpses of the water and the hills beyond as they had back then; just enough to make him want to see more. Sometimes, on long balmy summer evenings, cars lined the road waiting to enter the viewing area further along to watch the sunset over the magnificent view. It was there in the carpark on one such idyllic evening that he had made his marriage proposal to Niamh. That was when his life had felt idyllic… how things had changed.

This was also the stretch of road he'd driven along more recently – for a not so romantic reason. He was nearing the turn off that led to an old ruin outside the town's boundaries. The traffic was backing up, and since it was spring, it wasn't going to be tourists who where clogging up the road. Something was wrong. A driver ahead of him got out of his car to take a look further ahead. JJ shouted out the window,

"Can you see what the hold-up is?"

"Gardai stop point, I think," came the reply as the man got back into his car to move forward in the line of traffic.

Shit, he thought, rather wishing the man had said he could see a car accident. *They've found him*.

An image of Eugene's body leaning up against the stone wall where he'd left him forced his earlier thoughts to the back of his mind. He knew exactly the scene the Gardai were looking at.

JJ considered doing a U-turn and taking the long way back around the lake, but he was too close to the stop point and didn't want to attract attention. Instead, he tried to ease his nerves by sucking a hard-boiled sweet from a packet he kept in the glove compartment. The sweet split in two and the sharp edge cut the side of his tongue; a tiny slit of a cut that would linger for days. Sitting in his car rolling along in the queue of traffic he reminded himself why he had done what he had done and as always justified his actions. *It will only be another few weeks before it's all over,* he consoled himself as he neared the check point, *then I can get back to the life I've made for myself. I just have to keep it together for another few weeks.*

JJ met the first Garda just before the turn off to the ruin. He wore a luminous green visor and thick black gloves. He looked cold and miserable, standing in the road waving the traffic on as it approached him. JJ lowered his window.

"Keep moving," the Garda said impatiently as he continued to direct the line of traffic forward, no longer willing to engage with the general public passing by; fed up of their polite enquiries about what was happening. It suited JJ; he was relieved he didn't have to speak to him.

He tried to see up the sealed off avenue that led to the ruin as he passed by. When he couldn't, like all the other passing motorists, he attempted to catch a glimpse in his rear-view mirror, but disappointingly that also revealed nothing. The bend in the long avenue hid the ruin from any viewpoint, making it a good hideaway. Wasn't that the very reason it was such a popular spot for misdemeanours in the first place?

"Today's a shit day," he said to himself, wishing it was over.

Louise's revelations remained pushed to the back of his mind in light of this new, more immediate danger. The Gardai had found Eugene, and he prayed he hadn't left any incriminating evidence at the scene. He'd been extremely rushed and stressed that evening. Only time would tell.

JJ could see Eugene's dead face, white as a sheet. *Fucking idiot*, he thought.

It hadn't been part of his plan. It had been an unexpected obstacle, but the type of complication that he knew could lead to the undoing of the best of plans.

He felt no guilt about Eugene's death. Eugene had ended his own life; that wasn't his fault. In fact, he was still angry with him. It was because of Eugene that he'd forgotten to get rid of the old fidget spinner. It was long gone now anyway, somewhere deep in a rubbish tip miles away.

Oblivious to his predicament, people were carrying on with their daily activities as he drove down the main street a few minutes later. Waiting for the pedestrian lights to change, he saw Mary from the chemist dragging her screaming toddler across the road, one hand hanging on to him while the other held a scooter he'd abandoned shortly after they'd left home. She looked fed up when she raised her hand in recognition of JJ's face and shrugged her shoulders as if to say, *don't judge me*.

He barely saw her, never mind judged her. He was continuing to picture Eugene's body, examining every tiny detail, wondering if he had done a good enough job of making it look like he'd died in that spot. By the time Mary reached the far side of the road he was contemplating the extent to which Eugene's body would have decomposed during the intervening week, and if that would cover up any mistakes he might have made. And as the lights turned green, his thoughts moved to Eugene's parents. Had they noticed he'd gone missing yet? Eugene was well known for leaving home once in a while.

On the far side of town and nearly home, Niamh rang again. He stopped the connection.

At home with a whiskey in his hand, he picked up the phone to return Niamh's call.

"Hey Niamh, sorry, I was driving earlier when you rang."

"Ah, JJ, I just wanted to ask you: have you been anywhere with Harry lately where he could've picked up some paint on his shoes?"

JJ stalled. *What's this about?*

"What colour?" he asked.

"Olive green."

Fuck. More trouble loomed. He stalled some more, trying to decide how to answer.

"That's a dark green, isn't it? Are his shoes destroyed?"

"He's some on his trainers – the ones he had on the day we found him."

"Oh, right. Sure he could have got that anytime Niamh. I wouldn't go jumping to conclusions."

"I know, that's why I was ringing you," she said quite vexed, "But when I couldn't get you, well, I went ahead and phoned the Gardai. Better safe than sorry, and all that. They'll probably check with you soon. I told them I hadn't the chance to ask you yet. Do you know of anywhere the paint could have come from?"

JJ stood his ground, holding his glass tightly.

"No," he replied firmly, "OK, grand, thanks for letting me know. I'll tell them when they call. Have to go, talk to ya later."

He pressed the end call button and cursed.

He could visualise the tins of paint in his cottage. One of the lids upside down on the kitchen floor. What a stupid, stupid oversight. He remembered picking it up before Harry and Eugene arrived but he couldn't remember if he'd checked for any paint spills. He'd left the tin out in the shed with all the other empty tins of paint. He even remembered banging his head on the low door frame and cursing the smaller stature of earlier generations.

Fucking Niamh, he thought, *Jesus, can she leave nothing alone? She's worse than the Gardai; doesn't*

267

miss a thing. Will nothing go my way today?

"Fuck it," he said aloud, "That's a direct link to the cottage."

It all went wrong

Not long afterwards, JJ was pouring himself a second glass of whiskey when the doorbell rang, and through the living room window he saw the now familiar sight of a Garda car parked outside. In one quick gulp he drank the entire glassful, willing the burn in his throat to give him the adrenaline hit he needed for this next encounter.

They didn't stay too long but he thought they seemed more suspicious of him than before, asking him if he could think of anywhere Harry might have come into contact with the paint. He told them that he couldn't, which was straightforward enough, but then they said,

"Mr Hennessy, we would also like to let you know that we are exploring the possibility that the death of a young man located today at the old ruin may be connected to Harry's disappearance."

JJ didn't have to act surprised because he *was* surprised. How were they able to link Eugene to Harry?

"Oh," he said.

"That paint we were asking you about – we found a similar colour paint on the sole of the young man's shoes. Not a large amount, but we think it's the same one. It'll be a definite lead if the test result is positive."

Convinced that they were carefully assessing his reactions, JJ tried to appear happy about the news. Then the Gardai left, telling him they'd keep him informed of any further developments. He downed another glass of whiskey before they'd even reached their car. It was all going wrong.

A few more whiskeys later, he was slouched in his chair, recounting the day Harry had disappeared, his mind searching, attempting to find and fix the cracks appearing in his carefully crafted plan.

It had all gone well at first. Harry had been in the garden as usual: twenty minutes on the swing, wrapped up warm – just like Anna had told the Gardai. It was his transition activity from school to home and it settled him for eating his dinner. Patrick had been with him.

Even though the swing was easily visible from the kitchen window, JJ knew all he needed to do was wait for Anna to start preparing the dinner. Distracted by her kitchen activities, she would be less aware of Harry's movements. It had been easy to hide – the garden hedge was high and Niamh's semi-rural plot meant there were no immediate nosey neighbours to worry about. The back gate led to a short narrow track that joined a public walkway through the woods. Niamh loved it as it was easy to walk Patrick in the evenings. JJ had only needed a minute or two to get them out of the back garden.

"Patrick," he'd called quietly, showing him a lead over the top of the gate, "Walkies, Patrick."

Patrick had headed straight to him, his tail wagging and Harry watching. He'd been out the gate and on a lead in seconds. After a quick glance to check Anna was still busy at the cooker, JJ had produced the old fidget spinner.

"Harry, look what I have," he'd called again in a singsong, teasing voice as he spun the spinner.

Lights lit up as it spun, displaying their rainbow of colours, and Harry had jumped off his swing seat like a greyhound leaving the blocks. It'd been so easy to entice him to leave the security of his home. No-one had seen them as they drove off. It was the perfect setting for his plan.

With neither Harry nor Patrick perturbed by JJ's unexpected visit, it had seemed like nothing more than a secret access visit to JJ. *In a couple of days' time they'll both be back home with Niamh*, he'd thought. *It's the small price she has to pay to ensure my safety and her ongoing ignorance.*

At JJ's cottage, Eugene had been waiting. JJ recalled that he hadn't been happy about the lack of internet connection but he'd assured him he wouldn't be there for more than two days. What else could he say? *Young*

271

people are far too attached to their gadgets anyway, he'd thought, *and Patrick and Harry will be more than enough to keep him busy. They'll all be fine.*

He'd made sure Eugene petted Patrick, so the dog was familiar with him before he'd left, and he'd known there were lots of dog treats too; he'd even left sleeping tablets if things threatened to go off the rails. If only Eugene had followed the plan…

Thinking back, JJ realised it had been a mistake not to have checked Eugene's belongings. *I'd have found his stash if I had.*

Niamh had taken longer to phone him than expected that afternoon. She'd rushed home when she received the hysterical call from Anna, then started a search herself before phoning everyone she knew, including him, and lastly the Gardai.

"Fuck you Eugene," he said aloud as he slipped into sleep and the whiskey-induced nightmares began to vividly whirl around in his head.

Eugene was floating above him with a spinner made of a circular saw, each jagged edge adorned with short fiery torches. He was swinging it over his head on a thick rope, then dropping it down close to JJ's face. JJ could feel the heat of the torches. They burned his skin as they skimmed by but he couldn't move. He was paralysed.

Niamh was laughing in the background, a tin of green paint in her hands. It poured down her arms in

272

thick globules. She was pouring it into his mouth while Eugene held his jaw open. He was choking. Finn clung to his body, kissing his neck, and Harry stuck sharp pins into his legs. Stab, stab, stab – the pain was excruciating. He was dying. They were going to kill him.

JJ sat bolt upright in the chair. His phone was ringing. In his stupor, he answered. It was Louise.

"JJ, the Gardai are questioning Finn about that body they found, and something about paint? They're searching his house."

"Listen, Louise it's got nothin' to do with me. I don't want to hear about Finn again. He's your business, not mine. Now fuck off, it's late."

On the other end of the phone, Louise slapped herself on the head with the palm of her hand. What was she thinking? She'd phoned him in desperation but from his slurred words she knew he'd been drinking. *He's always drinking, the gob shite*. All the same, to say he wasn't interested and then hang up… He was a heartless human being.

JJ's head hurt. He switched off his phone to avoid any further calls and took himself to bed. The whiskey, as usual, was not helping.

273

Eugene's last evening

"I haven't much time," JJ had said that afternoon, when he'd arrived at the cottage with Harry and Patrick and handed the dog's lead to Eugene. "Here you go, give him a pet, you'll see he's very gentle."

Eugene had reached out to stroke Patrick on the head but when Patrick had looked up at him he'd pulled his hand back.

"He's fine," JJ had said impatiently taking the lead from him and walking off with Patrick into the bedroom, leaving Harry by Eugene's side. "I'll put him in Harry's room. Remember, all you have to do is keep Harry happy. That stuff there," he'd said, pointing at the things on the little table, "That'll keep him happy. If he gets upset, the sweets will help."

"Yeah, sure OK," Eugene had replied, looking down at Harry who'd seemed to be ignoring his presence, "Hey, Mr H, how do I connect to the internet?"

Deciding to play it cool, knowing full well that a

young man like Eugene would not like his response, JJ had said,

"You don't, the internet's non-existent out here, didn't I say that to you?"

Eugene wasn't to know that JJ had removed the Wi-Fi router earlier, not wanting to risk him being on the internet when he needed him to keep an eye on Harry. He'd been fairly sure Eugene would have refused to come if he'd known that in advance!

"No, you didn't."

"Here, I nearly forgot to give you these," JJ added, re-entering the kitchen and handing Eugene a brown envelope. "For Harry or Patrick, if you're having serious problems with them. Only one mind ya, do you hear me? Only one. They're sleeping tablets."

He'd kept going, knowing he needed to get out of there as quickly as he could.

"Harry's not eaten dinner yet. Beans are his favourite. OK, right… OK."

Before leaving, he'd bent down to Harry's eye level. Holding his son's hands, JJ had said, "Harry, this is Eugene, he's going to mind you for a bit. You be a good boy now."

But Harry had avoided his gaze too and JJ had quickly taken him by the hand into his bedroom, where he switched on the TV for him to watch. Once the cartoons had started, Harry put his fidget spinner on the little table and JJ left him there, content.

"All good," he'd said to Eugene, as he gave him Patrick's leash and walked on out the back door, over his shoulder adding, "I'll contact you by phone later. Do not under any circumstances phone me. I expect I'll be with Niamh or the Gardai most of the time, so no phoning me, no matter what. Just deal with it."

"Sure, sure, OK boss."

Then he'd left. Eugene had listened to the sound of the jeep's engine start up and fade away as JJ drove off. He'd not seen the usually suave, sophisticated JJ stressed before and it had unsettled him. Seeing him appear so vulnerable and raw scared him.

Why's he so nervous? he'd thought. *Am I putting myself in danger?*

Two weeks earlier, JJ had made it all sound so easy when he'd approached him for his assistance. Unable to tell Eugene the real motive for kidnapping his own son, he had told him it was a way to get back at his wife who was divorcing him. He'd said,

"It won't be for long, just a couple of days, long enough to break the bitch for dumping me. Then she can have him back."

He had offered good money, so Eugene hadn't given it a second thought until he'd heard about Harry's needs and his service dog, but JJ had somehow managed to reassure him about all that.

That afternoon, after JJ left the cottage, Eugene hadn't felt so reassured anymore.

Initially, he'd kept a safe distance from Patrick and Harry, sitting for a while at the kitchen table observing them, playing with the dog treats in his pocket as he watched, afraid to get too close in case he upset the child or his big dog.

A little later on, feeling braver, he'd got closer to deliver a tin of beans and a glass of milk for Harry's dinner. He'd also given Patrick a treat that had been well received, making him feel a bit more confident.

Eugene's head was in the fridge looking for something small to snack on when he'd heard the scraping and scratching of the video winding itself up in the player. Racing into the room, he had startled Patrick, who'd jumped up and barked. Frozen for a moment, totally petrified, Eugene had stood statute still, but Patrick hadn't barked again and he'd thrown him some treats to make sure he stayed calm.

"Good boy, good boy," he'd said, as he edged toward him and offered forth his shaky hand to pet his head. "Good boy," he'd said again, heart thumping wildly in his chest, "Let's see if we can fix this video."

Sat on the end of his bed, Harry had begun to swing his legs and bang them off the low table in front of him, where the remains of the tin of beans and the untouched glass of milk still rested. He'd also started to tap the back of his hand off his lips, a sign he was uncomfortable, but Eugene hadn't known that.

He'd been intent on getting the video working again,

delighted by how well it had kept the child occupied. In the end, he'd had to break the shiny brown ribbon that was caught in the mechanism to get it out, and not realising it was Harry's favourite cartoon, he'd not been too upset by the loss of one video.

Harry had watched as he picked a random video tape and inserted it back into the machine. When it started to play, annoyed with the choice made, Harry had grunted and kicked the table hard from underneath, lifting it off the ground and knocking some of the paper and crayons onto the floor, spilling the milk in the process. Eagerly lapping up the spill, Patrick had knocked Harry's fidget spinner off the table and under the bed.

Harry then flung his hands into the air and pointed towards the previous video, now in tatters on the bedroom floor. In a panic, Eugene had grabbed the broken video, hiding it behind his back, and when Harry got up to look behind him, he'd quickly sat on it.

"Gone," he'd said.

By then, with Harry on the verge of tears and Patrick's insistent nudging for more treats no longer possible to ignore, Eugene had started to sweat.

Giving Patrick all the treats he had to get him away from him, he'd put another video into the machine with similar results, before he'd remembered that he was supposed to hold things up for Harry to make a decision. Harry had been wailing by that time and Eugene grabbed two more videos.

278

"This or this?" he'd said, exasperated, but neither of them had been acceptable and tears of frustration had streamed down Harry's face as he shook his head and folded his arms. Shortly after, he'd started to bite at the back of his hand; fast jerking grabs at his skin with his teeth, drawing blood. Feeling queasy, Eugene tried to pull Harry's hand away but that had enraged him even more. Not knowing what else to do, Eugene reverted to holding up another two videos.

"This or this?" he'd said, getting increasingly desperate.

Harry's wailing and biting continued as Eugene held up yet more videos in rapid succession. Then, finally, Harry pointed at one. *Thank God*, Eugene had thought, *He's a fucking little time bomb waiting to go off.*

Once the cartoon had started, Harry's crying subsided and he stopped biting. Sitting back down next to Patrick he'd lain against him, seeking further solace from the touch of his soft, warm coat. Eugene again chanced to pet Patrick; he had been surprised how calm the dog had been compared to him, but Patrick was accustomed to hearing Harry's wails. Soon after, Harry fell asleep, using Patrick as his pillow, and Eugene quietly made his way into the other room.

Isolated in JJ's cottage, the three of them had been completely unaware of the frantic searching under way only a few miles away. At the cottage, there had been a peaceful truce.

By the time JJ arrived at Niamh's house that day – genuinely flustered and out of breath – Niamh had been readying herself to go back out, having stopped her searching to meet with the Gardai, and Louise was making consolatory cups of tea in Niamh's kitchen. She'd never seen JJ in a distraught state before; it was one of the few occasions she'd ever felt any softness towards him.

By seven-thirty p.m., back in JJ's cottage, Harry had woken up and was again watching his cartoons when Patrick wandered into the kitchen. Eugene had immediately jumped up and opened the back door, hoping he wanted to relieve himself – there could be no denying it, he'd been terrified of big dogs. Patrick had gone straight out and afterwards, to Eugene's delight, he'd returned to Harry's bedroom without approaching him at all.

Once he'd been sure Patrick had settled back down, and suspecting Harry might soon be getting hungry for his tea, Eugene had made him a sandwich. Harry had gone into the kitchen without prompting – on seeing the food preparation – and while he ate, Eugene stood drinking his coffee at a distance, not wanting to trigger the little time bomb again. The child scared him as much as the dog with his silent pointing, outbursts and self-harm.

Returning to his bedroom after his tea, Harry had no longer wanted to watch cartoons, and Eugene had nervously watched him wander around the room, picking up and examining different objects before putting them back down. When he started to pull at the polythene on the windows, Eugene had rushed in to grab his hand and stop him.

"No!" he'd said firmly, but Harry had just pulled his hand away and reached again for the polythene.

"No!" Eugene insisted more firmly, as he'd been advised to by JJ, but again Harry had just ignored him.

Deciding to try bribery, Eugene had gone back into the kitchen to get some sweets from the cupboard, but by the time he'd got back, Harry had already pulled half the polythene away from the window. The sweets were proffered and accepted and Eugene used that time to re-attach the polythene. Next, he'd tried to occupy Harry by showing him two books, but that hadn't worked, so he'd shown him paper and pencils, drawing a house for him with a tree outside and a matchstick man and woman. Harry had watched him draw, but then he'd begun to wander the room again. When he returned to the windows, Eugene was ready with more sweets, and when Harry had noticed the lamps and started to flick the switches on and off, Eugene had given even more sweets to get him to stop.

Eventually, nothing had pleased Harry anymore, not even sweets, and he hit a sugar high. His grunting turned into shouting then the shouting turned into screaming. Shortly after that, he'd begun to bite the back of his hand again. Patrick had been the only calm one among them. Eugene had felt his brown eyes watching him as if to say,

"You're doing it all wrong mate."

Not sure about what to do at that stage, Eugene left the room, leaving Harry there, thinking maybe he had made things worse by staying with him. Harry had been tired and wanted his fidget spinner, but with it out of sight Eugene had forgotten about it. As a way to soothe himself, turning towards the wall, Harry resorted to kicking at it hard; the contact and sound calming him down, and after a while the kicks became gentler as Harry settled again. Eugene, just glad the biting and screaming had subsided, left him to it.

By eight forty-five p.m. on day one, Eugene was reaching the end of his tether. He deeply regretted being so easily talked into this by JJ, knowing he was at a point of no return. He'd really wanted to take some of his stash to calm his nerves.

Although JJ had told him to keep Harry up until he fell asleep and to only give him a sleeping tablet if he woke upset during the night, Eugene had not been able to wait any longer and decided to enforce Harry's bedtime.

He stuffed a sleeping tablet into yet another sweet and while he waited for it to take effect, he'd stuffed another two sleeping tablets into a dog treat and fed that to Patrick, thinking he'd feel better if he was asleep too.

Forty minutes later, when both were sleeping soundly, Eugene had carried Harry to his bed and covered him with a blanket, leaving Patrick where he lay on the floor. He'd turned off the gas heater and had quietly shut the door just as his phone began to vibrate.

"How are things with you?" whispered JJ down the line.

"Grand, he's asleep now, watched videos all day."

"Good lad. OK, I'll call tomorrow."

After JJ had hung up, Eugene felt he could relax. Making himself comfortable, he'd propped himself up on his bed, rummaging through his rucksack until he'd found his needle, lighter and stash. After preparing his concoction, he'd expertly inserted the needle into a vein in his arm, inducing the utopia he'd been looking forward to all afternoon.

At some point during that night, he'd woken up, half drugged, at first not recognising where he was, and then he'd topped himself up with much less expertise. For good measure, he'd also taken some of the sleeping tablets from JJ's brown bag because he hadn't wanted to wake again until daylight. The cottage might have made a good party venue, but with only an unpredictable child and a beast for company, the silence and darkness had freaked him out.

Every sound had seemed amplified in the quiet, and he'd begun to fantasise that Patrick would wake from his sleep in a rage to devour him.

In no time at all, Eugene had lost consciousness.

The aftermath

The morning after JJ had kidnapped Harry, he'd excused himself as the family sat down to eat breakfast and phoned Eugene from the bathroom in Niamh's house. It was only six a.m., but Harry, an early riser, might have already been up by then. He wanted to check how the night had gone. The phone rang out with no answer. The second time he'd rung from the garden, after the Gardai had left, but again no answer. *Maybe Eugene has his phone on silent*, he'd told himself, *I should have warned him to keep it on.*

He sent a text message after that, telling Eugene to text back when he got the message – *not to phone.*

Fifteen minutes later, with no return text, JJ had started to get more anxious. *Something's not right. How much longer do I wait. I'll have to go out to the cottage,* he'd thought. *Fuck it Eugene, respond.*

When Niamh disappeared upstairs to shower, unable to sit it out any longer, he'd told her parents he was going to go home and shower as well. It had been as good an excuse as he could think of and no one had batted an eyelid at the suggestion.

JJ tried Eugene again in the car but there had still been no answer.

Back in his own house, he'd phoned and texted with no result. *Harry and Patrick should've woken Eugene by now,* he'd thought, cursing Eugene for putting both him and them at risk. *If I find you sitting with your headphones stuck in your ears, I'll have to restrain myself from beating the living daylights out of you… at least until another day.*

Is Harry OK? The sudden swell of emotion had taken him by surprise. The thought of Harry being harmed in any way… *will I be able to live with myself if Eugene's done something to him*?

He'd tried phoning one last time before picking up the keys to his jeep, parked in the garage the day before, after he'd brought Harry and Patrick to the cottage.

I'm going to kill that fucking Eugene if the phone's been on silent, he'd thought again as he backed out onto the road.

Like the previous few days, the fog had hung thick and heavy over the lake – an apt backdrop for deceit and skulduggery.

As he drove, JJ had cursed the poor state of the potholed road, which prevented him from picking up speed. His gut had told him something was wrong, and time was of the essence, while his brain told him there'd be a logical explanation. He'd wanted to believe his brain. A risky inconvenience was far better than a tragedy.

The roadside gate at the entrance to the narrow gravel lane leading up to the cottage had been shut as expected. JJ had kept his fingers crossed when he got out to open it, hoping the old wooden bolt would slide easily to allow him quick access. Over the years the elements had played havoc with the bolt, swelling the wood so much that at times it refused to budge. To his relief, it slid easily across and once he'd driven through he'd quickly got out to close it after him. With the cottage beyond view he stopped to listen before getting back into his jeep, but there'd been nothing except the usual rustling and bird song.

The lane was far worse than the road; the frost and rain had enlarged every pothole in its rough gravel surface. He'd rocked back and forth, moving as fast as he could but painfully slowly; a complete contrast to his heart rate which had been rising exponentially throughout the journey.

When JJ originally purchased the cottage, the estate agent had described it as secluded, and indeed it was. Keen to distance himself from Dublin, he'd wanted to find a remote location, somewhere that would allow him to let his past slowly recede into memory. It had been his first ill-gotten gain buy, and was as far removed from the concrete backyards of his youth as he could imagine. Once the gate was closed, no one could see anything beyond and only invited visitors wandered up the long lane. He loved the privacy.

He'd been sad to leave his cottage after he moved in with Niamh. Her house on the outskirts of town was deemed to be the most suitable for a family so the cottage had been rented out until recently. Before all this mess erupted, JJ had planned to move back in himself.

Both sides of the drive were lined with tall fir trees which were planted twenty rows deep, giving the impression of driving through a forest. He breathed in the scent of the firs through the open driver's window as he drove up the lane that day, the earthy scent a reminder of a place where he hadn't wanted to be. He'd known he was putting himself in jeopardy taking such a chance, but he'd no choice. *Eugene had better have a good reason for his silence.*

After rounding the bend in the lane, through the fog, the cottage had come into view. A linear, single storey, simple dwelling that would once have been a workman's cottage, possibly housing a large family within its three small rooms. Other than the bathroom and a little porch added by JJ, its original structure was unchanged. Even that day, in a state of fear, not knowing what to expect behind the facade, he still appreciated its simplicity as it sat firmly embedded in the mist which wrapped around it like a soft silk scarf.

The house had looked empty with the windows blacked-out at the front. *So far so good, that's as planned*, he had thought, but then he'd noticed the polythene on Harry's window, partially pulled down. Parking up outside the door, he'd turned the jeep so it faced back towards the laneway in. This was an old habit – always be prepared for a quick getaway.

Before his foot had hit the gravel, he'd heard Patrick. His low echoing bark had sounded quite ferocious, and in the stillness of the morning fog it was travelling too far. He had to quieten him. *Something's definitely very wrong.*

JJ had hurried around the back, preparing himself to deal with whatever he met inside. He'd known he would have to settle Patrick first, no matter what he encountered next. When he entered the kitchen, Patrick had run straight to him, almost knocking him over in his excitement to see him.

"Get down!" JJ had commanded as he pushed the dog back to the floor. Patrick, who had been locked in all night was itching to get out the open door and JJ let him go.

Fearfully, he'd turned towards Harry's room; within the darkness of the blacked-out bedroom he could see Harry sitting within a shaft of light cast across his bed, directly below the pulled down section of polythene. He was sitting, rocking back and forth with his blankets pulled up over his head, quietly sobbing. The sound had been one of defeat and distress but at least, from a distance, he had looked to be physically all right.

JJ had let out a deep sigh. "Thank God."

Glancing about, he'd called Eugene's name while heading towards Harry's bedroom; the remains of the previous day's sandwich were still on the kitchen table, and Eugene's door was shut. The cottage had felt cold.

He'd shouted Eugene's name again, as he cautiously entered Harry's bedroom, looking about suspiciously, but Harry had been alone and there hadn't been a sound from Eugene's room.

"Hey, Harry wee man, Daddy's here. It's all OK now," he'd said softly to his sobbing son.

Harry had looked like he'd been crying for some time. *I'll kill that fucking Eugene when I get my hands on him*, he'd thought, and for a second time that day he felt a surprising surge of emotion for his son's distress.

Having come back inside, Patrick had sought some attention from JJ, and had obediently returned to his bundle of blankets on the floor after a rub to his head and an instruction to lie down.

"Eugene, where are you?" JJ had shouted louder, but there had been nothing but silence from his room.

Knowing Harry's fidget spinner would be the easiest way to calm him, JJ had scanned the room looking for it from where he sat on the bed with Harry. Not able to see it, he'd leaned down, running his hand underneath the base, and that's where he'd found it, exactly where

290

it had fallen the day before. Giving it a whirl, he'd handed it to Harry.

"Eugene," he called again, looking back towards the closed door. Still no response.

Getting up from the bed, JJ had turned on the TV and pushed in the last ejected video, before lighting the gas heater to generate a bit of heat. Once Harry was ensconced, he'd reattached the pulled down section of polythene to the window. Then he'd fetched Harry a banana and a drink of milk, all the while listening for sounds of movement and keeping a watch on Eugene's door. With Harry settled, he'd headed back across the kitchen to find out if Eugene was still there, noting the mangled videotape in the open kitchen bin on route.

"Eugene, I'm coming in," he'd said, as he slowly turned the handle on the bedroom door and then quickly swung it open as far as he could to get a clearer view inside.

Eugene's bedroom window, unlike Harry's, remained blacked-out. In the greyness he could see Eugene lying on the bed, curled up on his side, facing the wall in the foetal position, still clothed with a blanket pulled up to his waist.

"Eugene, are you OK?" he'd said more calmly but there was still no response.

Gingerly he'd moved closer, penknife at the ready.

"Eugene, wake up."

Crunch – JJ had stepped on something in the

291

darkness and looking down, beneath his feet, he had seen the now broken syringe.

"Ah shit," he'd said kicking it sideways.

Eugene's arm felt cold, and when JJ had turned him over on to his back for a better look he could see his eyes were partially open and his jaw slightly slack. He'd known he was dead.

"No, no, no," he'd moaned as he pushed Eugene over to face the wall again putting his penknife back into his pocket. "Shit."

While trying to comprehend the situation he was in, Patrick had again appeared at JJ's side and had started to sniff at Eugene's corpse.

"Get back to bed Patrick," JJ had said sternly, pushing him back out the door and closing it to keep him out.

Standing over Eugene in the dimly lit room with his fists clenched, he'd stared down at the dead body in the bed as his mind raced. There was no choice, he'd have to get Harry out of there. He couldn't leave him on his own with Patrick.

Despite the scene before him and the turmoil in his mind, he'd concluded that his plan could still work. *It's just going to have to be a very short kidnap – a warning. Harry will have to be found today, not tomorrow or the next day. Lucky you Niamh*, he'd thought, *you'll be so relieved.*

JJ had been careful to shut the bedroom door behind

him before he returned to the kitchen to pour himself a glass of cool spring water from the tap. It had helped to bring more clarity to his thoughts. *Take it a step at a time*, he'd reassured himself while flexing his neck from side to side. *First things first, the boys need breakfast.*

He'd been very gentle that day when Harry had started to cry again, not wanting to upset him further. Bringing him into the kitchen he'd sat him at the table and from the cupboard he'd held aloft a bread roll and a cereal bar. Harry had pointed to the bar and JJ had given it to him, with some orange squash from the fridge.

After refilling his glass of water, he'd considered the search schedule they'd put together earlier that day with the Gardai, and he'd tried to figure out where the best place would be to leave Harry so he would be found without him being caught dropping the boy there.

Concentrating on working out his next moves, he'd not noticed when Harry returned to his video, face lit by the TV screen, leaning against Patrick who was sleeping soundly on his bundle of blankets. He'd been too busy thinking about what to do.

Better phone Niamh and the Gardai for an update and let them know I've gone back out looking. They'll be wondering where I am.

On the phone, Niamh had told him she was with Louise and that they were still with the search party in the fields near her home. There was another search in progress nearby, so he'd known it was too risky to travel

293

in that direction at that time. Bearing in mind all the searches scheduled that day, he decided that the old forestry road was the best option. He knew Louise and Niamh planned to check that route, and Patrick knew his way home from there; he'd bring Harry home whether or not they came across him. He couldn't risk leaving Harry closer to the town as he'd originally planned to – there'd be too many volunteers out looking at such an early stage. Deciding the safest time to drop Harry would be later that afternoon, he'd resigned himself to wait patiently until then. He had plenty of time – too much time, and worried the Gardai might want to meet him during the day; if so he'd have to chance leaving Harry for an hour or so, with only Patrick and a corpse supervising.

That afternoon, he'd spent the intervening hours occasionally checking in by phone and planning what to do with Eugene.

At four-thirty p.m., he made his first move.

"OK, Harry, let's get your coat and go for a walk."

Patrick had been wide awake once he heard the word.

After putting on Harry's coat and Patrick's harness, he'd taken both his child and dog to his jeep, leaving Eugene's dead body behind in the cottage.

Tying up loose ends

The short drive to the forestry carpark had been uneventful. JJ had felt secure enough, knowing where the searches were being conducted that day. His only risk lay in meeting a random walker, but with the inclement weather he'd kept his fingers crossed that eventuality would be unlikely.

Under normal circumstances it was a pleasant walk from the carpark, through the forest, back to home, but he'd been well aware that leaving Harry on his own without adult supervision was risky; at the very least the walk would take much longer than usual. That hadn't stopped him though. *Life's not perfect, is it?* he'd told himself.

Arriving in the carpark, he'd thoroughly checked the way was clear, then let Harry and Patrick out of the jeep. Harry was used to being connected to Patrick when they went walking so he looped the lead he had though Patrick's harness and attached the snap hook end to the drawstring of Harry's coat. Somewhat uncomfortable about the risk he was taking, leaving his child unattended, he'd at least wanted to be sure the connection would break in the event of an emergency. *It's the best I can do. They'll be fine,* he'd reassured himself.

He then knelt down in front of his son saying, "Now Harry, I want you to be a good boy and head home with Patrick. Daddy has to go somewhere."

Putting a handful of sweets in Harry's pocket, he'd petted Patrick on the head and commanded,

"Go home Patrick," pointing up the narrow pathway leading into the trees.

The fog had been starting to fall, but there was little he could do about that. *A bit of water won't kill the boy and Patrick will find his way despite the fog, he's well used to this route.*

As he got back into the jeep, the pair had stood looking at him and he'd become frustrated; it was too dangerous for him to stay much longer.

"Go home Patrick. Go home." he'd raised his voice as he started the engine, but a confused Patrick had stood waiting for JJ to join the walk.

"Go home!" he'd shouted, "Go home!"

It had been no use – they had both just stood looking at him with blank expressions.

Too afraid to wait any longer, he'd driven off, looking into his rear-view mirror as he went, hoping to see them walk away, but they hadn't budged.

Patrick will head home soon enough, he'd told himself as they disappeared from his sight.

Back on the main road, as he headed to the cottage to await the phone call to say Harry had been found, he tried to focus on his next move; the one last loose end to safely tie up – getting rid of Eugene's body.

JJ's normally peaceful, quiet cottage had felt eerily silent on his return, and he'd wished he could tear the polythene off the windows to let in some brightness and lift the mood. In the half-light thrown out by the little lamps, shadows on the walls and ceilings had become distorted into unrecognisable shapes, and his mundane objects had taken on the form of large foreboding illusions. *The sooner I can get the cottage back to normal the better*, he'd thought, but he had another few hours of sitting in the gloom before it was time to load Eugene into the jeep; a few more hours of anxious waiting, battling to suppress a panic attack.

Not wanting to see Eugene again until he had to, he'd sat trying to picture Harry and Patrick on their return journey home as a way to help re-focus his mind. Knowing the route, he'd been well able to imagine their whereabouts as they walked.

They should have cleared the densest part of the forest by now if they didn't hang around the carpark for too long, he'd thought. *Patrick's a trained service dog, he'll get him home*, he'd again reassured himself. *He'll have gone on his way quickly enough. He knows his job.*

JJ's main concern had been that Harry, a clumsy walker, might fall, but he'd pushed that thought to the back of his mind. *Soon I'll get a phone call to say they've been found.*

As he waited, he'd been unable to stop his eye from being drawn to Eugene's door, so headed outside into the backyard to clear up Patrick's morning mess. After that he'd gone around to the front of the property where he spread some taupe across the back of his jeep in readiness for Eugene's departure.Then, he'd wandered about aimlessly for a while listening to the sound of the gravel beneath his feet. He'd also sat on the front step admiring his little piece of heaven, refusing to think about the dead body that lay beyond the wall behind him.

The tops of the trees had become obscured by the falling mist. It had been quite beautiful to look at, but also a reminder that he'd left his son in the middle of nowhere with the weather deteriorating and the night about to close in.

"Come on, ring," he'd said to his phone.

JJ wished he'd used somewhere else for his ill-fated production. This folly was going to taint his cottage forever. He'd always have bad memories now – everything was spoilt. His cottage would no longer be his refuge; he'd never feel at peace here again. *I might even sell and look for somewhere else*, he'd lamented, feeling sorry for himself.

Getting up from the step, the stiffness in his knees had reminded him that despite his well-maintained appearance, there was no denying he was getting older. Moving Eugene wasn't going to be an easy task, but the time had come to put the boy's body into the back of his jeep. Stretching out to relieve the tightness, he had reluctantly returned inside to put on some gloves, before commencing the gruesome tidy up.

In Eugene's bedroom, JJ pulled back the blanket covering Eugene, releasing the stale smell of bodily fluids from beneath. He'd had to turn his head away to avoid the sudden stench.

Left by his bed, Eugene's trainers were an obvious starting point for getting him ready to go and JJ had put them on first. Next, he'd tried to get Eugene's jacket, which had been flung to the floor the night before, back on him. He pulled it over his bent arm and around his back, but rigor mortis had set in by then, and between the stench and the effort it all became too much of a struggle. Taking it back off, he'd shoved it into Eugene's rucksack with the other things he had brought with him.

After a moment to catch his breath he'd reached across Eugene and untucked the far side of the bottom sheet, flinging it over his body so he could pull it towards himself and the edge of the bed. Eugene's corpse had fallen to the floor with a hollow thud, laying there while JJ wrapped his broken syringe in a tissue. JJ took the syringe out to the jeep first, putting it on the front passenger seat. Then he put Eugene's rucksack and the bicycle from the shed onto the back seat. Finally, he'd returned to the bedroom to collect Eugene.

Gathering the sheet together from all four corners, he'd dragged him out, tugging him over all the bumps and obstacles he met on his way to the jeep. Once there, he'd climbed into the boot and tried to haul Eugene up, curled up in the sheet like a child in the womb, but Eugene had been too heavy and the sheet had kept getting caught on the catch of the boot. Frustrated, he'd jumped back out to think of an easier way to get him in.

Leaning him against the back of the jeep, JJ had pulled him up as far as he could, keeping the sheet wrapped around him. Then, bending down, he'd picked his body up like a large child. Cradled in his arms, Eugene became a person again. His corpse, so intimately close, had been something he'd wanted to avoid. JJ had felt the shape of his body, his head fallen forward against his shoulder as he carried him; this physical intimacy representing an act of compassion – compassion, an emotion he couldn't feel for Eugene. He had a job to do.

Once Eugene had been safely stowed in the back of the jeep, JJ covered him over with another blanket and shut the boot. Sweating profusely from his efforts, he took off his gloves and went back inside to scrub his hands.

Not able to face any more of the clean-up operation, he'd shut Eugene's bedroom door and paced the floor, waiting for the phone to ring and put him out of his misery. It was almost fully dark by then, and he had begun to think he'd have to take everything back out of the jeep and go and find Harry and Patrick himself.

He'd phoned Niamh again, she was on her way to the clinic with Louise; they were planning to head out searching again once they'd checked for messages from clients. He'd said he was still out searching. She'd sounded very dejected, and he'd tried to encourage her optimistic nature, knowing her trauma would end soon, but she'd appeared to be losing all hope.

Despite having lied to Eugene, saying he'd wanted to upset Niamh in revenge for their separation, he hadn't actually given her response to the situation much thought, too consumed with finding his own way out of the danger he was facing and knowing full well himself where Harry would be.

Finally his phone had rung – Harry found at last.

There'd been no time to waste. The ruin was the perfect place for the useless Eugene. It was a well-known hideaway for youngsters who experimented with drugs and drank cans of beer before tutoring themselves about sex. As it had been much later than he'd expected, he had to be quick, aware some of the local youths might be gathering now it was dark. He wasn't sure how often

301

the ruin was still used as a rendezvous for misbehaviour; new venues emerged all the time as the old ones were discovered by the general public or the Gardai.

The drive to the ruin was also the drive on the way back into town, so he'd known that if anyone saw him he could easily avoid suspicion. Everyone would be heading back, knowing Harry had been found.

A car had stayed behind him on the last part of the main road drive, happy to hang back in the dimming light. It had contentedly followed rather than led, not wanting to be the first to meet bright headlights on the winding road at dusk.

JJ had to pull in to the side of the road, pretending to answer his phone to get it to pass, praying the driver wouldn't be someone he knew who might stop to check he was OK. He'd been so close to getting it all sorted at that point. *To be caught now would be cruel*, he had thought. To his great relief, the red rear lights disappeared into the distance and once they'd vanished out of sight, JJ had continued on.

Glad to pull off the main road, he'd entered the lane which led to the ruin. There had been no cars or bicycles parked there so he drove the jeep as close as he could to the old stone walls. Before getting out he made extra sure that nobody was about. Crumbling stone covered in ivy had been all that greeted him. He'd been completely alone.

Once inside the ruin, he had looked back out through

302

the remains of a large window opening and could see his jeep parked just outside, congratulating himself on managing to manoeuvre it through the last few trees which now grew on the lane. That was going to make it easier to get Eugene to his temporary resting place, and right under the window where he stood had been where he decided he would put him.

Back at the jeep, he'd put on his gloves and opened the boot door, pulling the sheet containing Eugene's body to the boot's edge. With one last tug it had landed with another *thump* on the ground. JJ had no time to be worried by his conscience.

With renewed energy, he'd hauled the body across the grass and rubble. Above the sound of the sheet ripping as it caught on a piece of rock, he'd heard sounds from his past, echoing about him in the fading light.

The towering trees that rustled above and soft forest floor were a familiar backdrop. He'd heard punches and kicks as he dragged Eugene along, and voices that called out to him to, "Stop, please stop," but he wasn't going to stop. He would see this through to its end, driven by madness, like the bastards who'd murdered Kevin.

Eugene was rolled out of the sheet below the window opening. There were soggy, empty cigarette packets on the ground along with condom wrappers and empty cider and wine bottles. Someone had made a fire from bits of rubble and in the ash JJ had been able to identify at least one syringe and a few charred bits of tin foil.

He'd looked again out of the window opening to check that he was still alone, then propped up Eugene's body as best he could to look as though he'd been sitting and had fallen forward. He went back to the jeep and threw the sheet into the boot, then got Eugene's broken syringe and rucksack which he placed on the ground beside the body. It had been hard to see as daylight was fading but he couldn't risk turning on the jeep's headlights. He'd stood for a moment to consider the scene from a law enforcer's perspective.

Eugene's lifeless body sat propped against the wall; his broken syringe and rucksack, which contained his bus pass, social security card and wallet, were by his side. It looked plausible to JJ as the scene of an accident and it wouldn't take long to identify him. By all accounts, here was the body of a young man from out of town who had come to hide away and take drugs for a few days. Lastly, JJ had leant Eugene's rented bicycle against a nearby tree.

When he'd finished, he said, "See ya," to Eugene's body, as if he were an old friend just resting for a while. The deed was done and he'd felt safe again, for that moment at least.

When Niamh had phoned JJ to tell him Harry had been found, JJ had told her he was at the far side of the lake, some distance from the car, so she hadn't questioned the lapse in time before he made it to the clinic.

304

After he left the ruins that evening, on the outskirts of town, JJ met a group of tired volunteers heading back, sticks in hand. He'd stopped briefly to thank them for their support in searching for Harry and let them know he'd been found. Assuming he had been out searching all day himself, they had not been surprised by his stressed and sweaty state. He was devious when he needed to be.

Back at his house, he'd changed his clothes and shoes, a t-shirt the quickest thing he could pull on. Then he'd driven his BMW to the clinic, still perspiring from his efforts and high on adrenaline, to welcome home his son.

Harry's journey home

Even though it was only a three kilometre walk to the town from where JJ had left Harry and Patrick in the carpark, for any child without an adult, let alone a child with autism, it had been a long journey home.

Patrick had stayed in the carpark after JJ left, confused by his request, and he'd waited patiently for him to return. It was only Harry's increasing agitation that eventually moved him on along the old dirt road through the forest.

The pair knew the walk well; they'd often done it before, but never on their own. Starting at the far end meant they had a downhill walk and once they'd cleared the denser trees, they had an intermittent view of the town to encourage them to keep going.

In late spring, the little stream that ran beside the track blocked with weeds, forming stagnant ponds full of frogs' spawn. Harry knew all the spots, and even though that day he was tired, wet and seemingly engrossed by his fidget spinner – which he'd not let go of again – he'd regularly stopped Patrick to check for the tadpoles' arrival. He always did this on such walks and it was often difficult to drag him away. That evening had been no exception, and it had taken Patrick much longer than Harry's parents to encourage him to move on. Indeed, at times, progress had been very slow.

The tracks, saturated for weeks, made hiking boots a more appropriate choice of footwear than Harry's trainers, which had quickly become heavy with muck as they'd walked. Aggrieved by the extra weight, he'd stopped frequently to scrape away the mud, slowing their progress further, and with the fog thickening and the drizzle turning to rain at times, they'd done well to persevere.

Patrick had tried to quicken their pace once they reached the trails closer to the town where the ground was firmer and steadier, but Harry had objected to the speed, pulling him back and slowing him down. He'd been tired and wanted to spin his spinner. It was difficult to walk and watch it spin simultaneously.

As daylight began to disappear, Harry slowed significantly more than Patrick, but intent on getting home, the dog had successfully continued the tug-and-pull game the pair had played since their walk began.

On the home straight, approaching the main road from where there was a concrete pathway into town, Patrick stopped, as he always did, to give Harry a chance to check the curb side. It was a rise which he sometimes missed and fell over. They hadn't known it then, but their journey was nearly over.

Harry had pulled Patrick to a stop one last time, this time to get another of the sweets that JJ had put in his pocket. There were no sweets left, but no matter, because a few minutes later as the drizzle had turned to rain, entering the boundaries of the town, they had met Louise on her way to the forestry carpark; their cross-country hike over.

Under one roof

Louise was sitting at her kitchen table having scrubbed her house from floor to ceiling in expectation of a visit from Finn that evening. He'd texted earlier in the week to say he'd like to talk more. She'd been ecstatic at the time and had thought about little else until yesterday. So much had happened yesterday…

A body had been found, linked to Harry's disappearance. Then Finn's house had been searched for green paint, and she'd endured those difficult conversations with JJ – the first at lunchtime, when he'd discovered he was Finn's father, and the other later in the evening, when she had foolishly phoned him and been so cruelly rebuffed.

Life's complications aside, Louise remained desperate to see Finn again. The fact that she'd already broken her promise to him by disclosing their relationship to Niamh *and* JJ hadn't dampened her excitement. Getting the house ready for his visit had helped her keep those indiscretions out of her mind. This evening was a new beginning – another chance to gain Finn's trust. *Surely now, after the Gardai's search of his house, he'll accept my offer to employ a decent solicitor and allow me to be of some practical motherly use to him.*

A slight whiff of kitchen cleaner lingered in the air as she expectantly sat waiting for his arrival, nervously anticipating his knock on her front door.

Finn was due to arrive at six-thirty p.m., but as seven p.m. and then seven-thirty p.m. came and went without him, she began to worry he'd changed his mind. Maybe there'd be no 'happy-ever-after' for her at all?

Looking around, she wished she had pictures of Finn growing up displayed on her walls – pictures of a life they'd had together. A life lost to them because of religious prejudice and Ireland's social norms in her teens; she'd been so terribly afraid of being shamed.

By eight p.m., Louise was lying with her head on the table contemplating what to do. Deciding to send him a text message, she was desolate when it wasn't acknowledged, fearing he'd changed his mind and no longer wanted to be contacted by her. Envisioning the fisherman at the lake, she became quite frantic, thinking perhaps she'd made things worse – even unbearable for him? He was already under so much pressure. Was she, his mother, going to be the straw that broke the proverbial camel's back?

In desperation, Louise phoned her friend,

"He's not arrived Niamh, and I can't get in contact with him. He's not responding. What'll I do?"

"Go over," Niamh said immediately, "It can't do any harm, just go over. Maybe something's happened and he couldn't contact you? Maybe he's been arrested? You need to find out. There's no point sitting home worrying. Oh, and leave a note on the door to say you'll be back soon in case he arrives while you're gone."

Louise scribbled a note, put it in an envelope marked 'Finn' and stuck it to the front door on her way to the car.

Turning the key to start the engine, she looked up and saw the envelope with his name written clearly across the front. She'd got so near to getting him back – it would be unbearable if he disappeared from her life once more, yet as she reversed she watched his name fade out of sight.

A few minutes later, Louise saw Finn walking along the pavement near his home. He was heading away from her house, rather than walking towards it. With his hands in pockets and head down as usual, he was striding at a mighty pace. She became hesitant and slowed down. *What if he really has changed his mind, he might be irritated by my persistence. Turn around and go home*, a little voice in her head told her while another louder, more urgent one said, *get a grip, pull up by him and ask him why he didn't come over as planned*!

311

Louise gave her horn the slightest *toot* of recognition and stopped the car just ahead of him. To her surprise, Finn immediately left the path and came around the back of her car to the front passenger door. For a moment, she was once more afraid of him; afraid of what she didn't know.

A blast of cool evening air filled the car as he sat in the passenger seat, looking tired and annoyed.

"Hi Louise," he said flatly, "I'm sorry, I've been at the Garda station again. I think they really want to pin something on me."

"What?" she said, "Why? I mean, I thought they'd be ruling you out by now."

She was flustered.

They sat in the car at the side of the road, and he told her how they had questioned him about the body they'd found at the ruins.

"They said it appeared to be an overdose but the state pathologist thinks the body has been moved," he said.

He told her they were following this new line of enquiry, looking for a possible accomplice involved in Harry's kidnapping, and perhaps even a murderer.

"They wanted to know if I knew him – if I'd helped him get Harry and Patrick out of the garden. They said it had to be someone they knew well, or Patrick would've barked. 'Aid and abet' were the words they used. They've definitely got it in for me. I'm seriously fucked, they really want to stitch me up."

312

With that, he slumped forward with his head in his hands.

Louise could see his shoulders begin to shudder. Staring at the distraught man beside her, she wasn't sure how to respond. She wanted to reach out, to touch and console him, but was unable to connect on such a motherly level. Fearful, she was afraid her need to connect would be rejected and that Finn would be overwhelmed by the strength of her emotion.

"Sorry," he said as he wiped his hand across his face and sniffed, "What am I going to do?"

"Nothing," she said with steely resolve, "Nothing. You've done nothing wrong. They'll find that out eventually. For now, you're coming home with me."

Louise knew she was treating him like a child but hadn't the time to think about phrasing her invitation more appropriately, her urge to make him feel better taking over.

"I'll get you something to eat. You can stay in the spare room. I'm not having you staying on your own tonight when there's no need to be."

He was still slumped forward with his head in his hands.

"Erm… I don't know Louise, I think I just want to get home. Maybe another time."

Louise had already begun turning the car in the direction of her house.

"I insist. You can't go home to an empty house

tonight. Please Finn, let me at least make you something to eat."

He thought of his empty house where there was nothing of comfort waiting for him, and he let her carry on, too tired to resist.

"They can't do this," she said, "They can't keep bringing you in with no evidence. That's harassment Finn, pure harassment. You need a solicitor and a good one. I can help you with that."

"Sure," he said despondently, rubbing his hand across his jawline and around the back of his neck. "When the school hears about this, I'll never get my job back. I can't go back to prison, Louise, I just can't. I'd rather die."

He hadn't told Louise about his time in prison but he assumed she knew like everyone else.

Louise glanced again at the man beside her; this almost stranger who was her son. He was such a lost and desolate soul, and in that moment she knew she was truly his mother because if she could take his place she would. One thing was for certain; no one was going to hurt him anymore. He'd been through enough. It was time for her to step up, and she was more than ready for the task.

Finn felt somewhat reassured to have someone on his side again, it was freeing being able to discuss his concerns, but he was less confident about how that someone might act out her loyalty to him. He didn't need any more trouble, and Louise definitely looked like she was willing to stir up a lot of it. He was, in fact, quite taken aback by her ferocity, and a little nervous of the enraged woman driving him to her home, but what had he got to lose?

He sat quietly for the rest of the short journey, not wanting to add any more flames to the fire of fury he sensed burning within her.

Awkwardly, they both ate their sandwiches at her kitchen table. Neither was sure what to say but they felt solace from being together and that was more precious than any words right now. *Easy conversation might take more time,* Louise thought, *but I can wait*.

While she fussed about, tidying up, he took in his surroundings. Her house was more cluttered than his but it had a welcoming, cosy feel about it. *I like it,* he thought.

Finn wanted to ask her about the caul she'd mentioned when she first visited him. It was something tangible from his actual birth, in his opinion even better than a birth certificate, and was the reason he had suggested they meet again. After their tea, he summoned up the courage and requested to see it.

Taken completely off guard, Louise was unsure how to respond. That caul was her most private possession and although it was a part of Finn, the thought of showing it to someone else, even him… She just wasn't sure she wanted to, and he saw her hesitation.

"It's OK," he said, "You can show me another day."

That was all it took to push her into action. She wouldn't disappoint her son again and left him sitting in the kitchen, pondering the strangeness of it all, while she fetched it.

Upstairs, Louise reached into the back of the drawer and took out the envelope one last time, giving it a gentle caress. *It should be handed over to its rightful owner,* she thought. There was no need to keep a representation of her son, not now when he was with her in the flesh.

Back downstairs, she sat down beside him at the table and handed him the envelope, watching in silence as he carefully opened it to look inside. His hands shook a little. She could feel the emotion too. Removing the tissue, he slowly separated it to expose the tiny sliver of dried skin-like material.

Keeping his eyes on the caul as he spoke,

"So this was on my head when I was born – in England?"

"Yes, and I kept it safe all these years, but you should have it now."

Louise unwillingly began to cry, the emotion of seeing her son touch his own caul overwhelming her. Embarrassed by her reaction and aware of Finn's discomfort, she stifled her tears as quickly as she could. It was a momentous moment for them both.

"Keep it Finn, it will bring you good luck," she said

smiling.

"I can't, it's yours," he said looking towards her.

"No," she said, smiling even wider and still teary-eyed, "It's yours, and I don't need it anymore. I have you now."

Louise reached across and touched Finn's hand but he said nothing and pulled his away. The intimacy of her words and touch were too much. Covering the caul with the tissue, he returned it to the envelope that bore his name.

"Thanks," he said, "I'll take good care of it."

There was a short silence then Finn said,

"I think I'll head off to bed if that's OK? I'm—" He was about to say 'fucked' but corrected himself, respectful of the person whose company he was in. "I'm whacked.".

Louise wiped her eyes and asked if he wanted a glass of water to bring to bed with him. She fetched him a spare toothbrush and told him where the extra blankets and pillows were in his room if he needed them. Then she gave him not only a bath towel but also a hand towel. All the fuss was overwhelming Finn and he considered suggesting he return home, but afraid she'd be very upset, he stayed.

Upstairs he welcomed the privacy of the spare bedroom and sat on the bed for a while looking at the envelope, trying to come to terms with the idea of Louise being his mother before finally settling down to

317

attempt to sleep.

Lying on the bed in his biological mother's home, his head was full of thoughts; so much had changed in the last few weeks. He tossed and turned trying to quiet his mind and had resigned himself to not getting much sleep when he became aware of the distant sound of the television and Louise pottering about downstairs.

Gradually, those sounds transported him back to his teens and began to soothe his mind, just as they had when his parents were alive. He was glad he'd stayed, and unexpectedly, a short time later, he fell sound asleep.

Louise listened to Finn moving around upstairs. Used to living alone, it was strange having different noises in the house; stranger still that those sounds were being made by her son.

When all was quiet and she was sure he wouldn't come back down, she allowed herself to weep tears of contentment. Louise couldn't ever remember crying for that reason before.

It was late by then, but she picked up the phone anyway, wanting to let Niamh know all was well. Niamh was waiting for her call and keen to know how the evening had progressed. In spite of the renewed interest in Finn by the Gardai, she was delighted for her friend. Most of the conversation was about how angry Louise was with JJ for the position he'd put Finn in, but Niamh could still tell by Louise's exhilarated tones that she had found a new happiness in re-uniting with her son. Now all that needed to happen was clearing Finn's name as quickly as possible.

After her call with Louise, Niamh sat thinking about Finn and Harry. She believed Finn was innocent and was upset that Harry was missing out on his interactions with him in the school yard, yet there was little she could do about it. There were rules and regulations both she and Finn had to follow which would keep them separated for some time to come.

She didn't tell Louise that her suspicions lay with JJ. It made no sense to her at all. Why would he be involved?

After the Gardai had told her about the link between the paint on Harry's trainers and the body found at the ruins, Niamh had recalled, some time back, JJ saying he intended to re-decorate the cottage. He'd wanted to move back in. It bothered her, why he hadn't mention this to her when she'd asked about the paint… she was sure he'd started the project. *It must have come to his mind,* she thought. And that deception got her thinking again about the pinch marks and where on earth Harry had found that old fidget spinner.

But before she could start accusing JJ of anything underhand, she really needed someone else's opinion. Perhaps her mind was playing tricks on her? Louise was her best option but this evening was not the right time. Louise deserved her first evening alone with Finn without her suspicions adding to her torment. *Maybe I'll get the chance to talk to her tomorrow.*

Louise had also held back information; she still hadn't been able to tell Niamh who Finn's father was, or about her meeting with JJ the previous day. Telling Niamh the former was not a conversation to be had over the telephone – and so their respective secrets remained unshared for another day.

The following morning, Finn left early, leaving a note on the table to say he was heading home to change and would stay there because he didn't want the Gardai to think he'd gone into hiding. He signed off by telling her not to worry and thanked her for the company and sandwiches.

It was a simple handwritten note from her son, but as the first of its kind, it had an immense impact on Louise. She traced each letter with her finger and after she'd re-read the note several times, she took it upstairs and put it into an envelope, writing 'Finn' in capitals across the front. Then she put it at the back of the drawer in the same spot where his caul had once lain.

She sent him a text message.

'Hey Finn, you OK? Thanks for the note. I was worried when I saw you were gone.'

'Yep OK, thanks again. Talk soon', came the immediate response.

If hearts could sing, hers would have done so right then as she made the sign of the cross in the Catholic way and prayed he would be found innocent.

Today was the day: she was going to tell Niamh about JJ, but she couldn't do it at the clinic. Instead, she was going to suggest that Niamh visit her house after work on the pretext of talking about Finn. This evening, she'd find a way to tell her the whole truth.

It had to be told soon, before JJ got the chance to twist it. Niamh might be too hurt to listen to her side of the story otherwise.

Louise would not be able to deny that she had been a deceitful friend for many years, but she hoped Niamh would understand the reasons why she'd stayed silent about her relationship with JJ.

A deceitful friend, and an estranged husband – *are either of us worthy of her forgiveness?* she wondered. *We've kept her in ignorance for so many years.*

Louise wished she didn't have to tell her at all.

Past meets present

It was late afternoon. Louise still hadn't arranged to meet up with Niamh that evening and she was on her own in the clinic, continuing to struggle with her conscience. Should she or shouldn't she tell the truth? There were risks no matter what she decided. She kept changing her mind.

Her common sense was strongly resisting the urge to be open and honest, despite wanting to be. The consequences might be catastrophic for both of them. If only she could be sure that JJ would stay silent, there'd be no need to upset anyone.

Louise was at the reception desk when she heard the doorbell and looked up to see a rather gaunt looking elderly man enter the clinic. He didn't appear to have a pet with him, and he surveyed his surroundings before slowly approaching her. The way he studied her made her uneasy.

Although elderly, he had a menacing presence about

him; a sly shiftiness. Louise was instantly on her guard.

"Hello, I'm looking for Mrs Hennessy. I understand she owns this practice. She's married to a Jonnie Hennessy. Have I the right place?"

"Yes, you have, but I'm afraid she is out on a call. Can I take a message for her?"

Louise felt the hair on her arms rising. It was the mention of 'Jonnie' rather than JJ that set her pulse racing. No one here knew him by the name Jonnie, apart from her. Jonnie was his past, not his present.

"Ah… that's a shame. I don't suppose the man himself is about?"

"JJ?" she said, hoping he would correct himself, "Sorry, no."

The man raised an eyebrow, "Not Jonnie anymore then," he said with a mocking smile, "No bother, just passing through. Me and JJ, ha!" he said in a sardonic tone, "Jonnie that is, go back a long way. Haven't seen him in years. Maybe you could pass on a message to his missus for me, to give to him. If she – it's Niamh, isn't it? – could let him know that young Eoin was asking after him."

"Yeah, sure. I can let her know. Young Eoin," she repeated.

He seemed to find that funny and began to chuckle to himself,

"Yes, you have it all right, young Eoin."

Rather than turn to leave, instead he paused to

consider his surroundings,

"It's a nice place this. They've done well for themselves."

Then after giving her some more scrutiny he turned and walked back towards the front door. It opened before he reached it; Harry and Anna walked in with Patrick in tow.

"Ah this must be young Harry," he said patting him on the head as he went by. "Young Harry, young Eoin. Ha ha!" He continued out the door, chuckling to himself.

Louise's sense of unease was intense. Intuition told her this was no ordinary visit. She tried to appear unaffected by the encounter yet secretly she knew she needed a quick getaway.

"I've just finished up Anna. Would you mind waiting for Niamh? She won't be long. I'll shut the front door. There're no surgeries this evening."

She reached for her handbag and took her coat out from underneath the counter as she spoke to make it clear she expected Anna to agree to her request.

Louise drove straight to JJ's, questioning her thoughts and instincts the whole way there. *Damn JJ.* She had the feeling she was being pulled into something she wanted nothing to do with. It would have been so much easier to pass the message on to Niamh as requested; so much easier that is if she could be sure that message didn't risk opening JJ's, and consequently her own, Pandora's Box. Harry's short-lived kidnap had been the catalyst to lifting the lid. The momentum had begun, the lid was slowly opening and now she had to try her best to stop it from spilling forth its carefully hidden secrets.

JJ answered the door; he looked decidedly groggy. *He's always at the whiskey bottle*, she thought to herself rather self-righteously. Louise had given up drinking excessively in her twenties, and apart from the occasional lapse now and again she was relatively 'dry' compared to when she was young. She couldn't understand why JJ still drank so heavily. *How does he think it's going to help*?

He looked haggard; his dull complexion and dark eye circles suggesting a long drinking session. Surprised to see her and not in the least bit pleased, he sighed.

"Ah for fucks sake, what now? I thought you wanted to go back to how things were. We don't know each other or have you forgotten?"

"JJ, listen, we had a visitor at the clinic today. He asked for you – for Jonnie."

That got his attention.

"Can I come in for a minute? He'd a message he wanted Niamh to pass on."

JJ backed into the hallway but stood his ground.

"So why are you passing the message on then?"

She stepped inside, closing the door behind her. He smelt of stale alcohol and un-brushed teeth.

"Because she was out; because he knows you as Jonnie," she said with emphasis. "I was scared the message would start something, and that Niamh would be asking questions. I want the past to stay in the past JJ. I don't understand what's going on. It's all getting very weird. I didn't want Niamh getting involved."

She knew she sounded hysterical. Her fears were both illogical and logical to her. She didn't know the man in the clinic so that shouldn't have threatened her, but she knew what she was hiding and that had to be protected until she was ready to tell the truth.

It also crossed her mind the stranger might be JJ's blackmailer. He did recognise Harry after all and the way he had looked at her... *what if he murdered that young fella they found in the ruin? What if he knows I was JJ's alibi all those years ago? Does he know more about me too? Am I in danger?*

JJ looked more addled now and invited her to follow him as he walked back down the hall.

"Come on then. Tell me what he said."

Sitting on the couch in the living room, Louise recounted the message from the man and described him in detail.

"An old frail man, but rough-looking too, like someone who'd abused drugs for most of his life. He looked like a hardy aul homeless person. And he recognised Harry, JJ."

JJ was looking tense. Louise could see his jaw

tighten.

"He said to say, 'Eoin asked for you'."

"Eoin?" JJ repeated.

"Yes, Eoin. Actually, he said, 'young Eoin'. Is that the name of the young fella that went missing? I can't remember his name. He thought it was funny anyway, he was laughing to himself. If it's his own name, I'm not surprised; he's no spring chicken."

"Young Eoin," JJ repeated as he sat back into the armchair opposite Louise.

The tiny bit of colour in his face drained away. Louise thought he might faint.

"Are you OK?"

JJ was silent; but his features registered his horror.

"That's it then. It's all over," he said, eventually.

"What are you saying? What do you mean?"

He knew who'd visited the clinic – it was Long John – and he was in serious trouble. *Where has the bastard crawled out from?* He exhaled in his defeat. *She may as well know it all now*.

He began at the beginning and told her the entire story, sparing her no details.

"We put Eoin under the conservatory."

JJ went on to tell her about Kevin too; that he was beaten to death, and that it was the same day he'd received his first beating. He told her about many of the other crimes he'd reluctantly been involved with, none of them his fault he said, but he'd be convicted

327

nonetheless as an accessory to murder and for perverting the course of justice by maintaining his silence over the intervening years.

Louise sat opposite him motionless. Appalled by the stories he was relaying, she wanted to stop him but he was lost in the memories of his youth, and just kept going. Eventually his stream of thought slowed and she asked,

"JJ, why did he let Harry go then?"

JJ confessed that he'd instigated the kidnapping as a ruse to try to ensure it was Long John who was brought to justice if a body was dug up during the re-development of Dominic's Park. He explained to her that once he'd known the redevelopment was going ahead he'd searched for Long John but he hadn't been able to locate him.

"I didn't know if he was dead or alive," he told her, "And I couldn't check if the body was still there, that was too risky, and I couldn't get someone else involved to check for me either. I did the next best thing. I made it look like it was Long John, not me, who wanted the development halted. It was the only way I could think of to make it look like I knew nothing about what went on in that house when I lived there."

He stressed over and over – he had never wanted to be involved in any of it in the first place; he had been forced into it.

"But the law won't listen to that. If I'm implicated,

I'll be convicted for remaining silent. My silence is damning," he said. "I was only a young lad. They'd have to prove it. Without any evidence, I'd have a good chance of denying any involvement, they'd have to believe I was ignorant to what was happening in that place. There shouldn't be any DNA after all this time. I didn't touch the body and it was wrapped in plastic. Eoin has always been my greatest danger. He's the only person they can easily link to me. I was living there, standing on top of him every day, for fucks sake."

He even told her about Eugene. That wasn't his fault either. Eugene had overdosed himself but who would believe that now?

JJ incriminated himself by naming people and places like a man possessed, re-living his traumas right there before her, his face twisted and contorted by the memories; his sweat and tears flowing freely.

There was also a hardness in his defence of his actions; his strong belief that he'd been forced to learn how to survive and thrive and he'd won out in the end. Yet this steely determination was quickly followed by despair at the realisation that perhaps he'd met his match in Long John.

Long John was coming to get his revenge and after all these years he would be the final winner.

"If the Gardai were better at their job," he said disparagingly, "Then Long John would be in custody and I'd be safe. The state's never there to protect the likes of me."

Louise was the only person he'd ever confided in and despite his present predicament, being able to confess and regurgitate all the vileness within him brought with it a very brief period of relief, as though he'd vomited up a bad meal.

He was emptying his conscience and Louise knew she would be caught in the fallout. The more he spoke, the less safe she became. She tried again to halt the onslaught of confessions.

"Stop JJ," she pleaded, "Stop, I don't want to know any more."

Yet he couldn't; he'd lost all reasoning. His life was tumbling down around him and he had nothing more to lose. All he wanted was some recognition, some reassurance from her, from anyone, that he'd only done what he had to do. He wasn't a bad person.

Finally, he finished speaking. Louise couldn't put any words together, too shocked and completely thrown off balance by what she'd heard. They sat in silence for a few minutes while she frantically tried to consider a suitable response.

Leaning forward on the edge of the couch, she observed JJ rocking back and forth, bent over, clutching his knees, staring at the floor and deep in thought. Then with every muscle tensed in her body to stop herself quivering she said earnestly,

"You have to tell the Gardai JJ, you *have* to tell

them."

As soon as she spoke the words JJ began to unfurl himself. Lifting his head, she could see his facial expression and realised too late that she'd made a mistake. He'd recognised the enormity of what he had told her. He wasn't going to the Gardai.

He looked straight into her eyes, now filled with tears of fear. Rising over the horizon of the dark place he'd just been in, he regained his senses and his control of the situation.

She saw it, but there was no way to take her words back. She sat, terrified.

"Please JJ!"

"I'm not going to the Gardai," he said flatly, his eyes seeming to pierce through her, "And neither are you."

Long John

Unknown to either of them, Long John was parked in his car, a little further down the road from JJ's house. He'd stayed in the carpark after talking to Louise, hoping Niamh might return quickly, intrigued to meet the woman who'd married Jonnie. He wondered how much she knew about him and would have liked the opportunity to watch her expression when he passed on his message.

A life of crime had attuned Long John to a person's fight or flight response – he'd detected Louise's wariness when she'd spoken to him in the clinic and when he saw her leaving in an aggitated state only minutes after his exit, he was prompted to follow her.

With interest, he witnessed the interaction at Jonnie's front door, assuming she was relaying his message and wondering why she hadn't passed it on to his missus. *Who is she? His bit on the side? A quirky fetish*, he thought, *shouldn't the bit on the side be younger than*

the wife? Nice house though. He's done well for himself.
A wife and mistress. Yes, he's done very well for himself.

He wondered too why Jonnie had kept Louise at the door rather than invite her straight in. Even after she'd closed the door behind her he could see their shadows for a while through the small square window.

When their outlines retreated from sight Long John settled himself down to wait. He wasn't going anywhere, his eyes were trained on JJ's front door. As he waited he thought about what an ungrateful bastard Jonnie had been, and he hoped by now he was well aware of his visit to the clinic. *He deserves what's coming to him.*

Sitting in his car as it cooled, Long John imagined the look of horror on Jonnie's face when he realised it was him who had visited his wife's workplace. He hoped it would provoke one of Jonnie's panic attacks. At the very least, he wanted the news to instil an immense sense of fear in him – *he deserves that*. He wanted Jonnie to know it was him, Long John, who was going to kill him. *He should suffer a bit before he dies,* he thought.

Looking across at what he presumed was Jonnie's grand house, he remembered back to when Jonnie was a bright, plucky young teenager arriving at his school. Seeing a bit of himself in Jonnie, he had wanted him to do as well as he could. He'd known right from the start that he was too fragile to survive the underworld with

333

no support, but unfortunately for Jonnie, like his dead sister, he had been destined for bad things.

Lucky for him he was such a bright spark, he thought, *he's no idea how that protected him – how I protected the runt as well, as best as I was able. I did everything I could to keep him at arm's length from the worst of it. Who'd have thought he'd turn on me like this?*

He remembered how the boss had been unimpressed by Jonnie's less than enthusiastic desire to get involved in their profitable 'business'. Long John had been told to keep him in check or he'd be done with him. The boss threatened that he'd find another clever type to replace Jonnie, and had said he wouldn't be taking Long John's advice again. Long John had known what that really meant.

Stuck between a rock and a hard place, he had been desperate to ensure Jonnie's loyalty. It was the only way to keep them both safe. The only way to protect his own back.

He recollected how he'd initially tried to gain Jonnie's trust. How hard he had worked to make Jonnie like him, and how, when Jonnie had realised he'd been ensnared, that had no longer worked. *Well… that's what forced me to change track. Jonnie always had notions above his station,* he thought.

In the end, fear was the only thing that was guaranteed to keep him quiet, so as often as he could, he had terrified him in order to ensure they both remained safe.

In his car with the air chilling further, he recalled the beating Jonnie received the day Kevin was murdered; the 'lesson' that turned Jonnie completely against him. Ironically, the assault had nothing to do with him.

Jonnie initiated that beating himself with his bloody panic attack, but he blamed me for it all anyway. I should have known better than to feel anything for him. Once someone holds a grudge there's always revenge at some point. Hasn't time proven that to be true?

I did a good job of making Jonnie afraid of me, he thought, as he contemplated the extent to which Jonnie's fear had blinded him, despite his intelligence. Jonnie had never found out that Long John was not the real boss, not even after they'd parted ways. It was safer that way.

This deception had its downside in that Jonnie thought Long John orchestrated events that he had sometimes strongly disagreed with, but as far as Long John had been concerned, that went with the territory. His disagreement had never mattered anyhow, if it had been something the boss wanted. He knew Jonnie hated him for murdering Eoin, yet he'd not been in agreement with Eoin's death at all and had tried very hard to prevent it. The only upside to that event from Long John's perspective was that it had provided an opportunity to make sure Jonnie lost all hope of escaping. Burying a body inside his own house had been a last-ditch attempt to put an end to any ideas Jonnie had been hanging on to about setting himself free and squealing to the authorities. The body under their feet had once secured their future, but now Jonnie had wrecked it all.

He's very naive for such a smart arse, he thought to himself, remembering when the new gang commandeered their patch after their boss had died. It had been a dangerously tricky situation. Jonnie had thought he'd engineered the process of his retirement directly with Long John, but Long John as usual had only been the middleman. He'd had to negotiate all their survivals, not just Jonnie's 'retirement'.

Luckily for them, it was one of his own protégés who'd headed up the new squad. They could have easily decided to annihilate them all. Jonnie was fortunate the youngster had a great deal of respect for Long John and felt he owed him something. *Jonnie is a lucky man; he has no idea how lucky.*

Bitterly, Long John reminded himself that he'd saved Jonnie's skin on more than one occasion, and for what?

We'd all been getting on with our lives in peace and quiet, he bemoaned to himself, *if Jonnie boy hadn't decided to step out of line. Now it's my responsibility to deal with him. He's no idea of the backlash he's created with his little scam. He should never have drawn attention to the house like that. The fool! If he'd left things alone it would've been like all the other houses –*

just four walls and a roof that needed knocking down. Well, I'm not saving his ass again.

He thought of the many young men now in positions of influence who had been through that house. The Gardai would investigate each and every one of them now their suspicions were raised. What a mess the whole thing had become. *What the fuck is Jonnie thinking?*

With little else to occupy him other than the arthritis in his knees, Long John continued to justify what he planned to do, just as JJ often did. *It's his own fault. So busy trying to cover his own ass. Forgetting where his loyalties lie, just so he gets a few more years of the good life. He's forced me out of retirement, put my life in danger and is making me risk my freedom. For a smart guy, he sure as hell didn't think through the consequences.*

The privileged little shit. His education handed to him on a plate. I never got that opportunity in life. Lucky bastard. He wouldn't have lasted spitting time without minding. I'm the one who helped him get what he has.

Pulling a blanket from the back seat, he laid it over his knees to keep warm while contemplating the brutality of his own life. Seething in self-pity, he stared across the road at the large house with the tarmac drive, his knees aching. *Even now*, he thought, *before he dies, he's getting the upper hand on me in there with his central heating and his mistress. He's waiting to die in comfort.*

"For fucks sake, would she ever hurry up! How long does it take to pass on a message?"

His patience was waning. *If she's not careful, she'll find herself in the wrong place at the wrong time.*

Should I tell?

Niamh was at home with Harry after picking him up from the clinic, working her way through her own worries; the clues which seemed to indicate that JJ was involved in Harry's kidnap. It appeared absurd. It didn't make any sense at all, yet the more she thought about the spinner, the pinch marks, the paint and how quietly Harry and Patrick had disappeared from the garden, the more disturbed she became. Even the sweet wrappers she had found in his pockets were suspicious: they were Harry's favourite sweets. How would the kidnapper know unless they were close to the family? She was unsure what to do – was she being delusional or should she tell the Gardai her concerns?

Finally, she decided to tell them. It was not up to her to decide if she was putting two and two together and making three, and she was at the end of her tether with worrying about it all. Putting Harry and Patrick into the car, she drove towards the station.

Seeing the station's blue light ahead of her she began to doubt herself again. *What if I'm wrong?* Changing her mind, she drove right by. She couldn't do it. Surely JJ had nothing to do with his own son's disappearance? What was she thinking of? Her mind was playing tricks on her.

I know I've serious doubts about his parenting abilities, she thought, *but that doesn't mean he's got anything to do with kidnapping Harry. How ridiculous! The Gardai would have laughed me out of the place.*

Doing a U-turn further down the road, she returned home, feeling foolish and annoyed that she'd disrupted Harry's bedtime routine for such nonsense. But the merry-go-round of thoughts in her head continued, and she feared they would soon affect her sanity. She picked up the phone to call Louise.

Louise's mobile phone rang several times with no answer. Niamh left her a message.

"Hey, Louise when you get this, can you give me a ring?"

There was no returned call, not even by the time she had bathed Harry and put him to bed. As always, she sat on the landing outside Harry's bedroom door, running her fingers through Patrick's thick coat. Tired of her endless questions, she wished her phone would ring.

"If only you could talk," she whispered into Patrick's ear.

Once Harry was sleeping, she made herself wait

340

another half an hour before calling Louise again, unable to curtail her anxiety about what to do and needing Louise's opinion. Her mobile rang repeatedly and Niamh was about to give up when Louise answered in a breathy whisper.

"Hi Niamh, sorry I missed you earlier."

"No problem," Niamh answered, finding Louise's hushed tone strange, "Is everything OK?"

"Oh, yeah, yeah. What's up?"

Louise tried to lighten her voice but it was difficult with JJ leaning into her ear while she spoke, his arm pulling her as close to him as possible so he could hear every word. She could feel the dampness on her cheek from the condensation of his breath. He was restraining her, and she had a desperate desire to break free, yet his vice-like grip on her shoulder indicated this was not a risk worth considering. JJ was a frustrated and distraught man and she quickly needed to placate Niamh about whatever it was she was phoning her for.

"Sorry about this Louise, but would you mind calling over. I really need to talk to you about Harry and JJ."

JJ released Louise for a moment and drew his hand across his throat, making it clear she wouldn't be visiting Niamh that evening. Distracted by his action, Louise didn't answer.

On the other end of the phone, Niamh was surprised by the silence that followed her request.

"Louise?" she said, "Are you there still?"

"Ah, I'm kind of stuck this evening, Niamh. Can we chat tomorrow?"

Not used to Louise dismissing her like that, Niamh was instantly annoyed. *I wouldn't ask her to call unless I really needed her to. Where are your friends when you need them? What happened to having each other's backs?*

Her pride took control, preventing her from asking why she couldn't come over.

"OK fine," was her abrupt reply, "See you tomorrow."

Then, feeling a little guilty, in a more enquiring voice she added,

"Are you sure everything's OK?"

"Yeah, yeah, but I really have to go, see you tomorrow then?"

Louise hung up, leaving Niamh wondering what on earth was going on.

JJ took Louise's phone from her hand and switched it off. He put it on the fireplace, leaning it against a picture of Harry and Patrick.

Back in Niamh's house, the merry-go-round in her head went on. She couldn't dismount, and with no advice from Louise, she eventually decided she'd have to contact the Gardai. Unable to leave the house with Harry in bed, she phoned the station to ask if someone could come over to discuss the concerns she had about the paint.

342

Two Gardai duly arrived. They listened to her thoughts and neither of them laughed at her reasoning. They took copious notes but gave no indication of what they thought. They asked her for any possible reason as to why JJ might want to kidnap his own son. She wasn't able to help them answer that question as there was simply no reason she could think of.

When they were leaving, she remembered she had a spare key to the cottage but they declined her offer to use it, saying if they needed to search the premises they'd seek Mr Hennessy's permission or obtain a search warrant.

What's he going to say when he finds out what I've done? she worried. *How will I ever re-build any parenting relationship with him after this? Do I even want to?*

The Gardai knew they couldn't enter JJ's cottage without a warrant or his permission, but after they left Niamh's house, they reasoned there was nothing stopping them from dropping by the cottage on their way back to the station to check it out from the outside.

They had no problem entering the premises; JJ had left the gate open after he'd exited with Eugene's corpse in the boot. Driving slowly up the gravel lane they hoped they wouldn't see any lights on in the cottage. Sure enough, there were no lights and no car.

"It's an eerie place, isn't it?" the driver said to his colleague, "Let's try knocking, no harm in double-checking."

They got out of their patrol car and walked towards the door. As they approached, they immediately noticed the blacked-out windows. When knocking received no response, they decided to look around the back. There, they found the curtains fully open.

Although there wasn't much to see inside, their torchlight revealed enough to prompt further investigation. It looked like someone had stayed in the cottage recently. They could see mugs and plates on the kitchen table, and an empty tin of beans on the floor in one of the bedrooms, with videos and lots of paper and crayons scattered about.

"This is supposed to be vacant," one said to the other, "But it sure looks like someone's been using it recently."

Not wanting to jeopardise any possible court action by intruding further without consent, they agreed they should head back to the station to inform their sergeant of what they'd seen there.

Before they got back into their car, they couldn't resist having a peek in the shed which stood to the side of the cottage. It had no functional door to speak of, so theoretically they weren't breaking and entering. There, they saw tins of paint, including two of an olive-green colour, just like the paint found on both Harry and Eugene's trainers. They took a picture to show the sergeant, and delighted with this fresh lead, the pair

344

headed straight back to the station to report their findings.

The sergeant decided to seek a warrant rather than JJ's permission, he didn't want to risk the removal of any evidence by JJ in the interim. They'd give him the chance to hand over a key, but if he refused or had to 'locate' it, they now knew Niamh had one.

While they organised a warrant to search the property, Louise remained hostage in JJ's home, and Long John continued to sit across the road in his car, impatiently waiting to get on and deal with his problem – Jonnie.

Inside and out

Outside, sitting uncomfortably in his car, Long John decided he wasn't going to wait much longer for Jonnie's mistress to leave. His arthritis became painful when he sat still for too long these days and Jonnie wasn't worth suffering for. Another hour was all he was going to give it. If the mistress wasn't gone by then, well, that would just be her tough luck.

*

Inside, the situation was tense. Confessing all to Louise had only served to further complicate things for JJ. He was afraid to let her leave, but didn't know what to do with her, and Louise, knowing she'd made a wrong move earlier by suggesting JJ contact the Gardai, was desperately trying to retract what she'd said.

"I'm not going to say anything to anyone, you know that don't you JJ? I mean, I've too much to lose, don't

I?"

"Shut up!" he shouted back at her, "Shut up. Just sit there. I need to think. What did she want to talk to you about me and Harry for anyway? It's none of your business," he spat.

"I don't know. I have no idea."

He started to rant again, revisiting his past; a past she'd known nothing about until this evening. *Please stop,* she thought, *please don't tell me any more.*

JJ even explained to Louise why he'd been so rough with her that day years ago, in the supermarket carpark. He apologised, telling her he'd been traumatised by the events of the previous day and that she, unfortunately, had been on the receiving end of his agitation. He said he knew she wouldn't be able to understand but he thought she should know nonetheless.

Please shut up JJ, she reiterated in her head, *I don't want to understand you, it's easier to keep hating you.* Yet despite herself, the more he explained, the more she began to understand, albeit not endorse his actions, and even though terrified, she optimistically hoped the apology was an indication that he would eventually let her leave unharmed.

"You've had a charmed life, after all," he continued, "Having a baby and giving it up was a breeze compared to what I've had to endure. Why'd you come back anyway when he was an adult? Couldn't you have kept him when he was a baby if you'd wanted?"

347

Louise didn't answer; she let him rant on. Niamh was his next target.

"Fucking Niamh," he said, "She seems to think she has it hard too but she got the most charmed life of us all. She just doesn't see it. She doesn't know what stress is. Sitting judging us all, she's no idea."

Under normal circumstances, Louise might have pointed out the stresses of running a business, alongside single-handily raising a child with autism, but this was most definitely not the time or place for that debate.

As she listened to his ranting, she realised that he was trying to understand how he'd reached this point in his life. She observed as he became increasingly lost, almost childlike, unable to comprehend why it had turned out the way it had; seemingly trying to forgive himself for his actions while simultaneously abdicating all responsibility.

If she hadn't been so afraid, she'd have felt sorrier for his predicament, but her fear of him far outweighed any other emotion. It was clear to her that he could be violent if he needed to be, and she was directly in harm's way should he choose to react in that manner. She sat as quietly as she could, waiting for him to calm down, suspecting he'd soon have to come to a decision about what to do with her. She was acutely aware that her time to persuade him to let her go was running out.

JJ was tiring, his adrenaline all spent. He was a broken man, much like Finn in her car a mere day earlier. Carefully, watching his every facial expression, she began to try to reason her way out. He looked in her direction when she spoke but he seemed to be almost looking through her rather than at her.

*

Outside in the cold of his car, Long John had no doubts about what he had to do and was impatient, waiting for the opportunity to complete his task. He'd have to move soon or his aching joints would become unbearable.

It was getting dark outside and he opened his car window a crack to let in some fresh air, afraid he might doze off if he didn't. He often needed a nap in the evenings now. *Twenty more minutes, that's all I'm giving it. I've had enough of this. I'm too old and too tired*, he thought.

One or two bullets, he thought to himself, *what does it matter? I just want to get it done and disappear. All this hanging around is bound to stir up suspicion.*

Reaching across underneath the passenger seat, he took out a pistol. He went back a second time, this time to retrieve a silencer, hardly needing to look at what he was doing as he secured it in place. Long John's gun was loaded, ready to go, and he was counting down the minutes.

*

Inside, Louise seemed to be on the right track. JJ hadn't told her to shut up, and he was listening now, or at least appeared to be. The thought crossed her mind that he was letting her talk while he decided the best way to kill her, but she tried not to dwell on that suspicion.

She sympathised with the awful situation he was in, and she said she could now understand how much stress he had been under all these years. She told him she'd no idea he'd lived such a different life to the one he outwardly portrayed. She said how very sorry she was for him.

"So you see Louise, I'm in a corner. I'm always in a corner," he said.

"I see that, but JJ you know I would never say anything don't you? It would be of no benefit to me to see you arrested. It'd only lead to our story being made public. Neither me or you want that. I can't bear the thought of people knowing about you, me and Finn, talking about us as though we've betrayed Niamh in some way. I'll stay silent to protect them and me. You too. I won't say a word."

He was still listening and thinking. She could see he was thinking, so lying, she continued,

"I'm glad you told me all this. You were right. I see that now. You had no choice. You should leave, get a flight out of here. You're in danger JJ. I see there's no point in going to the Gardai now. They aren't going to be able to help you. You should get away and quick – tonight – get a flight out of here."

"You're right," he said, to her surprise, "You and me are in this together now Fairy. You and me."

Louise wanted to be sick. How had he heard 'we are in this together'? Had he really been listening?

"Have you somewhere you can go?" she asked, trying to ignore what he'd just said.

What am I saying? she thought immediately, *I don't want to know where you might go. I want to get as far away from you as I can.* He glared at her. *Shit, I've said the wrong thing again.*

"Somewhere to go? No, I have no fucking place to go! Have you?" he asked, sarcastically.

She hung her head, defeated again, and they sat in silence.

*

Outside, Long John was buttoning up his coat and searching the area for bystanders. The way was clear. *It's a quiet little town*, he thought to himself.

*

Inside, Louise looked around. She could make a run for it, but from where she sat she'd never reach the door in time, she wasn't agile enough. Her phone was switched

351

off and too far away, so that wasn't an option either. Surely if he was going to let her go, he'd have done so by now? What was he going to do? She was desperate and decided to plead.

"JJ please, I need to go. I promise I won't say a word, for God's sake, you know I won't. Please, I have to go now. My car's parked outside, you know how people gossip. I'm so sorry, I can't help you. You're going to have to make your own decisions about what to do, but please, I'm not part of that. You'll have my silence forever, I promise. It's in my best interest. I have to go," she kept stressing, "I have to go," and then began to cry.

What else could she do? She was going to die and the thought of how he might do it terrified her.

JJ stood up.

"For fucks sake, shut up. You can go."

It was as if a light bulb had switched on in his head – he'd suddenly remembered something – and he no longer wanted her there.

"Of course… you go. I know you won't tell. If you do, Finn gets it. You know all about my contacts. It won't be me, it'll be an unfortunate 'accident'. You can keep your mouth shut when you want to, you've lots of practise, don't you Fairy?"

He was acting as though he were in a hurry, wanting her to leave. Was he playing games with her? He'd said she could go. She wanted to jump up and run but was too fearful, so she waited for further permission.

"Get up, get out, fuck off, you're no help to me. Hurry up!" he shouted.

Louise jumped up with such suddenness that she lost her balance and fell back onto the chair. She pulled herself up immediately. Standing, she tried to compose herself.

"Yes, I'm good at keeping secrets, JJ. I absolutely promise to keep yours."

"I'm not worried Fairy, you're in it with me now. You and me together, joined by secrets. Finn's life depends on your discretion."

Sensing her freedom was within reach she managed a more confident response.

"I know that. There's no need to talk like that JJ. I told you – I won't say a word."

He was by her in an instant, swivelling her around by the shoulders and pushing her in the direction of the door. Picking up her handbag with one hand he shoved it at her chest while marching her along from behind.

As she approached freedom, Louise reached for the unfamiliar lock but her hand was trembling and she couldn't get it to turn. JJ's hand appeared over her shoulder.

"Let me help you," he said coldy, as he squeezed her hand firmly and released the lock to open the door. Fresh air entered the gap and hit her in the face. She was almost outside, so close to getting away from him. Just a short walk to her car and she'd be free.

Pulling the door towards her, she had to step back against JJ to get out, the closeness she had once yearned for as a young woman now repulsing her. She felt his fist in the small of her back. He pushed her out, saying in his silly sing-song voice,

"There you go Fairy, off you go, fly away."

Louise jerked forward, surprised by the force of his fist and heard the door shut behind her. He was gone – just like that – and she was outside. A car drove past as though all was normal. She stood for a second in disbelief and then the urge to get away took over. Gathering her strength, she fumbled for car keys as she made a beeline for the car. Focused solely on the safety of her vehicle, Louise stumbled into one of JJ's bins at the side of his driveway, bruising her hip as it rattled against the impact. She didn't feel the contact, and she didn't stop. The car represented safety.

Her keys were in her hand. *Beep* – she saw the orange lights flash indicating her doors were unlocked. She was by the car and opening the door. Inside, she'd be safe.

A little further down the road, Long John readied himself for action. *At last*, he thought, *about time. She doesn't know how close she came…*

Louise's hands were shaking so much she couldn't get the key into the ignition.

"Come on, come on," she encouraged herself, resting her head on the steering wheel.

Then, with a final determined effort to halt her

shaking hand, she managed to start the engine.

Bang, bang, bang. Louise literally leapt out of her seat. She looked across and saw JJ knocking hard on the passenger door window. Her heart thumped.

"Wait," he called, pulling the door open.

She was unable to move, her foot stationary on the accelerator.

"You forgot your phone," he said, throwing it onto the passenger seat before stepping back and gesturing for her to go.

Her feet followed his command, one foot hitting the accelerator while the other released the clutch. The door slammed closed. As though driven by a learner driver, the car jumped forward before shuddering to a halt.

"For fucks sake," JJ said, standing in the dark.

As she sped away, in her rear-view mirror, she saw him turn to go back inside his house. She also thought she saw a shadow. In hindsight, she'd think later that perhaps it was someone crossing the road…

Louise was shaken but alive and relieved to be free at last. She drove straight home.

Time's up

Long John got out of his car so quickly he pulled a muscle in his leg. He cursed as he stretched it out and hurriedly limped across the road.

This was the best chance he was going to get and he wasn't going to miss it. Another few minutes and it'd all be over. He'd get on with his life again, and JJ wouldn't know what hit him. If he was quick enough, he wouldn't even have to ring the doorbell.

Feeling his gun in his hand, held low by his side, he approached JJ from behind as silent as a panther stalking its prey in the shadows.

Walking back toward his house, the door still ajar, JJ could see through to the kitchen where his computer was. Fairy was right – he'd book a flight. *It's the safest thing to do*, he thought. *Once I'm away and hidden, I'll work out my next move. Fairy won't have a choice but to help if I need her to. We're partners in crime now. It's good to share*, he was thinking as he walked those last few steps towards his door. *Fairy will stay quiet, her mother's instinct will ensure that. She won't risk losing her job or Niamh either, not just after she's found her greatest prize – Finn.*

JJ was unaware of Long John approaching; Long John was readying himself for the encounter, every fibre in his body on alert, his gun now held up at shoulder level and his finger on the trigger. Only fifteen more feet and he'd be where he wanted to be, directly behind Jonnie.

Back at his front door, JJ noticed a coin and a crumpled tissue on the step and bent down to pick them up. They had fallen from Louise's bag when she was retrieving her car keys. *Never pass a coin – it's bad luck to leave it.*

Long John stopped in his tracks as JJ bent down to pick up Louise's dropped items. He didn't move an inch. He wasn't quite as close as he wanted to be, and when JJ straightened up to rub the coin between his thumb and forefinger, Long John closed the gap between them. He was now directly behind JJ.

It was only then that JJ heard the sound of movement behind him, and looking towards his hall he saw the second shadow thrown by the porch light.

He knew his time had come. He knew who was behind him. There was nothing he could do. Long John pressed the pistol to the side of his head and JJ automatically raised his hands in surrender. In his ear,

JJ heard him whisper,

"Hey, Jonnie boy, long time no see."

He didn't turn.

"Long John," he said calmly as he continued looking ahead into the hallway at the shadows on the floor.

Even though his hands were already raised in submission, they didn't protect his fall as he fell face first onto the tiles, obliterating his own shadow in an instant.

The dead body that now lay in the doorway was that of a ruthless man, but it was also the remains of a young lad desperate to do better than his parents; a boy, unable to escape from the brutality of his randomly allotted life, who'd learnt how to survive within it. Jonnie had been a bright and ambitious teenager who'd put his faith in people who'd betrayed him; a boy who had wanted more.

Long John was the only person to see him drop to the ground and he didn't wait around. He scurried back to his car, massaging the pulled muscle in his leg as he walked. Inside he switched on the radio and turned the volume up high, shoving the pistol back under his seat. Then, he drove off, out of sight. He didn't even glance across at the house as he went by, not wanting to see Jonnie's body lying slain in the doorway. The deed was complete and his work was done.

Rest in peace Jonnie.

Life after JJ

A Garda car drove right past Long John not long after he'd murdered JJ. He saw their car approaching in his headlights and for a moment thought he'd have to make a run for it, but they passed by with no interest.

Pulsating all over after gunning him down, he changed stations on the radio until he found a tune he liked and increased the volume in an attempt to calm his post-murder jitters. He needed a drink, but that was at least a forty-five minute drive away in Dublin and he dared not stop until he was there, in more familiar surroundings.

The Gardai arrived at JJ's house shortly after they drove past Long John, to issue him with the warrant to search the cottage. It was left in the car as they ran towards the body lying on the doorstep. One called for backup and an ambulance while the other scanned the immediate area, shouting into the house in an attempt to establish if there was any imminent danger in the vicinity.

It was obvious JJ was dead. Blood was pooling on the floor, just as it had done the day his sister jumped from her bedroom window onto the concrete below, his hair sticky and matted with the red hue. Having been partially blown away by the close range of the pistol, his face was incomplete, but still unmistakably recognisable as JJ. It was a gruesome sight.

The victim was warm. This had only just happened, and the recentness of it shook the young Gardai. They'd seen deceased bodies before but only like that of Eugene's which had been dead for some time. It was rare to come across a body so maliciously murdered that had been speaking and breathing only a few minutes before.

The Gardai positioned their car sideways across the driveway to hide JJ from immediate view and further back up was requested. They showed great respect for the dead man; regardless of their suspicions about him, this was no way to die.

Niamh phoned Louise in a shocked and bewildered state. It was approaching midnight but Louise answered the phone instantaneously without any attempt to hide the fact that she was still wide awake beyond her usual hour. Niamh didn't seem to notice.

In an extremely disturbed state and unable to settle herself, Louise had been rocking back and forth on her bed, much like JJ on his armchair earlier that evening, when her mobile rang. She'd had two showers and a couple of glasses of wine by then; her face was bloated from crying.

Seeing Niamh's name light up on her phone, she pessimistically pressed the call receive button, expecting her to be in a distressed and angry state, assuming JJ had told the truth, and her past had been exposed. Before she could say, "Sorry," Niamh spoke without preamble.

"Louise, JJ's been shot! He's dead!"

Louise hated herself for it, but she immediately felt a great surge of relief, her shoulders involuntarily relaxed. That feeling of relief still disturbed her whenever she cared to think about it. She was horrified too of course, but there was no denying the relief.

With Niamh in tears on the other end of the phone, Louise consoled her as best she could before heading over to stay with her until her family arrived. She told her nothing about the evening she'd had with JJ nor about the visit from Long John earlier in the afternoon. Niamh didn't need to know. JJ was dead and she soon realised she might never need to disclose her relationship with him at all.

After Niamh's parents arrived to look after their daughter, Louise took her leave. She didn't sleep at all in what was left of that night; she lay on her bed and stared up at the ceiling, whispering repeatedly,

"I'm safe, it's all over. Me and Finn are safe," as she

tried to work out the best way forward.

JJ had burdened her with a lot of information about his life and his involvements and she wasn't sure if she was still in danger because of what she knew. She had information that could avenge a lot of wrongdoing; that could be used to bring about justice and closure for countless victims. She also knew exactly what had happened to Harry and why... but Louise hadn't been lying when she'd told JJ she wouldn't tell. She really did have too much to lose. His death hadn't changed that. If anything, it had reinforced it.

By morning, having pondered his life story and her present predicament, she was feeling some tiny measure of empathy for the father of her child. Now that he was gone and his ominous threats removed along with him, she was able to acknowledge what had been a tragic existence.

She concluded that fear and despair had fuelled his deranged plan, and he'd paid the price. He wasn't a good man, but he wasn't a completely evil one either. He had done what he thought he needed to do to save himself – until he couldn't save himself anymore. Wasn't that what she was going to do too?

Despite her new understanding about his plight, she still hated him for pulling her further into his web of deceit. *I've more secrets than I've ever had, but even if telling those secrets benefits others, I know very well they'll ruin Finn's and my future, possibly even Niamh's too,*

362

she told herself. *If fate hadn't brought me to JJ's house, I'd never have known any of it. JJ had no right to unburden himself to me, so it's best to pretend those few hours never happened – the past is better left in the past. It had nothing to do with me anyway.*

She decided if the Gardai found a body in Dominic's Park and it was Eoin, and as JJ's alibi they sought her out, she would stick to her original story. She wouldn't tell them anything else and she'd plead with them to keep her ill-fated relationship confidential. If she was lucky and a body wasn't found then it was unlikely anyone would come looking for her. With a bit of luck there'd be no need to tell Niamh anything; no need to distress Finn with the truth either, and she could have the life she'd always wanted.

Long John had enjoyed a pint or two in Dublin the evening of Jonnie's murder, and snorted a few lines later that night. He'd hoped it was the last time he'd have to kill someone. He was too old for it, and although his feelings no longer ran very deep – drug-induced relief having long ago diffused all his emotions – it still upset him when he had to kill another of his young protégés. A small part of him registered the inhumanity of it, despite his attempts at bravado.

On the day of JJ's funeral, reporters respectfully kept their distance, but his murder was big news. Leaks had already emerged about his suspected connection to Harry's kidnapping and the death of Eugene O'Sullivan.

Niamh, already sick and tired of fending off eager reporters fishing for information, was embarrassed by the media attention and angry at JJ for his part in that. The day of his funeral had become a day to get through rather than a day to mourn or remember the deceased, not that she wanted to anyway.

Louise on the other hand surprised herself and others by shedding some tears. She was unable to stop herself. There was some sympathy in those tears, knowing what she now knew, but mostly they were a mixture of guilt, relief and fear. Guilt for withholding the truth, relief that JJ was no longer a threat to her, and fear about the possible danger she was in. As she stood by his graveside, linking arms with Niamh, none of the mourners could have guessed that she was praying the investigation would die with him.

That afternoon she scoured the faces in the small crowd, nervously looking for any sign of the elderly man from the clinic, sure he must have seen her leaving JJ's house that night and suspecting he was the shadow she had seen in her mirror. Louise was terrified he might return, thinking she was also a threat. If he knew the information she had now, he'd surely want her dead too. It was totally JJ's fault that she would be looking for Long John's face everywhere from now on, and she knew that fear would never leave her.

Unsurprisingly, Finn didn't attend the funeral. JJ had only ever been a cause of trouble to him and he had no sympathy for the man. The day of JJ's burial, Finn visited Twitch's grave in the back garden. He looked down to where his companion was buried and he told his little dog,

"Eat the arse off him if you see him up there, in the sky."

He wouldn't get his day in court, but JJ had got his comeuppance anyway.

Finn wasn't completely off the hook with regards to the investigation, but he was coping better with Louise's support, and the engagement of a solicitor was resulting in a more conservative approach by the Gardai.

He was the first suspect to be taken in for questioning after the murder, but CCTV footage showed him in the town at the pedestrian crossing waiting to go into a shop at the time of the shooting.

Little had Finn known that when he'd crossed back over the road a short time later, with a six-pack of crisps and a litre of milk in his hand, Long John had been queuing four cars back, waiting for the lights to change to green. He'd been swearing about, "Fucking pedestrian crossings," growling to himself about how roads were made for cars.

It didn't take long to conclusively link JJ to the kidnapping. The green paint and DNA proved Harry and Eugene had been at the cottage and when the Gardai examined his jeep they were able to link him to Eugene. All that was left was to find a motive, but that was where the trail went cold.

Niamh was totally devastated when the truth was exposed, and spent the next few weeks derailing JJ's character to Louise. Sometimes Louise tried to offer a more balanced view, but it was difficult when Niamh knew nothing about the truth and she had to be so careful not reveal what she knew. She wished she was more ignorant of his past; then like Niamh she'd be able to continue to dislike JJ with the same verve. How much easier that would have been.

Instead, Louise remained silent, watching, listening and supporting Niamh in every way she could – other than by putting her and the Gardai out of their misery by telling the truth. She was so attentive that at times it irritated Niamh.

"For God's sake Louise, I'm fine, you don't need to cook dinner anymore… No, Harry's fine with me tonight… No, I don't want to close the clinic for a few weeks… I'm fine, honest, I'm fine."

One evening, she was listening to Niamh repeat back to herself what she was hearing on the phone, as was her habit. Niamh was speaking to the Gardai and Louise's eavesdropping revealed something about the planned search of Long John's house. She couldn't grasp the detail, and anxiously waited for the call to end.

Niamh casually told her they were going ahead with excavating Long John's old house at the end of the week and that they were pinning their hopes on finding some clues there. She was excited about the idea, hoping the old house would deliver the answers to all her questions, completely unaware of Louise's predicament.

Long John's house held Louise's fate in the balance, just as it had JJ's. There was absolutely nothing she could do except keep her fingers crossed and wait. Was this, she wondered, the beginning of her own downfall?

The nine o'clock news

Bellingham & Company wanted to distance themselves from their association with JJ and the search of number fifteen, Dominic's Park. They were keen to progress with the demolition and eager to begin the re-development of Afton Way – a complex of apartments with a crèche, gym, shops and medical centre – the quicker the better. Unhappy about the possible negative consequences of their new complex being associated with murder they were being fully cooperative with the Gardai's search plans so as to hasten their investigation, naturally hoping nothing would be found

Long John's house had no special position or traits to make it stand out from any of the other houses in Dominic's Park, but it would to be the first to fall, and it was the only house on the estate the Gardai were interested in. They were present to supervise the proceedings and were pinning all their hopes on finding something conclusive for their investigation. They needed to find a motive.

After all this time it would be a real cause for celebration to finally find some compelling evidence to convict Long John. Suspected of being involved in Dublin's gangland culture, it disgusted them that he'd been able to maintain his heroic public image for so long.

After JJ's murder, Long John had successfully gone back in to hiding, and unperturbed about todays search, he lay in a semi-conscious state, on a couch in an acquaintance's flat.

A group of reporters walked the boundary of the cordoned off site, hoping for a new headline to add to the the story so far, having been tipped off by an informant who was part of the clearing team. They paced back and forth, their cameras and long-distance lenses slung across their shoulders, unable to see through the rows of houses yet to be demolished.

It was eight-thirty a.m. on a bright spring morning. The sun was shining and the birds chirping; an unseasonably warm day, warm enough for a t-shirt, with not a hint of fog or icy winds. April had arrived and the radio DJ played songs about long summer days, encouraging the nation to dream about the better weather to come. On the site the workmen had removed their heavy winter jackets, keen to take advantage of the of pleasant weather.

Accompanying them were a number of Gardai,

369

including a dog handler. They stood chatting waiting for the demolishion equipment to arrive. Keen to start her day's work, the sniffer dog twirled herself in small circles at her handlers feet as if chasing her tail.

"How much longer?" the handler said to one of the Gardai, "I thought the site would be ready before we arrived."

"Some problem attaching the grapple or the hammer or something," came the reply, "They won't take long once they start. You can take her for a walk if you like. Probably better if you do."

The dog handler didn't need persuading and quickly disappeared through the narrow alleyway opposite the site. Unlike the others, he was used to such situations; it was just another working day for him. Realising the delayed start probably meant he'd be late getting home, he took his phone from his pocket to phone his wife. She was going to be disappointed – they'd planned on eating in the garden, wanting to take full advantage of the last bit of afternoon sun.

In the distance, the rumblings of machinery could be heard trundling down the narrow street; the same street JJ had slowly driven along only weeks before to re-visit his past.

The caterpillar tracks of the hydraulic excavator clipped and crushed the edges of the already broken pavements, squashing the weeds which sprouted from the cracks. The little hardy plants survived the impact, unlike the less resilient but sturdier-looking concrete slabs. Fractures appeared in the boundary garden walls, crumbling in parts as the ground moved below. One after the other the small square front gardens were thrown into shade by the enormity of the machine. It was quite a melancholy sight to see the estate that had housed countless generations of Dubliners succumb to the shadow of their executioner.

Louise was at home trying not to think about what the day might reveal, but she couldn't stop her mind from racing. She too felt like she was in the shadow of an executioner and hoped and prayed that the secrets at number fifteen would die today and the rise of Afton Way would keep them buried forever.

Niamh was spending some time in Dublin with her family. The story had gained too much traction in the media for her liking; it promised scandal and speculation was rife. With heightened public interest in any new information, Niamh was well aware reporters would bombard her when they heard of the Gardai's search. She wanted nothing more to do with any of it. Her life was getting back on track and she didn't want it to be derailed again.

Finn was spending his day cleaning up a second-hand bike he'd bought. He'd no interest in what was happening today. JJ was just a bad memory. Next week he was looking forward to returning to work at St. Teresa's school, with no inkling whatsoever that his favourite pupil was actually his half-brother…

The first of the large excavators stopped in front of number fifteen; the long hydraulic arm with its mighty hammer began to shudder its way through the wall and pulverise the front of the house.

Once the gable walls toppled the rest of the house fell. Dust and dirt filled the air. The sound of smashing glass, breaking timbers and falling brick walls obliterated the uplifting sounds of nature on this beautiful spring morning.

After the excavator had demolished the house and moved the larger pieces of debris to one side, it reversed back down the street.

The area was sprayed in a haze of water to help settle the dust before the sniffer dog was sent in to run over the rubble of the collapsed building. The dog didn't pick up a scent of anything amiss.

It was time for the heavy yellow diggers to move in. They pushed, shoved, reversed and spun around, shifting the rubble until the concrete foundations were partially exposed. The sniffer dog was sent back in, but again found nothing.

The diggers gave way to the workmen who operated heavy-duty pneumatic hammers. With their ears and eyes protected, these gloved men with their steel-toed dusty boots set to work. Their entire bodies vibrated as they drilled down, cracking the foundations wide open. It was hot and slow work. The foundations had to be cleared one section at a time, and each section had to be inspected by the sniffer dog. By lunchtime, the first section of the house had been examined, right down to soil level.

After lunch, full-bellied and with the sun high in the sky, the workmen continued. The sniffer dog no longer circled excitedly. In between her bursts of work, she lay in the shade of a Garda car to escape the sun's heat, a half-drunk bowl of water nearby.

Another section was cleared which again exposed nothing. This search could turn out to be complete folly.

It was late afternoon by the time the workmen reached the back kitchen section. The dog had moved across to the space once occupied by the conservatory. She sniffed around one of the idle diggers' wheels. Her handler called her back but she was interested in something.

"OK," he said, "Let's clear that section there. Can you move your machine?" he asked the driver of the digger.

He duly reversed as instructed and the sniffer dog headed directly to the vacated spot, excited now as she sniffed the cracked concrete. She stopped and stood still. There was something there. Her handler called her back.

"Good girl, good girl," he said as he led her away, patting her excited body while continuing to praise her efforts; his hopes of getting home before the sun went down completely were rising.

One of the men with the concrete drills moved in and carefully began to penetrate the surface. Then others with hand shovels took over. Fifty minutes later, one of them shouted,

"I think I have something!"

Protruding from the subsoil was a piece of black polythene. Slowly and carefully the surrounding rubble and soil were removed to expose what was hidden below.

To the layman there wasn't much to see. The workmen had expected to find something shocking like a polythene bag containing a skeleton, bits of bones or maybe even a skull. None of that was there, just pieces of torn black polythene, nothing macabre at all. They stopped their excavation and sent the dog back in. She maintained a keen interest in the spot so it was cordoned off for a more in-depth investigation, the black polythene the only tangible evidence.

Before the workmen left for home, they stood for a while in silence, looking down at the hole they'd dug. Those who had faith in the dog's senses pondered who may have been disposed of in the spot, while others considered their efforts a waste of time.

It had been a long day, and with little to show for it, other than a demolished house.

The reporters who'd been outside the site on and off during the day waited for them, hoping for a comment

374

or two as they left, but the trustworthy workforce said nothing. Noticing the Gardai weren't leaving, the reporters decided to wait a little longer and their persistence was rewarded with the arrival of the forensic team. The long day spent watching and waiting had been worth it after all. The Gardai gave them a statement to say the site was of significance and a forensic investigation would follow. By nine p.m. this new information was part of the evening's news.

Louise was too afraid to phone Niamh to ask what information the Gardai had given her about the search, afraid any uncontrolled response might raise some suspicion about her. She was perched on the edge of her settee waiting patiently for the news. An empty bottle of wine sat on the coffee table beside a newly framed photo of Finn. She felt fuzzy and a bit disconnected as she sat perspiring, her fingers firmly crossed.

The familiar voice of the newsreader announced,

"Gardai have confirmed that no human remains have been found in a house in the former Dominic's Park Estate…"

Her heart leapt with joy. She couldn't believe it. *Poor JJ*, she thought, *he died for nothing. The body has already been moved. Thank God!*

Louise reached for her glass as the newsreader went on to remind the public of the story so far in relation to JJ's murder, Eugene, Harry's kidnap and the continuing search for Long John. She took a gulp of wine, grateful that she wouldn't have to disclose anything to Niamh or anyone else.

Louise was raising her glass to herself in celebration when she heard the newsreader say,

"The investigation remains ongoing. A more in-depth forensic search will be conducted over the coming days."

She lowered her glass back down to the table.

"God damn him anyway!" she cried aloud as she stood up, too upset to remain seated.

No pity for him now, her thoughts turned to how stupid he had been to panic. *He should have known Long John would never leave the body behind him under the house when he left. What was he thinking?*

There was no corpse. *If he'd done nothing at all, an apartment block would be getting built there now, there'd be no forensic team combing through the rubble. He and I would still be strangers to each other*, she thought.

She couldn't even cry. The position she was in seemed so ludicrously unreal. JJ had turned her life upside down again. She'd become a criminal, just like him, incriminating herself by her silence.

She wasn't going to tell the truth though, there were too many consequences for her, and she wasn't going to let him ruin the life she had now either. *I'll just have to get on with it.*

Reaching down, she lifted the glass once more and

began to swirl the last dregs of wine around. Louise watched as they rose to the top edge, teetering, close to spilling over. Almost losing control of the momentum, she stopped swirling and drank it down.

There's another bottle in the fridge, she thought.

Acknowledgments

Sincere thanks to Kirsty Jackson and the Cranthorpe Millner team for accepting my manuscript, to all of you who worked to help create the final product & a special thanks to my editors Victoria Richards and Michelle Jenkins.

To everyone involved, thank you.

CPSIA information can be obtained
at www.ICGtesting.com
Printed in the USA
LVHW111528260822
726940LV00015B/218